Alan R. Kerr was born in Auckland, New Zealand. He was brought up outside Belfast in Northern Ireland where he still lives, and divides his time between the United Kingdom and Cyprus.

EASTERN TRADE

Alan Kerr

EASTERN TRADE

Vanguard Press

VANGUARD PAPERBACK

A CIP catalogue record for this title is
available from the British Library.

ISBN 978 1 78465 186 2

Vanguard Press is an imprint of
Pegasus Elliot MacKenzie Publishers Ltd.
www.pegasuspublishers.com

First Published in 2017

Vanguard Press
Sheraton House Castle Park
Cambridge England

Printed & Bound in Great Britain

For Lucy

(A little rescue dog)

Our time together was brief,
but I think of you every day.

Acknowledgements

A word of thanks to the following people: Philippa Donovan of Smart Quill Editorial, who provided an in-depth independent professional edit of this book's first draft. Suzanne Mulvey, Commissioning Editor of Pegasus Elliot Mackenzie Publishers Ltd, who gave me the opportunity to break into the world of published books. My partner, Kate, who continued to encourage me during stare at the wall times, and my sister Julie and brother-in-law, Stephen, for the finishing touches before publishing.

"Why, Sir, you find no man, at all intellectual,
who is willing to leave London. No, Sir, when
a man is tired of London, he is tired of life,
for there is in London all that life can afford."

Samuel Johnson, 1777

Chapter 1

He hit the call disconnect button; it was not his usual mobile phone but one he had purchased cheaply from a high street store. He glanced at the clock on the facing wall; it was one that reminded him of his school days, a stained wooden surround with glass, Roman numerals and a hand which hesitated every second. It was a few minutes before six and to his right a large flat screen television sat bolted to the wall, with its volume muted and tuned to a financial news channel, which showed a ticker of company prices that moved right to left along the bottom of the screen.

He gently shook the ice in his crystal tumbler, before draining the remnants of his Scotch and pushing the swivel chair slowly backwards, standing and taking the few steps to look out from the window of his nineteenth storey office. The street below was full with traffic. Taxis and buses ferried people around the city and not without the occasional blare of a horn from the same frustrated drivers. Roads around the financial district of London were narrow, with some dating back to the middle of the seventeenth century, even before The Great Fire, and were now far from suitable for the traffic that the city needed to contend with today.

With it being a Friday evening in early November, most people within the Square Mile either left for the weekend or headed for the sanctuary of the many pubs, wine bars and restaurants that the city had to offer. The clocks had lost an hour the previous week, but it was as if someone had flicked a switch as winter had arrived in earnest.

Through the gloom, he could just make out the Thames and beyond, on its southern bank, the newly opened, and impressive, building, the Shard. At one thousand and sixteen feet, it was by far the tallest building in the city. His company was relocating to the Shard sometime in the New Year, a move that he wasn't overly thrilled about, as he had always considered the centre of London's financial district to be the few streets that surrounded the Bank of England. Nevertheless, this was new London, and more of these structures sat piled as drawings in architects' offices across the country and beyond. It would be slow progress, but these New York style skyscrapers meant that, once again, the city was open for business, as if it was a signal of sorts, one that ended the recession. A recession that would live long in the memory for a generation or more.

With the capital recovering, the rest of Britain would follow, bringing an influx of foreign business, with the Far East being among the leading contenders. It was this thought which shot a shudder through him. The Far East meant China and Hong Kong and he recalled the difficult board meeting that he had left a few hours previously, not that he primarily disagreed with the other directors or anything to do with company business. What had concerned him was the stylishly dressed Oriental man who was now attending company board meetings. He had protested furiously, but the rest of the board had out-voted him, claiming that the man, known as Lee Chiang, was the best person to guide the company towards expansion into the east of Asia.

The knock at the door jolted him back to the present. A pretty face appeared around it, along with shoulder-length hair, soft blonde curls and then a smile, which belonged to Carol, his long-term sometimes-suffering personal assistant. She was in her mid-thirties and of average height, divorced with two teenage boys, but kept a cheery exterior each day despite his daily demands. Maybe she had underlying problems; if so, she did not bring them to the office.

'Is there anything more you need, Mr Harrison?' she asked.

'No, thank you, Carol, you may go.'

'Good night then, sir.'

'Goodnight, Carol, have a good weekend.'

'Thank you, sir, and you.'

She made to close the door, but he interrupted. 'Carol?'

She reappeared, still smiling. 'Yes, sir?'

'Are there any cars?'

'Eh, no, Mr Harrison,' she replied. As if there may be a problem, as if she may not be able to catch the 6.23.

'Never mind,' he replied. 'I'll get a cab.'

'I can order one for you sir.'

'No you will not! You'll miss that train.'

Carol smiled. 'Thank you, sir.'

'I'm sure I'll be able to hail one on the street,' he said. 'Goodnight Carol and thank-you for your loyalty to me and the company.'

'You're welcome, sir,' she said. 'Goodnight, Mr Harrison.'

Carol closed the door, but paused, frowning, while keeping hold of the handle. It was an unusual remark. Thank you for your loyalty to me and the company, he had said. Mr Harrison could be demanding at times, but he was fair, and more than good to her, plus her salary was higher than any of the other PAs and with very generous bonus payments. She shrugged as she moved away from the door and returned to her desk, grabbing her handbag, before she took the few steps along the corridor to the lift. She pressed the down button and checked her watch: she should still be able to make her train with a few minutes to spare. A ping announced the lift's arrival. Once inside, she pressed for the ground floor, but glanced up as the lift doors closed, towards the far oak door, which remained ominously silent and still.

After Carol had left, Harrison once again sat down. He swivelled his chair and while holding onto the desk rolled into a comfortable position. He was surprised at how long he had been standing, as his laptop now displayed a screensaver with the company logo, one, which faded in and out. He hit a random key and it disappeared, now replaced with the spreadsheet he had previously been working on. His mind, however, was elsewhere. The photograph frame on his desk was that of his wife Natasha and her horse Admiral. She was standing beside the jet-black horse, stroking its nose while smiling at the camera. He was still convinced the damn horse was smiling too. His mind went back to that March day three years ago, when Admiral bolted, after a transit van travelling too fast along the country lane spooked him. Natasha had held on for as long as she could, but was eventually thrown and landed in a field, breaking her neck and dying almost immediately. Admiral galloped towards the main road, where a passing heavy goods truck struck the poor shocked animal, killing it. With a lump in his throat and tears in his eyes, he touched the glass frame of both rider and horse. She would have been forty-two in September past and he had been six years her senior. Some nights he would dream of Natasha riding Admiral as they galloped along a stretch of sandy beach at the edge of the surf, with her hair shimmering in the sun, smiling and the white dress she sometimes would have worn trailing behind her.

They were childless, so he sold the house after Natasha's death at a reduced price: five bedrooms and stables with an enviable view of the South Downs on the outskirts of Midhurst. Now, he lived alone in a comfortable Edwardian mid-terrace in St Johns Wood, north of central London and only a five-minute walk from his beloved Lords Cricket Ground. To be able to hear the sound of leather on willow, during warm, balmy, summer afternoons, drinking a beer or two, with his club pals, whilst watching Middlesex or England was his own little slice of peace and relaxation.

He sighed and, putting both hands to his face, rubbed his eyes. It had been another long day, but not in hours: he had become accustomed to being in the office until after six p.m. It was long due to the incessant unnecessary board meetings, along with tense discussions, and always in the corner Lee Chiang, impeccably dressed in one of his Savile Row suits. The smug bastard claimed to represent some Hong Kong investment corporation, which wanted to buy a large proportion of company stock. Harrison was suspicious of Chiang, as he had been unable to clarify several issues, such as who the main financial backers for his company were and, more to the point, how the finance was raised. Harrison bounced Chiang's name off many of his contacts within the city, and they had warned him to stay well clear of the Oriental man and his possible connections with Chinese crime gangs. When Harrison mentioned Triads to an acquaintance over lunch, the reply was enough to convince him that Chiang was indeed corrupt, although as yet nothing had been proven. Chiang, however, had charmed the rest of the board, claiming that without his influence it would be practically impossible to expand into China and the Far East.

Harrison, though, when pressurised by the board, had refused to budge, but unlike voting for Chiang to remain during meetings, there wasn't any possibility of excluding Harrison from company business, so his stalling on this occasion scuppered any deal Chiang had to offer. Harrison also believed that Sir John would be just as unwilling to accept any business offer from Chiang, but, unfortunately, the chairman was convalescing at his villa in Tuscany after a long illness. Something else, though, was playing on Harrison's mind. If the stories of Chiang's crime connections were true, would he go beyond the law to get what he wanted, and what was it that Chiang needed so badly from his company?

Harrison gently massaged his forehead as he felt the beginning of a headache move across from his left temple. He saved the program and logged off the computer, giving it time to shut down before folding the screen down onto itself. He then opened the desk drawer to his right and slid the laptop in, before closing it again. He took a set of keys from his trouser pocket, selected the correct one and locked the drawer. He picked up the television remote, pointed it at the screen and pressed the off button, watching as the screen went blank, before replacing the remote back onto the desk. He stood once more and arched his back, stretching the lower muscles as he pushed in his chair. As he took the few steps to the coat stand, he once again glanced out of the window. Large streaks of rain now splattered the glass and he hoped he wouldn't have too long to wait for a cab.

As he opened the door, he turned and had a quick look around. Happy that everything in the office was in order, he switched off the light and went into the hall, closing the door behind him. Carol's empty desk sat to his right. He crouched slightly and put the key into the lock, turning it before trying the door. As only he and Carol had keys to the office, he was confident that no one else could access his office over the weekend.

When it arrived from the upper floors, the lift contained a man and two women, all in their mid-twenties, relaxed and most likely going for an after-work drink. He bade them a good evening and they returned with awkward smiles.

'Is it ground you wish to go to?' the young man asked.

'Please,' he replied.

Harrison moved to the back of the lift. Being six feet four inches tall, he tended to tower over most people, although the young man was just a few inches shorter. Harrison thought back to when he first joined the company twenty-five years previously, not long out of university and about the same age as these three young people. He remembered his first day, arriving full of enthusiasm, working in the city and for the company his father was chairman of.

Harrison senior had punched the hours to push the company to where it was now. He oversaw the flotation onto the London Stock Exchange, and later fought off takeover bids as profits and dividends soared. Sadly, the workload eventually took its toll, because at the age of just sixty-three, his father was found dead, slumped across his office desk after suffering a massive heart attack. The chairman's reins moved to John Warricker, and now fifteen years on, it was Sir John suffering from ill health. To Harrison, Sir John had been his mentor, having worked under him while his father was alive, and although Harrison secretly thought that one day he himself would become chairman, those hopes seemed to be slowly disappearing with the arrival of Lee Chiang.

The lift slowed as it reached the ground and when the doors opened, Harrison allowed the three young people to exit first. They bustled out excitedly, with their voices echoing throughout the marble foyer. Harrison walked slowly across the floor; he said good night to the security personnel and passed through the revolving doors into the night air.

He shivered as he turned up the collar of his coat, searching each pocket for his gloves. A soft, black, lined, leather pair that had been a gift from Natasha a few weeks before her death. As he walked across the square, a coffee shop was closing for the day, with a staff member stacking chairs and wiping tables. Light from inside and soft music drifted outward from the doorway. A fine mist of rain was now falling and people criss-crossed the square, some with umbrellas others increasing their pace to get to wherever they needed to be. Harrison passed under an archway in the far corner of the square, the sound of traffic growing louder as he heard the whine of an engine as a bus left a stop. He stood at the pavement's edge, looking left and then right hoping to see a cab. After a few seconds, one appeared from his right, travelling in the direction he needed to go. He raised his left arm and leaned slightly into the road, waving a gloved hand, but it failed to slow. A second cab appeared, once again from his right, and again it failed to stop.

'This is a lot more difficult than I thought,' he whispered.

The falling rain stung his eyes, while the headlights from the traffic blurred his vision. He tried once more; this time a cab on the opposite side of the road was dropping off a passenger. He checked that the road was clear and ran across, dodging a cyclist without lights and getting a mouthful and a finger in the air for his trouble. A woman had gotten out of the cab and was paying the driver. Harrison waited patiently until she was gone.

'Can you take me to Holland Park?' he asked, watching his breath rise in the cold evening air.

'Sorry, guv, I'm late for a job in Whitechapel. I only took the lady because she was going the same direction,' the driver replied.

Harrison grimaced.

The driver smiled apologetically and added, 'If you only want Holland Park, it's about twenty minutes on the Central Line.'

The driver made a gesture with his finger behind Harrison and down the street. He glanced around to see where the driver was pointing and saw a sign for the underground.

Harrison thanked him.

'No problem,' replied the driver, as he pulled his cab away from the kerb.

In the distance, he could see the glow of the station, the area busy with traffic and people. A large group were huddled under a canopy of a building for shelter along with luggage of various kinds. As Harrison approached, they made a move towards the kerb. He saw a bus or a coach approaching, signalling to stop an express of some kind, its destination showing as Stansted Airport. Ahead of him stood the railway station with its large curved glass roof. He hurried up the few steps to its entrance, where a newspaper hawker handed him a free *Evening Standard*. Harrison couldn't remember when he had last been on the tube or used this station – Liverpool Street.

When he and Natasha had lived on the Downs, he would have got a cab from the office to Paddington, then the train to Billingshurst, before driving the rest of the way to Midhurst.

Now, he would take a cab the short distance to St Johns Wood, or be chauffeur-driven by one of the car companies they used.

From a side street, the driver and passenger of a Volkswagen Transporter van had watched as Harrison spoke to the cab driver. As he walked towards the station, the passenger turned around in his seat and knocked on the panel behind. A few seconds later the rear roller shutter was raised and out jumped a young Oriental woman, wrapped up for the cold, wearing a little backpack with shoulder straps and holding a guidebook of London. A man of similar age and looks immediately followed, carrying a London street map. The two of them could easily have been mistaken for students or tourists. They crossed over the road and, keeping a safe distance, followed Harrison into the station.

As he descended the station's steps, Harrison removed his gloves, took out the cheap mobile phone he had used previously and re-dialled the last number, hearing it picked up on the second ring.

'Hi, it's me,' he said. 'I'm running slightly late. I couldn't get a cab, so I'm using the tube.'

'Okay, see you soon,' came the reply.

He pressed End, putting the phone back into his pocket, and stepped off into the station concourse. It was a vast area, with people hurrying in every direction. As he looked up at the departure board, he saw that trains were departing to towns and cities throughout the country. His eyes darted across the station, before they eventually settled on a sign directing him left for the underground trains, but he needed to buy a ticket, single, and one way.

With ticket in hand, he descended a second escalator, this one almost perpendicular, taking him further underground. A rush of warm air rising hit his face as a train departed a platform. He stepped off the escalator and made his way towards the westbound platform, now full of city workers. Some wore earplugs attached to phones, others flicked through magazines or newspapers and one middle-aged woman stood engrossed in a novel. An electronic sign above the platform displayed the arrival of a train in three minutes, with its destination as Ealing Broadway. Any train travelling west suited Harrison and, as he glanced up at an old station clock suspended from the ceiling by a pair of what seemed like even older chains, its minute hand twitched forward to 6.47 p.m.

The young couple moved swiftly through the station, using their Oyster Cards and keeping Harrison just in view. As they descended into the bowels of the station and before she lost her signal, the woman sent a text message from her mobile phone.

A second rush of warm air preceded the screeching and squealing brakes of the approaching train. Harrison waited until it had completely stopped before choosing which carriage to enter. He took a seat running lengthways along the side of the carriage, while a young Oriental couple sat down facing him, studying a map of London. The woman looked up at him briefly and he politely smiled in return before opening his paper. He went straight to the sports section, as he was attending the autumn rugby international at Twickenham the following day and was looking forward to meeting up with some old rugby pals.

The carriage though, was warm and the rocking momentum, along with the hypnotic rhythm of the track, soon made Harrison sleepy. He closed his eyes and began to drift as the carriage rocked from side to side. There was a sudden jolt as the train slowed on its approach to another station. He opened his eyes and found that the seats opposite were now empty. He spotted the station name, scanned the tube map on the carriage wall and saw that he had only two more stops to go.

The carriage was almost empty, as he went back to his newspaper, flicking through the first few pages, but not absorbing much in concern to the headlines. The one news item which did catch his attention was on page seven of world news. Iran was enraged with Israel over the incursion of two of its naval ships into Iranian territorial waters in the Persian Gulf and the firing of warning shots over an Iranian coastguard boat. The Israeli Government responded, claiming the naval ships were ensuring the safe passage of oil tankers bound for the Jewish state. Harrison was about to read more on the story when the train arrived at his station. He got up from his seat and exited the carriage, rode the escalator up to ground level and walked out onto the road.

It had stopped raining, but as he slipped on his gloves, the cold once more nipped at his face. He turned right from the tube station, passing a row of shops. A dry cleaner's, its lights on and people inside with the smell of warm moist air streaming out through the open doorway. A hairdresser was open late for business, and beside that, a small cosy restaurant with candles on the tables and plenty of diners. As he walked to the pedestrian crossing, traffic flowed more freely, now that the early evening rush was over. Once on the other side, he turned left and then right into a quiet tree-lined street along a carpet of fallen leaves made wet by the rain.

The young couple had boarded the train and sat facing Harrison. When he closed his eyes and after the train had arrived at the next station, they got up from their seats and left the carriage, before re-boarding, but this time in the carriage next to Harrison's. They had an idea of where Harrison would leave the train, but where they sat they would clearly see if he left the train sooner. When Harrison eventually got off at Holland Park, they followed, but again kept a safe distance behind to avoid suspicion. They also walked past the same row of shops that Harrison had, but when they reached the pedestrian crossing, they did not stop to cross; the young woman again removed the mobile phone from her pocket and dialled the same stored number. She spoke a few words into the handset and then ended the call, before the two of them continued walking and disappeared around the next corner.

Harrison continued along a street with elegant three-storey detached houses, many having being built at the turn of the twentieth century, although the majority were now converted to apartments. The white stone buildings had matching garden walls and gate pillars. Black-painted wrought iron railings lined the walls, with the iron twisted a third of the way up and topped with speared tips which set the railings off beautifully. The gates were similar and the gardens were simple and neat, many with shrubs and decorative coloured stones. Others had ornamental matching trees still small enough to remain in their pots. He noticed the expensive cars parked at the kerb on either side keeping in line with this up-market part of west London, and apart from an elderly Oriental woman walking her small dog, the street was empty of people. Approximately halfway down on the left he found the house. The gate, in need of some oil on its hinge, creaked slightly as he opened it. He walked up the short-flagged path with low-level lighting, pressed the fifth button on the intercom system and looked up at the security camera angled down at him. When the door buzzed, he pushed it open and stepped inside, with it swinging shut behind him. The woman with the little dog watched as he entered, before she continued with her walk.

The building's interior was warm, brightly painted and smelt of fresh timber. There was an entrance hall with four doors, two on either side of the corridor. To his left sat a wooden staircase, highly polished with a mahogany banister. He climbed the first three steps before making a sweeping right turn and continued up to the first floor landing. Ahead of him stood the door with a number five upon it. He took off his gloves and gave the door a gentle knock. After a few seconds, a shadow drew over the peephole sitting within the door two-thirds of the way up. The door opened slowly inwards, by an attractive woman of average height. She was the wrong side of thirty, closer to thirty-five or maybe older, but with an hourglass figure, and auburn hair tied back which showed off her sculptured face. The woman was wearing a black lingerie lace top with shoulder straps and matching thong with her cleavage heavily exposed, while her erect nipples pushed the lace away from her breasts.

She smiled when she saw Harrison, and said, 'Good evening, David.'

Chapter 2

Harrison stepped over the threshold and closed the door. He knew the woman as Leila and he followed her along the warm, bright hallway that smelled of fresh cotton and was neatly decorated with prints of a New York skyline. She led him to a huge room off to the right with ambient lighting, containing an Italian chestnut three-seat leather sofa and a low-slung teak coffee table, which sat upon a geometric weaved rug. A large gold leaf-framed mirror hung on the wall above the sofa and underfoot the wooden floor was solid and polished. To Harrison's right sat a bed larger than a double but not a king, covered with a red and white duvet along with matching pillows and cushions, and positioned in the centre of the bed, laid out flat, was a large white towel. The curtains that ran almost from ceiling to floor were drawn and taking centre stage, hanging from the ceiling at either end of the room, were two small crystal chandeliers.

'Would you like a drink, David?' she asked.

'Please, Scotch and a little water.'

Leila smiled. 'I was able to find the… what is it you say, malt?'

Harrison stared at her. 'Glen Mhor?'

She nodded and removed the bottle from a sideboard, unscrewing the lid and pouring a little into a crystal tumbler, before opening a small bottle of Scottish spring water and adding some to the glass, then walking seductively towards Harrison, handing him the glass and kissing him gently on the cheek. The routine was the same. He received the drink, she kissed him and then he removed an envelope from his inside pocket, which she took gracefully.

Leila turned towards the door. 'Take time with your Scotch, David, I shall return shortly.'

Harrison watched as she left the room. Leila was around five feet eight inches tall and their first meeting had been by chance. Two months previously, he had been having dinner with clients in a plush West End restaurant, when he paid a visit to the rest room and on his way back almost knocked over a beautiful woman in the lounge. Slightly shaken, he insisted she sat down while he brought her a drink. The woman stated that she was due to meet someone for dinner, but they had failed to show. The woman had captivated Harrison, so he handed her his card. She then returned with one of her own. He was, though, somewhat puzzled, as the only print on the card was that of the woman's name – Leila, a website and, below, a telephone number. When he returned home later that evening, he typed the web address into his browser and saw an even more attractive and scantily dressed Leila staring back at him from his computer screen.

The Scotch was good. Glen Mhor 1980. A single Highland Malt, which cost over £100 a bottle, and from a Scottish distillery that now no longer existed. Leila was high class: she enjoyed a luxurious lifestyle and, at £250 per hour for her escort services, she needed to provide such a service. This was Harrison's fifth visit, his first meeting with Leila being a two-hour dinner date and then one hour alone with her in this luxurious apartment, that had set him back £750. An extravagance yes, but on a salary of £1.2 million per year it was one he could afford. Leila was also a listener, but Harrison knew she was careful not to ask too many questions, when at times he spilled out problems about his work. Although Leila knew the type of business he was in, she did not know the name of his company and, as such, the discreet liaison was even more appealing.

Harrison took off his coat and sat on the edge of the bed. When Leila returned, she was still wearing her lingerie top, with her hair now down around her shoulders, but minus her thong. He felt a tightening in his groin. Leila, he thought, born of the night. He had searched the meaning of her name. Her dark hair, eyes and olive skin had lived up to such a definition. From what Leila had told him she was aged thirty-eight, born in the Middle East, but had not divulged the exact location of her birth, and Harrison, being the true gent, had not pushed.

Leila sat astride him, loosening his tie and unbuttoning his shirt. He moved his hand down and gently caressed his fingers between her legs. Finding her warm and wet, she released a gentle moan. She delicately and sensually slid her hands across his chest, bending down, kissing him on the lips and sliding her silky tongue into his mouth. With quick movement, she undid his belt, lowering her head and brushing her hair against his chest as she unzipped the fastener with her teeth. She reached in, taking out his erection, and began slow movements with her tongue up and down the length of his shaft. She took him in hand, opened her mouth, pursing her lips around him before he slowly disappeared inside. Harrison, flat on his back, felt all the tension from his life leaving him. He found comfort in these surroundings. Did he feel guilty after these meetings with Leila? The first time yes, the second slightly, but by his third visit any guilt that he had felt was gone.

She removed Harrison's trousers and shorts, taking a bottle of oil from a small bedside table as he rolled onto his front. She poured some of the oil onto his shoulders and upper back, working it into his muscles. He let out a relaxed sigh as she massaged the oil into his skin, slowly moving from the back of his neck along his shoulder blades, then down into the small of his back, gently pressing before working her fingers into his backside. Harrison, fully relaxed, felt sleepy. It had been too long since he last felt like this. Sliding her hand beneath him, she cupped his balls gently massaging them. When she was finished, he rolled once more onto his back with Leila hovering above him. She again took hold of his erection, unrolled a condom over the top of it, before guiding him underneath as he gently slipped inside her. She lifted her top, pulling it over her head, exposing her fully erect nipples. Harrison pinched both, before lightly caressing each breast with his hands. She began slow, gentle movements on top of him, and with the room warm, little beads of perspiration began to appear on her chest. She leaned forward, kissing Harrison full on the lips, before he pulled her down, slipping one of her breasts into his mouth while suckling on the ripe erect nipple. As the momentum between them quickened and their bodies gyrated together, Leila squealed with pleasure, as Harrison, unable to hold back any longer, exploded inside her.

As their movements gradually slowed, Leila, pushing the hair away from the front of her face, rested her head on Harrison's chest, closing her eyes. He lifted a hand and began stroking the top of her head, feeling happy and contented. She raised herself up on one elbow and with the tip of a finger drew a figure of eight along his chest, curling the hairs around it.

'How was your week, David?' she asked.

'Where shall I begin?' he sighed.

'The beginning is always good.' She smiled.

Harrison chuckled at the humour. He adored her accented English and how she genuinely appeared interested in him. He felt somehow compelled to engage in this pillow talk, as if, once unburdened, his troubles would disappear.

'Poor David,' she purred, after he had finished, stroking his cheek with her warm, soft hand, her body smelling fresh and clean but absent of scent. 'Rest, David, while I shower,' she said.

Harrison smiled and nodded. He yawned and, with his eyelids heavy, he soon floated away.

He woke with a start, not knowing how long he had been asleep, but the clock on the bedside table told him that it had only been for a short while. He got off the bed, stretched and reached for his shorts. He stood bare-chested, seeing his reflection in the mirror, and pulled in his stomach. He was still reasonably fit and his weight had only increased by a few pounds since his mid-twenties. He got dressed, straightened his tie, and again used the cheap mobile phone to order his minicab, one for the usual pick-up point, the corner of the next street and only a two-minute walk away. The apartment, though, seemed uncannily quiet. He opened the door and stepped into the hall.

Leila appeared barefoot from the bathroom, wrapped in a cream towel, showing a little cleavage, with her hair straight and wet.

Harrison smiled, as beautiful as ever. 'I've ordered my cab,' he said.

She walked up to him, stood on tiptoes and kissed him on the cheek. 'I hope we will see each other again soon, David.'

'I'm sure we will,' he replied.

Harrison opened the door, pulling it closed behind him, hearing the snib move across the lock, as he trotted down the stairs. On the ground floor, he opened the front door and once more stepped out into the night. It was colder now, though the rain from earlier had cleared. A light frost had formed, glistening on the path towards the gate. He carefully retraced his steps out onto the pavement, turned right and began walking towards the next corner. A few of the parked cars from earlier had gone and the street remained deserted of people. On the opposite side of the road, parked a few yards up on the left, sat a white box van, with livery on its side advertising a laundry in Soho. In the distance, Harrison could hear the hum of traffic on the main road, but apart from that, it was quiet and he was alone.

The four male occupants of the white van watched as Harrison had exited Leila's apartment. Each of the four wore dark boiler suits zipped to the neck with ski masks covering their faces, and only their eyes, nose and mouth visible. Quickly and silently, three of the men exited the van. They moved stealthily across the wet tarmac, gym plimsolls on their feet, making ground on Harrison without a sound, one of them carrying a long black police-type baton. When he was almost upon Harrison, he swung the bat low, as if on centre court at Wimbledon, returning the ball with a backhand, a sweeping shot across the body.

Harrison, suddenly aware of someone or something behind him, stopped to turn around, but in that millisecond of thought, he was hit hard across the back of his knees. His legs crumpled and he lurched forward, grappling at thin air, landing hard on his shoulder. Someone grabbed his wrists and held them high above his head, while another took hold of his legs. He tried to kick himself free, but the hold was firm. He opened his mouth to yell, but someone put a gloved hand over it. Harrison, wide eyed, with his pulse racing, could only make out silhouetted figures. A mugging: let them take what they want and then seek help, he thought. He tried to relax and close his mouth, but now he was being prevented from doing so.

In the faint light, Harrison could make out one of his attackers holding a syringe. He tensed once more, struggled and tried to move his head. Whoever these people were, robbery was not what interested them. He prepared himself for the needle as the syringe entered his mouth, but it didn't contain one, and all Harrison felt was a cold odourless and tasteless liquid squirted into the back of his mouth then trickling down into his throat. He tried to prevent himself from swallowing, but it was impossible.

The driver of the van slowly moved it parallel with Harrison. Once the three attackers were satisfied that he had swallowed the liquid, they left him on the pavement and climbed into the van. The vehicle then drove slowly away to avoid suspicion. The address on its side was of a non-existent street number in Gerrard Place, Soho, and the telephone number would have got the caller through to an empty warehouse fifty miles away in Chelmsford, Essex. The vehicle registration number belonged to a seventy-two-year-old man from Aberdeen, who died four weeks previously, when his Jaguar car was involved in a collision with a tractor on the A90, Forfar Road, three miles from his home.

Harrison rolled onto his side. He was cold and wet. He used a nearby tree as a crutch to support himself as he slowly and unsteadily tried to stand. Vehicle headlights suddenly turned into the street and he wondered if it was his minicab. He staggered a few yards with his mouth now dry and his head throbbing, as the world around him spun. He had trouble putting one foot in front of the other as his legs abruptly turned to jelly. His breathing was laboured, and now he could hardly get a breath. A sharp pain stabbed his chest. He slumped against a parked car. 'I must keep moving,' he told himself. It took all his strength to do so. The vehicle had stopped two hundred yards away and he was just able to make out a taxi sign on its roof. 'I must get help,' he said, his voice now not much more than a strained whisper. He fumbled at his coat for his mobile phone, but a second sharp pain stung his chest, this time a terrifying one, forcing him down onto his knees. He dropped the phone and tried to reach it, but couldn't move, before he fell against the wing of the parked car, sliding onto the ground. The phone on the pavement began to vibrate, its ringtone silenced, but the light on its small screen flashing. It was the minicab company. The phone continued to pulse, like a heartbeat, whereas his own was now becoming irregular. He closed his eyes, finding the vibrating sound from the phone soothing. It began to fade as Harrison gradually became unaware of his surroundings. The darkness behind his eyes slowly brightened as he began to feel a deep warmth. A figure appeared in front of him, hazy at first, before becoming clearer and more solid. It held out its hand and he felt compelled to take it. It was a woman's hand, her smiling face lit up with a halo of light behind. He felt himself reaching out to her. 'Natasha,' he managed to say, as his spirit departed his body.

One of Harrison's attackers pressed the number nine on his mobile phone three times: an emergency number. He asked the operator to send an ambulance to the corner of Holland Court and Netherby Way, as he believed a man to be suffering a heart attack. Due to the amount of poison administered to him, the caller knew that by the time the paramedics arrived, Harrison would be dead. The poison was sufficient to bring on a cardiac arrest, similar to a technique carried out by intelligence services throughout the world. The victim would appear to die of natural causes, but any autopsy would fail to record foul play.

The man cancelled the call and dialled a second number, one stored on the mobile phone. When the call was answered, he spoke three words: 'It is done,' and terminated the call. He clipped off the back of the phone, taking out the battery and slipping out the small sim card, snapped it in two before throwing half out of the window. He then replaced the battery and its cover. When the van had driven a further half mile, he dropped the second part of the sim out of the window. Once the driver reached the main road, he turned left, taking them towards the M4. Fifteen minutes later he turned anti-clockwise onto the M25, following a path south of Heathrow Airport to an industrial estate outside Staines. There he parked the van inside an empty warehouse before switching vehicles and the four of them returned to London in a dark Toyota Avensis.

The man had taken the call at his desk in a small second-floor office. He wrote the message on a slip of cigarette paper using a pen with a very fine nib. He then took a cigar from its tube and rolled the paper around it, before replacing the cigar and screwing on its tiny lid. He handed the cigar tube to the young woman patiently waiting, who put it securely inside her jacket and left the room. The young woman descended the narrow staircase onto the street below, one full of London theatregoers and diners from nearby Leicester Square. She began walking the few hundred yards for delivery and shivered with the cold, wishing she had brought her scarf. The aroma of cooked meats and spices hung in the air and close by was the Pailou, a type of arch, which stood at either end of the street and which was a focal point of Chinatowns throughout the world. The young woman continued until she was almost upon the structure, before peeling off left into the doorway of a plush restaurant. She nodded at the maître'd and continued towards the rear of the almost full dining room until she reached a door marked for restrooms. The door opened onto a stairway leading down into the basement. She did not care much for being underground as she found the whole experience claustrophobic. The male and female restrooms were ahead of her, but a short corridor to her right led to a similar-looking door.

When she gave the door a gentle knock, it was opened inwards by a young Oriental man in a dark suit. He pointed to a table in the centre of the smoked-filled room; it was the only one occupied, covered with white linen, and upon it sat the remains of a meal, which the two seated men had finished. She saw a waiter standing at a hatch in the far wall putting dishes onto a dumb-waiter. When the young woman approached the table, she handed the little cigar tube to the suited man to her left. The man to her right was overweight and of Middle Eastern origin. Iranian, she believed. However, that didn't prevent him from enjoying a Western lifestyle.

She felt his eyes crawl over her skin as the man to her left unscrewed the tube and tipped the cigar onto the table. He unrolled the cigarette paper, turning it slightly to the light, before a faint smile slowly appeared on his lips. He nodded for the young woman to leave, which she did without much hesitation. The man dipped an edge of the paper into a lighted candle, allowing it to burn, before dropping it into the ashtray. He took a cutter from his pocket and sliced an end off the cigar before lifting the candle to it. When he was happy the cigar was alight, he blew a puff of smoke into the air.

'Cuban. Bolivar number one, possibly the finest cigar you can buy, Mr Shakiba,' he said.

'Good news, Mr Chiang?'

Chiang inhaled deeply on the cigar, before blowing out rings of smoke and watching as they rose slowly towards the ceiling. After a short pause, he replied, ‘It appears our little problem has been resolved.’

Chapter 3

One month later

Mickey Ross waited until the man climbed into the passenger seat of the Renault van. The driver didn't waste much time in accelerating away along the narrow residential street, almost before his passenger had securely closed the door. Mickey had snapped a few photographs of the man as he waited and one as he got into the van, then another of its number plate. He slipped his London black cab into drive, checked his mirrors, indicated and pulled out onto the street. The van thirty yards in front barely slowed as it coasted the speed ramps around the south London streets close to Charlton Athletic football ground. Mickey followed, as the van turned left on to Woolwich Road, now crammed with Friday morning commuters travelling towards Greenwich. The nondescript white van was a Transit type with roof bars, although this morning one would have had difficulty knowing its colour as it was masked by a film of road dirt and grime. Added to that, on one of its barn doors some wag had scrawled, *I wish my girl was this dirty.*

The traffic bottlenecked near Deptford, as drivers jockeyed for position on the approach to the Rotherhithe tunnel. Mickey, feeling slightly exposed, decided to create a little space between himself and his quarry, so, dropping back slightly, he allowed a small car to filter in front of him.

The two men in the van were not hardened criminals, but Mickey, as a private investigator among other things, had been hired by a local authority to check out the passenger of the van, a Mr Ainsley Taylor, who they believed to be a benefits cheat. Taylor's circumstances did not concern Mickey; he just needed to provide evidence that Taylor was in fact working. As of yet, all Mickey had were a few photographs of Taylor at the front of his house and of him hopping into the van: not enough for his client to build a case against him.

At a set of traffic lights, the van turned right towards Surrey Water, but the little Ford Fiesta in front of Mickey stalled and became caught on amber. He cursed as he watched the van disappear around the side of a London bus and away from view. Mickey waited until the lights changed back to green, before following the path of the van, hoping somewhere to pick up a clue to its destination. A few building sites occupied Surrey Quays and he was sure that the van would end up at one of those sites. Mickey, now parallel with the Thames, glanced across to the Isle of Dogs and the high-rises of Canary Wharf, a place where not that long ago he once worked.

It was only by coincidence, as he passed by a filling station, that he eyed a dirty white van parked on its forecourt. He found an old gated entrance a few yards further along, pulled in and stopped. It could have been any white van among the thousands in London, but keeping an eye on his rear-view mirror, he watched as a few minutes later the van left the station forecourt and sped past him. He did a quick check of its number plate and whispered, 'Got you.'

The van made a right turn into Grove Street, leading down to the banks of the river. Ahead of them, Mickey spotted a tall yellow tower crane with its jib stationary, hanging out over the water's edge. The van slowed as it approached a stretch of wooden hoarding, bumping up onto the kerb as it came to a stop. Mickey slowed and parked a little further back, picking up his digital camera with zoom lens from the passenger seat. The driver of the van climbed out first, a tallish man in jeans wearing a hard hat and high-vis vest. Taylor then followed from the passenger side, similarly dressed as the driver and appearing to be ready for a day's work.

Mickey snapped away, hearing the click, click, as the camera recorded the men entering the building site.

'Nice one, Ainsley, you weren't wearing those when you left the house,' he said. Happy with his shots, Mickey sent the photographs by Bluetooth to his smart phone, before attaching them to an email and then forwarding the file to his contact in social services.

'Another cheque in the post,' Mickey said, as he swung his cab around, making his way north towards Euston station.

The sudden blast of the horn woke him.

'C'mon, Mickey! Wakey! Wakey!' It was Kevin the driver sitting behind. 'Who are you this morning, mate, Alan Sugar, Sherlock Holmes, or a cab driver?'

'You're a card, Kev,' replied Mickey.

'Put her in gear, mate, we'll make a cabbie out of you yet. There's a couple of trains in shortly; maybe it'll get both of us away,' added Kevin.

Mickey had dozed off after his early morning exploits around south London, but now he slipped his cab into gear, cruised forward and narrowed the gap to the cab in front. Mickey Ross was thirty-three and a little under six feet tall. To Mickey, the little was extremely important to him: he was, in fact, just under half an inch below six feet and over the years he had used various ways of measuring himself. Now, he had gotten used to the fact that he just missed out on the magical figure six, or maybe was just resigned to it.

Outside, it was a few degrees above freezing, a crisp and clear bright morning, with London gearing up for the festive season. Mickey, having drunk a few cups of tea since his early start, found that his bladder was beginning to suffer.

'Hey, Kev!' he shouted, 'I'm nipping to the toilet!'

'You better be quick, old son, or I'll drive around you.'

'Now, Kev, you Hammers know your place,' Mickey shot back.

'Piss off!' he mouthed, still stinging after Mickey's team Spurs had beaten West Ham the previous week.

The drivers' room was close to the taxi rank, a Portakabin that sat separate from the station. It was a durable one-piece construction, grey in colour and made from galvanised steel, which offered protection against any extreme weather. Roughly thirty feet in length and ten feet wide, it contained a kitchen with running water, a kettle for making hot drinks and a microwave oven for food. A short corridor ran off to the left leading to the toilets. In these days of equality there needed to be two separate doors, one for men and the other for women. The gents were empty. As soon as he closed the door, his phone rang. The caller ID showed an unknown number so he cancelled the call. As he stood at the urinal his phone rang again; this time he answered, but a little abruptly, touching the Bluetooth in his ear.

'Hello, am I speaking with Michael Ross?' a pleasant female voice enquired.

'Who is calling?' replied Mickey, now feeling slightly embarrassed at having answered so sharply.

'I have some work for a private investigator.'

Mickey sought business through word of mouth and with cards he handed out to passengers that he picked up in his cab. Private investigating was a skill he acquired from his student days at Cambridge, and driving the London black taxi suited his cover. Mickey Ross, cab driver, former city analyst and private investigator. It was usually at this point the caller asked if he was any good. He generally tailed unfaithful spouses, benefit cheats such as earlier that morning, and snapped a few photographs before filing his report.

'Is it convenient to talk?' the caller asked.

Mickey looked down at what he was doing and, trying to keep the smile from his voice, answered, 'I'm in the middle of something right now, would it be possible to call you back?'

'Okay,' she replied. 'I'll text my number to you; it's not the one I'm currently calling you from.'

'You didn't give me your name?' Mickey asked.

'It's Lauren King,' she replied.

Mickey had left the sleepy Cornish fishing village of Portreath in his late teens after securing a place at Cambridge on an economics course, by scoring top grades at school. It was at Cambridge that he met Sophie, a law student, and they stayed together throughout their time at university. They were both in their mid-twenties by the time they graduated and while Mickey was hired by a large American investment bank as an analyst and trainee Forex trader in Canary Wharf, Sophie began working in commercial law in the city. It wasn't long before Mickey was earning a substantial salary, enough to clear the mortgage on the house that he had purchased in Woodford, North London. It was an ideal location, typically suburbia. Life was good, the money better, but, having a sensible head on his shoulders, he still saved more than what he spent, unlike Sophie. As an analyst, Mickey monitored other financial institutions such as banks and he was beginning to see that figures from some of those banks did not add up.

He sensed a storm approaching, but not on a par with what was about to strike. He advised Sophie to curb her spending, but Sophie being Sophie, told him to quit worrying and to enjoy life.

'You're such a stick in the mud, Michael!' she scolded.

It was a pity that Mickey hadn't shown the same concern regarding his own employers.

On a pleasant morning in the middle of September 2008, Mickey took his normal route to the tube station and boarded the same train that he had done for the previous four years. He exited Canary Wharf station and arrived at the office block where he worked, only to be greeted by a mass of employees who had been denied entry to the building. People were standing around in confusion, until a few of them shouted and pointed to the electronic ticker wrapped like a ribbon around the outside of the Thompson Reuters building, because stuttering across in red letters and for the whole of the world to see, was the news that Lehman Brothers had filed for bankruptcy.

From Euston, Mickey got a short run to Whitehall, and, remembering the phone call from earlier, pulled into Charing Cross Station and checked his phone, finding an unread message.

Hi, Michael, please ring me on this number when you are free to do so, regards Lauren.

He saved the number, edited Lauren's name as the contact, and dialled. The phone rang five or six times and he was about to cancel the call or expecting it to go to voice mail when it was answered.

'Am I speaking with Lauren?' he asked.

'Who is calling?' she replied.

'It's Michael Ross.'

'Michael Ross?' She hesitated, trying to remember: a woman who, dealt daily with many people. 'Oh, Michael. Yes. Sorry. Thank you for returning my call,' she replied softly.

'You said I could help you with a little PI work,' he prompted.

'Yes, again I am sorry. This may seem very cloak and dagger, but can we meet?'

Mickey required more information, so he pushed, 'Would this be a marital issue, Lauren?'

'No, no, Michael, it's nothing like that,' she replied. Hearing the smile in her voice, Mickey said, 'Sorry, but I had to ask.'

'Of course you did. The issue at hand is more, sort of business related,' she said.

'A large or small business?'

'Large, in fact it's listed on the Stock Exchange.'

'If there's a problem with fraud or insider dealing then it would be better to contact the Stock Exchange direct,' he offered.

'I had thought of that,' she said, 'and the other regulatory bodies that are in the city, but, I don't have any hard evidence.'

Mickey knew about that and he knew how it worked: you needed to supply the Stock Exchange with reams and reams of information, before they would even consider possible abuse.

'I understand you are a former city boy,' she said.

'I was an analyst at Lehman's,' he returned.

Mickey switched off the cab's engine and listened. There was little if any background noise, not even a slight echo. Lauren could have been in the sitting room of her home, or in a carpeted suite high in the sky in some office block or other.

Now intrigued, Mickey asked, 'When would you like to meet?'

There was a short pause before she spoke, this time closer into the handset and slightly quieter. 'There will be movement on this company on Monday, Michael. So, if it is suitable for you, I would like to arrange a meeting tomorrow, Saturday.'

Spurs were at Newcastle, but he didn't fancy the long journey to the northeast.

'Tomorrow suits me fine,' he said. 'Have you a place in mind?'

'I'll be at Il Divo wine bar in Covent Garden at one p.m.,' she said firmly.

'One p.m., Covent Garden, Il Divo, got that,' he replied.

'See you then.'

Before he could say anything else, she ended the call. But how would he recognise her? Would she be wearing a strange hat or standing holding a bunch of flowers? He discounted both thoughts almost immediately and decided he would wait until he arrived at Covent Garden.

Chapter 4

Friday morning turned to afternoon with the sky above an ominous shade of grey. The cold wind had strengthened and the threat of snow was in the air. At around five p.m. Mickey took his final fare of the day. He followed the line of the river and left central London with his two passengers, travelling the thirty-minute journey to the city airport at Docklands. Ahead of him stood the metropolis of Canary Wharf on Canada Square, with its pyramid glass roof and flashing beacon that warned off any straying aircraft. On either side and standing almost as tall were its neighbours HSBC and Citibank, with Barclays just behind. Together, these four huge monoliths towered over the rest of the development on the Isle of Dogs and stood as if sentinels lit up against the night sky, guarding the eastern approach to the city.

It reminded Mickey of his final day at Lehman's. He and the rest of his fellow workers were eventually allowed into the building and escorted up to their desks to collect any belongings that they may have kept there. Each of them was handed a flattened cardboard box, which once made up wasn't much larger than one that came with a pair of shoes. Mickey didn't keep much in the way of personal stuff at work. On his desk, he had a little globe of the world that he would sometimes spin during brief moments of boredom or frustration, and, beside it, a miniature detachable plastic model of a British Airways Concorde that had been a gift from a client. On his desk partition, he had stuck a few photographs of nights out at the pub from his university days, and one of him and the guys from his floor here at Lehman's, after a team-building paintballing event in Waltham Forest.

He heard a sniffle and looked up to see a female colleague he vaguely knew as Dana or Donna at another cubicle in tears, filling her box and more with enough items that would have covered a market stall. Mickey decided he could carry or shove his belongings into his coat, so he ditched the box.

Outside, as he crossed the concourse, he stopped and looked up at those same four buildings in Canary Wharf, feeling suddenly dizzy and nauseous, as if someone had sucked all the air from the atmosphere. Added to that, the world's media had arrived, along with a dozen or so paparazzi photographers, snapping at the now former employees of Lehman Brothers. Satellite television vans were parked haphazardly, with dishes aimed at the sky and reporters with microphones in hand, preparing for a live feed to the studio and poised for the inevitable, 'Bob, behind me you can see…'

He was unable to venture underground for a train, but Mickey desperately needed to get away from the madness and take the quickest route out of Dodge. He hailed a passing cab and jumped in the back.

'Where to guv?' the driver asked.

'Eh…? Somewhere towards St Paul's, please,' he replied, off the top of his head.

A soothing piece of classical music trickled from the cab's speakers and in that solitary moment of thought, Mickey decided that he couldn't go back and that he wouldn't ever again seek employment with another bank or financial institution. He sat back in his seat, closed his eyes, breathed out and smiled.

When he eventually gathered his thoughts, Mickey asked the driver to drop him at a pub in Whitechapel instead. It wasn't the most inviting of establishments, more of a spit and sawdust kind of place, but Mickey wasn't fussy and after that morning's shenanigans, he was in need of a drink. He went inside, took a stool at the counter and ordered a pint.

Across the room, two lads in their early twenties were playing pool, with one balancing a pint precariously on the edge of the table.

'If that pint spills on that table, I'll shove that cue up your arse!' the barman barked.

The two lads laughed, one lifting the pint, while the other gave the barman the finger.

'Bloody kids,' the barman said to Mickey, wiping the bar counter. 'In here every day, couldn't tell you the last day's work they ever did.'

Mickey took a mouthful and smiled. 'This is good beer,' he said.

The barman, a tall broad man in his sixties, looked at him quizzically and asked, 'Son, are you lost?'

Mickey laughed. 'No, why do you ask?'

'It's the way you're dressed; we don't normally get you city lot in here.'

On a ledge, high in the corner of the room sat an old portable television, tuned to a news channel with its volume set low. A female reporter was delivering her piece from outside Lehman Brothers.

'I just got canned,' Mickey said, nodding at the television.

'No shit!' replied the barman, pouring another pint and sitting it on the counter. 'On the 'ouse, mate.'

'Cheers.'

On his way home, Mickey phoned Sophie. She was initially shocked and offered some sympathy, but it wasn't long before she asked, 'What will our friends say?'

'Stuff our friends,' Mickey slurred. 'They're your friends anyway, not mine.'

'Have you been drinking, Michael?'

'I've had a few.'

Sophie sighed. 'You can get another job in the city, can't you?'

'We'll see,' he replied, and ended the call.

For the next few weeks, Mickey traded his own personal account. He traded technically, reading the charts, avoiding fundamental news releases and macro-economic data. He would get up at six a.m. and check for any major geopolitical stories that had developed in Asia or the Far East overnight, and how, if at all, they would affect the stock markets of Europe and the United States. Wall Street and the German DAX were heading south and across the world commodities were continuing to slide lower.

Before long, he began to get cabin fever and Mickey knew he needed a new challenge. It was during a liquid lunch one afternoon with a few former city pals that one of them happened to mention he was learning The Knowledge, to be a London cabbie. Mickey listened and afterwards decided to enquire further into it, and maybe rekindle an old passion of his, a little private investigating.

Sophie was horrified at the thought of Mickey driving a black taxi, believing it was beneath him. He retorted by suggesting that maybe she thought it was beneath her.

He pinned a street map of London to a wall in the kitchen and each morning while having breakfast he'd sit and study it. He bought a second-hand motorcycle to learn the streets from a bloke in Tower Hamlets, a red Honda 100cc, £200, and a bargain. For an extra tenner the guy threw in a full-face and slightly battered helmet, though Mickey didn't know how good it would have been if he had gone head first into a bus.

At weekends, he would rise early and whilst the roads were quiet use his mountain bike. Mickey was amazed at what he saw and learnt when he lifted his head, now being a resident tourist in London. He jotted down street names, calculated routes, fascinated by the amount of side streets and alleyways with bizarre and historical names, such as Adam and Eve Court, Hanging Sword Alley, and Swallow Place and Passage.

It was after one of these trips, and while they were having coffee in the kitchen, that Sophie asked, 'Are you really going to do this, Michael?'

'Yes, Sophie, I am,' he replied.

'If you want a job there are any amount of companies in the city looking for your experience. You'll not earn that kind of money being a taxi driver.'

'I've had my time in the city, Sophie, and I don't want to go back to the stresses of it all again, and, to be honest, I'm quite enjoying my freedom. Anyway, there's always your salary.'

'But that's my money!' she shouted. 'I don't want a dirty old taxi sitting in our driveway!'

'It won't be dirty and it won't be old.'

'It won't be there at all, because if it is I won't!' she screamed, storming out of the kitchen.

'Fine,' Mickey whispered, sipping his coffee, 'you know where the door is.'

Two years after he started, and on a hot day in July, Mickey passed his final exam. He was now officially a London black taxi driver. Two days after that, he bought a black cab and parked in the driveway, before meeting a mate for a drink in Spitalfields, close to the financial district of the city, shortly after six p.m., just around the time that Sophie would be returning home from work. It wasn't long before he got the inevitable text message from her.

'*There's a taxi in the driveway*!' she said.

'*I bet it looks well beside the Jag*,' he replied.

Sophie owned a new Salsa Red F type V8 Jaguar convertible, a gift from her daddy, which went with her lipstick, apparently. The cost? £79,950. She only had to pay the £2500 fully comprehensive insurance each year; but Sophie enjoyed her comfort, and refused point blankly to use the tube or buses, as she complained they were full of smelly people invading her space. Maybe it also had to do with her law firm owning a shed load of parking spaces in Middle Temple, close to the Victoria Embankment. Sophie also drove most weekends to visit her parents in Sevenoaks or One-oak, as Mickey often teased, after six of the famous oaks toppled during the great autumn storm of 1987.

When he arrived home a few hours later, slightly worse for wear, Mickey discovered that the Salsa Red F Type V8 Jaguar convertible with matching lipstick wasn't parked beside his London black taxi. Then again, he didn't expect to see Sophie's house keys on the doormat and on closer inspection neither did he believe that her three wardrobes and two chests of drawers would be empty, probably courtesy of a Stobart truck.

He went into the kitchen, opened the fridge and took out a beer. He flipped the lid, taking a long slug and toasted Sophie. He picked up the *Evening Standard* and opened the patio doors. It was a beautiful warm evening and, with the birds chirping in the background, he began leafing through the newspaper to the want ads. He soon found what he was looking for, because next day Lucy moved in. She needed a new home and came with a collar and lead, a couple of bowls and a few tins of dog food.

Mickey dropped his fare at London City Airport and handed his passengers a card for any return journey, before swinging his cab around and heading for home. He flicked his wipers on, as a heavy sleet shower engulfed the city. Close to home, he stopped for a takeaway and a couple of beers, before giving a passing thought to the following day's meeting with the mysterious Lauren.

Chapter 5

Saturday morning began with his usual six a.m. alarm call. The patter of feet on the stairs, the bedroom door being nosed opened and then the leap onto the bed, before a sniff and finally a wet tongue on his face. Who needs an alarm clock when you have a five-year-old West Highland Terrier?

'Okay, okay, Lucy,' Mickey surrendered, throwing back the covers and flinging his feet onto the floor. He put on his slippers and peeked through the blinds. Outside the cul-de-sac was quiet and although it wouldn't be light for another hour or so, somewhere on a leafless tree, a brave little bird was clearing its throat. Mickey used the bathroom and got rid of his bed-head while Lucy played hide and seek on the stairs. He slipped on a dressing gown and went downstairs, with Lucy the more energetic following behind, then bounding across the hall at the bottom of the stairs and beating him to the kitchen, before pawing at the patio doors.

'Braver girl than me, Lucy,' Mickey said, as she ran outside and squatted on the grass. The overnight rain had gone, but the early morning air was cold and crisp. In the distance, he heard the faint sound of a train, and while Lucy nosed in the undergrowth, he closed the door and filled the kettle.

Whilst the water boiled, he switched on the television, one he had fixed to a wall at the far end of the kitchen, and tuned it to a financial news channel. It was just after two p.m. in Hong Kong and the female anchor was discussing with an economist in Beijing the rumblings of poor economic figures out of China. The report was due on Monday and any downturn could negatively affect world markets.

When the kettle boiled, Mickey brewed a pot of tea as Lucy scraped at the door. The news ticker showed that commodities were down and Wall Street had fallen lower before the previous evening's close. Oil had been steady, but in the final hour had fallen by 2.5%.

He went to the fridge. 'Damn! No milk this morning, Lucy,' he sighed.

A fall in Chinese output could be detrimental to the worldwide economy, but Mickey was surprised that oil was down by such an amount in the final hour of trading.

After he gave Lucy her breakfast, he took her for a walk to the nearby park and as they were alone, allowed her to roam off the lead. He was meeting Lauren at one, and as the sun began to peak above the horizon with the clouds pink marshmallows in a mackerel sky, he began to think about what to ask her and reminded himself to bring a notebook, one that would fit neatly into the inside pocket of his coat.

It was at Cambridge that Mickey, while reading one of the university newspapers, spotted a vacancy for a trainee private investigator. It was a small advertisement tucked away at the bottom of one of the pages, as if it didn't want to be found. He needed the extra cash and thought it would be a bit of fun, so he phoned the number and the man who answered asked if he could come along to his office that very afternoon. The three-storey eighteenth century building was on a curve in a narrow cobbled pedestrian street. A little sign above the doorway with Bridge Private Investigators upon it, directed Mickey to a rickety staircase with threadbare carpet that led him to the first floor, where an old fluorescent tube blinked from the ceiling as he reached the top of the stairs. He tapped on the half-glass door, opened it and was greeted by a short, round, middle-aged man with a beaming smile. He vigorously shook Mickey's hand, asked him a few questions and five minutes later offered him the job. The salary was average, but it helped.

One of his first jobs was to investigate a lecturer whose wife thought he was shagging a student. She turned out to be correct, except the student in question was male. Mickey worked casually as a private investigator throughout his years at Cambridge and missed it when he graduated.

On their way home, Mickey remembered to buy milk, stopping at the local newsagents and adding a copy of the *Daily Telegraph,* which Lucy carried home in her mouth. He made another brew, took some cereal and read the paper. The business section mentioned the previous day's jitters on Wall Street, but nothing momentous. There was also an article on a UK technology firm called Viarad, whose share price had fallen through the floor after it had failed to secure a multi-million-pound Government contract to supply software to the Civil Service. He read a little more on it and as it was Saturday turned to the sports section.

As Covent Garden was not heated but undercover, Mickey decided to change into warmer clothing, similar to what he would have worn during the winter months when he worked at Lehman's. He took the ten-minute walk to Woodford station, passing a few of his neighbours who were taking advantage of the clear day by decorating the outside of their homes with fairy lights and other festive items. It was a good call to walk as the park-and-ride was full of cars with Christmas shoppers making their way to Oxford Street or the enormous shopping complex at Stratford.

Woodford underground station was an over-ground station on the Central Line, with the electronic sign above the platform displaying the arrival of a train in four minutes travelling towards Ealing Broadway. The station's platform was crammed with people, but Mickey managed to squeeze onto one of the benches beside a little girl and her father, who had been keeping her amused with a game of I-Spy. After a few minutes, in the distance and on the sweep of the bend, the train appeared, meandering along the track. The little girl quickly forgot her game as the train pulled level with the station.

Mickey changed for the Piccadilly Line at Holborn and came across a guy not much younger than himself strumming a guitar attached to a small amp and singing the Van Morrison hit, *Brown-Eyed Girl*. The acoustics vibrated off the tiled wall of the underground walkway, as Mickey tossed him a few quid while the busker nodded his appreciation in return, with the coins landing on his guitar cover. At Leicester Square he exited the station and headed towards Covent Garden.

A Christmas market had opened close to the park in the centre of Leicester Square and nearby a long queue of small children with parents and guardians snaked its way along the side of a theatre advertising a Christmas pantomime. Mickey hadn't walked through the area for a couple of years and the last time probably would have been with Sophie.

On a warm summer's day, a few weeks after she left, Mickey phoned Sophie's mobile. With it switched off, as she was probably at work and with him not prepared to leave a message, he telephoned her office landline instead.

The woman who answered sounded as if she had either a boiled sweet or a marble in her mouth. 'The Honourable Society of the Inner Temple. How may I help you?' she asked.

'May I speak with Sophie Montagu, please?' Mickey asked in his most posh voice.

'Who shall I say is calling?' she replied.

'It's a Michael Ross.'

'Please hold.'

There was a short pause as Vivaldi faded in, with an appropriate version of 'Summer', from the *Four Seasons* suite.

A minute or so later, the woman returned. 'I am extremely sorry, Mr Ross, but Miss Montagu is in a meeting and unable to take your call. Do you wish to leave a message?'

'Yes, thank you. Could you please tell Miss Montagu I have an urgent message for her, that she has my number and if she could return my call as soon as possible,' Mickey replied, before hanging up.

Thirsty from cutting the back lawn, he grabbed a chilled beer from the fridge, sat outside and waited. With the phone beside him on the patio table and Lucy beneath, in the shade gnawing on a bone, Mickey began drumming his fingers. It wasn't long before the phone rang.

It was a private number, but he gambled, 'Hello, Sophie, that was a short meeting?'

She ignored the comment. 'You said it was urgent.'

'Your post keeps arriving at your former address, in other words, mine!'

'What type of post?'

'Oh, the usual fan mail, credit and store card bills. By the way do you have a forwarding address?'

'I'm in Chelsea.' She hesitated.'

Mickey had heard she was dating some broker called Simon who worked at Credit Swiss and who just so happened to live in Chelsea.

'Does he follow them?' Mickey asked.

'Who?'

'Simon.'

'How'd—'

'I'm not a recluse, Sophie, and before you say it, I'm not jealous.'

'They win things,' she said.

Now Mickey was confused. 'Who?'

'Chelsea!' she exclaimed. 'They win things!'

Moreover, Spurs do not, thought Mickey.

A vapour trail from an aircraft high in the sky was expanding outwards, creating a white fluffy cloud.

'Shall I post your mail to Simon in Chelsea?' he asked sarcastically.

'No, you will not! Post them to Mummy's instead,' she abruptly replied.

Lucy had wandered onto the garden and began digging in the soil, looking for somewhere to bury her bone.

'Don't do that, Lucy!' Mickey shouted.

'Who the hell is Lucy?' Sophie asked.

'My dog.'

'In our house?'

Sophie didn't like dogs. Then again, Sophie didn't really like anything or anyone. 'Excuse me! If I remember correctly, it was you who put the keys through the letterbox. Anyway, Lucy is a well-behaved animal and doesn't snore.'

'You mean she sleeps on our bed?'

'On your side.'

'You're disgusting! Post my letters to Mummy's!' she yelled, before slamming down the phone.

Mickey laughed. 'Nice one, Lucy.'

He went inside, found a large envelope, shoved all of Sophie's post into it and wrote on its front, *C/O Miss Sophie Montagu. The Honourable Society of the Inner Temple, London.*

The streets and pavements were narrow and full of people as he walked through Long Acre. The low sun had cast the street in almost constant shadow with the brown and red brick buildings that lined the route appearing in silhouette and darker than their colour suggested. As he turned right at Covent Garden tube station, a mass of people came streaming from the doorway of the nineteenth century, blood-red, listed building. The underground station had limited exits: you either rode to street level in one of the four massive lifts or trudged up its one hundred and ninety-three steps. It was the main reason Mickey had stayed on the tube for an extra stop.

Street artists scattered the covered market's approach, many head to toe in body paint, standing or sitting as still as statues, only moving slightly as a gesture when someone rattled a tin with a coin. Mickey checked his watch and saw that he was early, so he paused to watch a female artist juggling with three little multi-coloured soft balls. She was wearing a pink fluffy ballet skirt and a black leotard with the straps crossing around her back. A large crowd had formed and she was out of breath and flush from running around. Mickey watched as she continued juggling with one hand, before kneeling to pick up a unicycle, climbing upon it to cycle around the square, while still juggling.

Mickey smiled as he turned and walked into the Victorian market, passing the tall Christmas tree with its giant blue and red baubles that each year took centre stage close to the market's entrance. Within, sat lines of stalls, some selling a variety of prints of London scenes, others with gold and silver jewellery, precious gemstones and a general blend of arts and crafts. Stallholders with rosy cheeks and red noses cupped steaming hot drinks to their mouths on a cold December day while wrapped up with various types of knitwear to keep warm. The market's interior, brightly decorated for Christmas, had a continuous flow of people criss-crossing the floor. As Mickey entered the inner market, past the restaurants and the little shop units, he stopped at a handrail overlooking the sunken area below. Dotted across the floor were a few aluminium tables and chairs, occupied by two, three or four people, some sipping wine from large stemmed glasses. Others had their bottles standing chilled, though today was cold enough to skip the ice. A version of *Silent Night* flowed from one corner, as two young women dressed in black with violins neatly positioned under their chins glided their bows effortlessly across the strings with a third seated at a double bass; and were quite possibly students from the School of Music hoping to earn much-needed extra cash from the seated patrons.

Mickey suddenly became aware of someone standing next to him.

'Beautiful, isn't it,' she said, 'makes me wish I was still at university.'

'I was thinking something similar,' Mickey replied.

'Hello, Michael.'

Mickey turned slightly towards her. 'Lauren?'

She smiled. 'I have a table booked. Shall we?'

Chapter 6

Mickey followed Lauren as she moved away from the rail. She was an inch or so shorter, although her boots made her taller than she would have been in a pair of flat shoes. He could tell she was of slim build, even with the khaki quilted jacket she wore. Her long brown hair had been tied neatly into a ponytail and a pair of blue designer jeans hugged shapely hips and long legs. They descended a flight of steps onto the floor below, with Lauren leading the way carrying a large black Armani dome bag.

She approached a friendly waiter standing at the bar. 'I have a table booked for two under the name of Ross,' she said, glancing at Mickey. 'I know I've taken a liberty, Michael, but I thought it would be easier to give your name,' she whispered.

Mickey frowned, but said nothing.

They followed the waiter inside, under cover and away from the main floor, to the only available table, a corner one set for four, in an alcove with a pebble-dashed wall. The waiter removed the reserved sign and two glasses, while Lauren took a seat with her back to the wall, facing outwards.

'Would ma'am wish to see the menu?' the waiter asked.

Mickey was ready for lunch, but by the look of the food served, it obviously wasn't a burger and chip place.

'No thank you, we won't be eating; but may I have a glass of Shiraz, please?'

'And sir?'

Mickey, not one for wine, especially at lunchtime nor on an empty stomach, added, 'Sparkling water with lemon and without ice, please.'

'Certainly, sir.' The waiter smiled, nodded at Lauren and added, 'Ma'am,' before turning away.

Once the waiter was out of earshot, Lauren clasped her hands in front of her, smiled and said, 'Thank you for meeting with me, Michael.'

'I hadn't any plans,' he returned. A faint smell of her perfume drifted across the table, a pleasant fragrance, one that he knew, but couldn't put a name to. 'I do have a few questions,' he said, 'such as, why did you use my name to book the table?'

'I do apologise, Michael, but first allow me to explain why I invited you here and then I will tell you who I work for.'

The waiter returned with the drinks on a silver tray, placing a coaster each in front of them, followed by a large stemmed glass of red wine for Lauren and an empty twelve-ounce glass with a slice of lemon for Mickey. The waiter cracked open a small bottle of sparkling water, half-filled the glass and set the remainder on the table.

'Is there anything else ma'am requires?' the waiter asked.

'No, thank you,' Lauren replied.

The waiter once again smiled and walked away.

Lauren breathed in the wine's aroma, took a sip, before giving an agreeing nod of her head, and said, 'Very nice.'

Mickey sipped his drink and replied, 'Carbonated water with a hint of lemon.'

Lauren smiled, enhancing her high cheekbones. She was wearing a touch of lipstick with just a little make-up. When she spoke, he could see that her teeth were straight and white, though crow's feet were beginning to appear at the edge of her hazel eyes. Mickey put her age at between thirty-five and forty, not because that was how she looked, but how she dressed, with her coat zipped three-quarters of the way up and a Litton dog print scarf around her neck.

She bent down, removing a beige manila folder from her bag, placing it on the table, and took out a black and white photograph, sliding it towards Mickey. 'Have a look, but don't pick it up,' she said.

The photograph was of a suited man in his forties, tall, of solid build, but not fat. He was walking and carrying a business-type bag but not a briefcase. On either side of him were two other men, similarly dressed, but indistinguishable, as the man in the centre of the photograph was the only one in focus. He was smiling and in conversation with the other two. His jacket buffeted in a strong wind and strands of hair stood to attention on his head; it was a captured moment in time.

'He looks familiar,' Mickey said. 'I could have seen him in any financial magazine or newspaper.'

'His name is David Harrison.'

Mickey nodded. 'On the board of PetroUK, with oil interests in the Persian Gulf, North Africa and if they are successful the Falkland Islands. I'm not surprised that Argentina wants them back.'

'*Was* on the board, but I am impressed, Michael.'

'*Was*? You mean he resigned?'

'No, Michael. He's dead.'

Mickey took a mouthful of water. It was cold and refreshing. 'What happened?'

'Heart attack,' she said, letting it hang for a second, before adding, 'apparently.'

'So you think it wasn't a heart attack?' Mickey responded.

'He was a very fit man, Michael. David recently ran The Three Peaks in The Dolomites, the London Marathon earlier this year and The Marathon de Sables the year before.'

'Yes, but even extremely fit people can succumb to a heart attack. From what I remember his father died of something similar,' Mickey offered.

'That's correct, Michael, but Harrison senior spent most of his later life at the office burning the midnight oil; his son didn't, he had a good work-life balance.'

'Maybe heart disease runs in the family.'

'David had regular medical checks.'

Lauren removed a photocopied medical report from the same folder and passed it along the table in front of Mickey. It showed frequent visits to a Harley Street clinic, but his doctor did seem concerned about Harrison's health, prescribing him with antidepressants in the spring of 2010.

'David's wife Natasha was killed in March of that year,' she said.

'How?'

'Riding accident. She was thrown from her horse and broke her neck.'

'Shit!' he said. 'Sorry.'

She waved away the remark. 'I hear a lot worse every day.'

'Did they have children?'

'No children,' she said, taking a sip of her wine.

'Siblings?'

'David has a sister, Emily. She lives in Perth, Western Australia, and flew back to attend the funeral, but has now returned home.'

'Did you speak with her?' he asked.

‘She was here for two weeks. Emily spoke of David’s concerns of outside influences interfering with the running of the company.’

‘Did he tell her who or what they were?’

‘No, only that pressure was being applied from other board members to allow a certain individual to sit in on board meetings. She didn’t elaborate.’

‘And you don’t know who this individual is?’ Mickey asked.

‘Not as yet, Michael.’

‘You haven’t mentioned their mother?’

‘Mrs Harrison is eighty years of age and in Kings Meadow Nursing Home, Buckinghamshire. She has Alzheimer’s and doesn’t know David is dead; if she were told, it would be like a new death every day. She is deeply cared for. David paid for the best care for his mother and she has a personal nurse assigned to her. His estate will continue to pay for his mother’s care for the remainder of her days.’

Mickey nodded, and became suddenly sad for a woman he had never met or known. He thought of his own parents in their cottage on the coast overlooking the harbour in the little Cornish fishing village of Portreath. Both of his parents were retired: he pictured his mother in their conservatory with her paints and easel, while his father would be at the bottom of the garden in the shed with his wood-turning lathe making pots and bowls. They both would sell their creations at spring and summer craft fairs around the county for a little extra cash. A hobby mostly and a social occasion.

‘Michael?’

Lauren jolted him back to the present. ‘Sorry. I was thinking. If it wasn’t a heart attack, then what do you think actually happened to him?’

'Michael, I work for an organisation called Chameleon. You will not find a website or a contact number for Chameleon anywhere. There are only three people in the world who are in possession of Chameleon's telephone number. The Director of Chameleon, the Chief Executive of the London Stock Exchange and the Home Secretary. Whenever one of these people leave office the number is changed.'

Mickey looked at her, nodded and said, 'Go on.'

'David Harrison was found dead in Netherby Way, not far from Holland Park underground station.'

'Who found him?' Mickey asked.

'A minicab driver.'

A roar of laughter erupted behind him, along with hand clapping and cheering. Mickey turned in his seat just in time to spot a waitress carrying a large birthday cake in the shape of the number forty. The cake had as many candles lit atop it. She approached a long table with a dozen or so people seated around it, where a chorus of Happy Birthday followed, along with more cheering and clapping as the embarrassed woman stood and blew out her candles.

Mickey waited until the noise level dropped before whispering, 'It wasn't me who found him, if that's what you're implying.'

She smiled. 'I know it wasn't you, Michael. I do know the difference between a minicab and a London black cab. David was found on the pavement slumped against the wheel of a car. The taxi driver spotted him as he turned his cab.'

'Did he live there?'

She opened a white envelope, the type you would receive an invitation or a small birthday or Christmas card in, and took out a business card, passing it to him. It was quite an innocuous card, blank on the rear, but on the front, was printed the name Leila, along with a telephone number and a web address.

'David lived in St John's Wood and we believe he visited this lady,' she replied.

Mickey noticed Lauren's use of the word *we*, realising for the first time that she was in fact working for an organisation or company, and if this Chameleon group existed, he was eager to find out exactly who or what they were. He twiddled with the business card, bending it slightly and passing his finger over the embossed lettering. He knew exactly what Leila was, as similar cards such as this were in circulation around the pubs and wine bars of the financial district, but he wasn't about to share this knowledge with Lauren, so he shrugged and asked, 'Who is she?'

'She's an escort or, to put it another way, a high-class hooker.'

'You think Harrison was visiting this woman Leila?'

'We pinged her mobile signal and it registers a hotspot in the vicinity where David was found.'

'Was he arriving or leaving?' he asked.

Lauren handed Mickey a ticket for the underground.

'According to the time on the ticket, David bought it from a machine at Liverpool Street Station at 18.43 hours and exited Holland Park Station twenty-seven minutes later. He was found dead at 21.16 hours, which leaves a gap of around two hours. We can only presume he was with Leila, but the timeline works in.'

'So, he was walking back to the tube?'

'No. He ordered a minicab for the street corner, the one who eventually found him. The taxi company said David was becoming a regular.'

'Anything else to make you believe he was attacked?'

'He had small cuts on both hands as if he had fallen,' she replied.

'A heart attack would do that.'

'There was also a faint lash on the back of both of his legs as if he'd been hit from behind.'

'Okay, he was hit from behind and then what?' Mickey asked, with a slight hint of irritation. He could hear the distant sound of children's voices singing *Jingle Bells*, possibly replacing the violinists and the double bass player who had maybe taken a break or packed up and gone elsewhere.

Lauren ignored Mickey's impatience and asked, 'Michael, have you ever heard of Halothane?'

'No,' he replied.

'It's a clear, odourless liquid used in general anaesthetic,' she said, 'but an overdose can bring on a cardiac arrest.'

'Do you think Harrison overdosed himself on Halothane?'

She shook her head.

'He was poisoned then?'

'That is the line of enquiry we are following,' she replied.

'Okay,' he nodded, regretting his sharpness.

Lauren passed Mickey a company report; a photograph on its front cover showed a silhouette of an oil pump, also known as a nodding donkey, used for pumping oil to the surface from onshore wells. It had been taken while the sun was low, as the sky behind was the colour of burnt orange. 'PetroUK made a profit of two point three billion pounds last year and have a market valuation of six point two billion pounds,' she said. 'The share price as of Friday's close was £2.64, and they paid a dividend in September of seven pence per share. David and the three other directors, Roger Mildenhall, Harold Goodwin and Geoffrey Burbridge, own a substantial amount of PetroUK stock.'

'How much is substantial?' Mickey asked.

'Altogether? Forty percent, a ten percent share each. Sir John Warricker, the chair of the company, owns twenty percent, a further eight percent is held by a private equity firm called Black Castle, with seven percent in the hands of private investors and the remainder held within the company.'

Mickey was calculating in his head. Seventy-five percent of the company was privatised. 'What will happen to Harrison's allocation?' he asked.

'David died four weeks ago yesterday and the announcement was made to the Stock Exchange the following Monday. Two days from now it will be exactly four weeks since that announcement, and the shares are due to be sold on the open market at 9.05 a.m.'

Mickey raised his eyebrows. 'How many shares?'

'One hundred and sixteen million,' she replied.

'Quite a tidy figure.'

'Directors Mildenhall, Goodwin and Burbridge want it executed that way. Sir John is ill, but he has faith in the remaining board members and believes they will abide by the rules and regulations of the London Stock Exchange.'

'You doubt their commitment, Lauren, is that it?'

'It's not my place to say, Michael.'

'Who is the newly appointed director?'

'No one has been appointed yet.'

'And the broker for Harrison's shares?'

'Cook and Compton in Bishopsgate.'

Mickey knew of them. 'So, what do you need from me?'

'I want you to find out who it is buys the majority of David Harrison's stock and why he was killed,' she replied.

'I haven't told you my fee.' He smiled.

She stared at him for a few seconds, returning his smile, and then reached into her bag, retrieving a black rectangular plastic box with a flip lid, the type that a woman would receive a necklace or a chain in, except when she opened it, the box didn't contain a piece of sterling silver. Instead, it contained a key about four inches in length, with a heart-shaped head, indented along its tubular barrel, which sat upon a slip of paper similar in length but fingertip width. She closed the box again, but left it on the table.

'Michael, this key opens a safety deposit box on the Brompton Road in Knightsbridge. On the slip of paper, you will find a six-digit code that is necessary to enter the room in which the box is contained. The concierge on duty holds a second key and both keys are required to access its contents.' She paused before continuing. 'I trust you have photographic identification with you, as they are expecting you to arrive before six p.m. today. Everything else that you need will be there, including fifty percent of what Chameleon are paying you.'

'And if I'm not happy with what you're paying?' he asked.

'Then walk away.'

'How do you know that I won't just take the money and run?'

'We don't believe you would do that, Michael. We have researched you thoroughly; in fact, Chameleon knows just about everything about you, where you live and that your former partner Sophie left you for Simon and, just to give you an idea of how much we know, Simon will be fired on Monday.'

'Really?' Mickey replied, trying to remain calm, but feeling a chill run down his spine.

'We needed to be thorough, Michael, but we trust you.'

It didn't sound like it, but Mickey didn't reply.

Lauren put everything back into the manila folder and slid it across the table. She finished her wine, before standing with her bag over her shoulder. Mickey began to follow, but she motioned for him to remain seated.

'It's been good to meet you, Michael. I hope everything that I have told you is of use. In addition, within the safety deposit box is a new telephone number for you to contact me on. You don't mind paying for the drinks, do you?'

She put her hand out for him to shake and then she walked away.

Mickey caught the eye of a passing waiter and signed an imaginary bill with his hands. The waiter smiled and nodded. Mickey looked at the closed folder Lauren had given him, sipped some more water and stared at the wall behind where she had been sitting. He was trying to absorb everything she had told him, replaying the scene in his head, as if rewinding an old VCR tape and pressing play.

He took out his notebook and pen and wrote in the centre of the page near to the top, the name Harrison, drawing a vertical line about an inch long from Harrison's name. He then added a horizontal one almost the width of the page touching the end of the vertical, before adding five more short vertical lines pointing down and writing Mildenhall, Goodwin, Burbridge, Warricker and Black Castle, as if sketching a family tree, before joining them all up to the single common denominator, PetroUK.

On a separate page Mickey wrote Holland Park, the area where Harrison was found and by whom. He added Leila, the escort, and as an afterthought wrote down Lauren and Chameleon, before putting his notebook away. He took the key from its box and studied it. Along its barrel and between its heart-shaped head and indents, was engraved a three-digit number and a name. He rubbed a finger across its barrel, tilting it towards the light and being able to just make out the numbers two, six, seven, with the name Lansborough of London beneath it. As he waited for the bill, Mickey searched for Lansborough safe deposits on his smart phone. It took a while for the search page to load, as the wine bar didn't provide the courtesy of free Wi-Fi. When the address did appear, it showed as 315 Brompton Road, with the map roughly pinpointing its position. He paid the bill and decided to go straight over, as his curiosity had overcome his hunger.

Chapter 7

It was a little after two p.m. when he left Covent Garden. Outside, Mickey had difficulty walking against a tide of people now making their way into the square, and although the sky remained clear with the remnants of a winter sun, a cold easterly breeze now blew up from the Thames. He started towards Leicester Square underground station with the manila folder tucked neatly under his arm, wondering why David Harrison had been killed, if that was, in fact, what had happened to him, and the significance if any of the information he was now in possession of.

Mickey again caught the tube on the Piccadilly Line, continuing west towards Heathrow and travelling the four stops to Knightsbridge. He didn't believe that anyone would be following him, but Lauren had sowed a few seeds of paranoia into his head, and as he studied his fellow passengers, he decided to jump off the train a stop earlier at Hyde Park Corner.

He exited the station and crossed the busy road, walking for a hundred yards or so before crossing back over the road and entering the park. He took a short stroll along the side of the Serpentine, stopping to glance behind a few times, with only joggers from the local running club, dog walkers and loved-up couples for company. Satisfied that he didn't have a tail, he left the park and hopped on a bus travelling towards Chelsea. He remained on board for fifteen minutes before jumping off at Brompton Road close to the Knightsbridge junction. Traffic was at a standstill and with a little over three weeks until Christmas, the expensive boutiques were enjoying a bustling trade and not a pound shop among them. Shopping, though, was the furthest from Mickey's mind. He had an idea of what he was looking for and having memorised the number it was going to be opposite or across and down from the most famous shop of them all, Harrods.

He found it after only a few minutes, a discreet-looking unit, with the glass in its front window giving off a green laminated glow that was different from the rest in the block. Mickey had an idea that the glass would probably be toughened and bullet-proof, ballistic with its thickness ranging from three-quarters of an inch to three inches. The door would be the same, constructed using polycarbonate thermoplastic and layers of laminated glass. He glanced in as he passed, the name Lansborough of London printed across the window. Inside stood four three feet-high stainless steel security bollards, as if on display and evenly spaced to protect against a ram raid. Behind, was a security shutter, grey in colour and possibly made of toughened aluminium that was similar but stronger to one on a residential garage. The building appeared secure. Its walls, ceiling and floor were probably coated with a thick steel plate. Mickey considered the fact that he would be walking into a bombproof shelter.

Across the road he spotted a burger bar; his empty stomach had now gotten the better of him, and with a few empty stools at the window, he dodged the traffic to the other side and went in. He saw that four tables were in use, with the bar area to the right creating a simple floor plan in the shape of an upside down L. It had cosy lighting, with pink painted walls decorated with Venetian glass-framed prints of canals and gondolas. He took a seat just inside the window at a ledge facing onto the road and picked up a narrow half-folded laminated menu, scanning its contents. A young blonde waitress approached him with Erika on her nameplate and her hair in a bun. In accented English, she asked if he would like a drink. He ordered a bottle of Coors Light and a Hawaiian burger with fries.

He could see Lansborough's clearly from his seat, but had not yet seen any movement from within the shop. Mickey suppressed a yawn while waiting for his beer. It soon arrived, along with a frosted glass. He thanked Erika, who assured him his burger would not be long. He poured the cold beer, taking a long drink, which had a soft wooden taste. A few minutes passed and a well-dressed middle-aged couple stopped in front of Lansborough's. The man pressed the buzzer, and a few seconds later he pushed open the door and they both stepped inside. Mickey's burger arrived and he began eating while keeping an eye on the shop. It was when he was forking the last two chips that the couple exited Lansborough's, having been inside for little over half an hour. He now had an idea of the length of time he would probably need to spend there.

He felt his inside pocket for his driver's licence and fingered the little box which contained the key and code, before taking it from his pocket, opening it and noting the six digits on the slip of paper. He then put everything back into his pocket, lifted the manila folder and paid his bill, a reasonable price for stylish Knightsbridge.

It was almost dark, with a sharp nip to the air, as he made his way to the pedestrian crossing. Traffic, though, was moving a little better and with the combination of the neatly decorated shops and the illuminated street lighting along with the many Christmas shoppers, the area had a pleasant festive feel. As Mickey walked up to the door of Lansborough's, he spotted his reflection silhouetted and that of the traffic on the mirrored glass, thinking if there were any security cameras paying him attention, he couldn't see them. He pressed the buzzer and after a few seconds, the door buzzed and he pushed the handle and went inside.

When the door clicked closed behind him, he found himself in a short hallway with brushed matting, maybe six feet in length. A second solid door stood in front of him with a security notice riveted at eye level. It requested Mickey to look into the camera, one he could not fail to miss, situated above the door with a large lens reminiscent of a Cyclops. It gave the feeling as if something was staring straight through and not at him, as if this one-eyed monster was sizing him up before allowing entry to its den. He stood for a few seconds, before the inner door buzzed him to push it open.

Mickey entered a room quite unlike the exterior of the building. It was pleasantly warm, with his feet sinking into the expensively laid carpet. The ceiling and walls were covered with teak wood panelling. Two black leather sofas sat at ninety degrees to an equally positioned glass coffee table and neatly fanned out upon it were several upmarket glossy magazines. From one wall, he could hear the faint ticking of a period clock and on either side of it were black-and-white prints of London from an earlier era. Apart from the five feet-high counter with its toughened Perspex glass rising to the ceiling, it was a room straight out of the 1940s.

For the first time since he walked in, Mickey spotted a tall, suited, grey-haired man on the other side of the glass.

'Good afternoon, Mr Ross,' the man said, as Mickey approached him.

Mickey, turning his head slightly, was surprised that the man already knew his name.

'Ms King informed us of your arrival. I do, though, need your identification for confirmation, please.'

Mickey passed his driver's licence through the narrow gap in the glass, one similar in depth to that found in a bank or post office. The man glanced at it and then disappeared into a room in the back. Mickey took his time to look around. Set among the ceiling lights were four dome-shaped cameras, covering each section of the room and absent of any blind spot.

The man reappeared at the end of the counter, Mickey hearing a click as a section opened, with the man passing through it.

'Mr Ross, my name is James Madeley. Will you follow me, please?' he said, as he returned Mickey his driver's licence.

'Thank you,' Mickey replied.

Madeley was taller by about three inches, aged mid to late fifties with a warm smile and deep blue eyes. He was broad, but not fat, nor skinny either, and smartly dressed wearing a dark suit along with a red and black tie, which contained diagonal stripes and a vaguely familiar-looking motif. Madeley held himself well as they walked along the narrow corridor, a walking style that suggested ex-military. Although Mickey appeared to be the only other person in the building, he was convinced the two of them were not alone. At the end of the corridor, Madeley typed a four-digit code into a wall panel. From a lower floor and within a shaft, the sound of creaking and clanking announced the arrival of a lift. Madeley ushered Mickey inside, followed and pressed for the lower ground. When the doors closed and with the lift drifting lower, Mickey couldn't help feeling he was descending into some Orwellian underworld.

Chapter 8

Madeley was not one for small talk, choosing to stand beside the lift door, while fixing his gaze on a point close to the ceiling. Mickey took another look at Madeley's tie. It consisted of a crown upon a buckled belt, tied in a loop with a few words in Latin.

'Grenadier Guards, Mr Ross. The Falklands, two tours of Northern Ireland and the first Gulf War,' he announced proudly without breaking his gaze. 'And you?' he enquired.

'Cambridge and the City, Mr Madeley,' Mickey replied.

Thankfully, the lift reached the basement with the doors opening into a room with a polished wooden floor and grey painted walls. A few feet away a man roughly the same age as Madeley sat beside an x-ray machine and a walk-through security scanner. Beyond this, was a short corridor and at its far end, Mickey could see an enormous steel door with huge hinges and a wheel similar to what would have been on a ship or a submarine when keeping an area watertight. Madeley asked Mickey to empty his pockets, remove his coat and shoes along with his belt, watch, and any other items that he had on him, such as the manila folder and his smart phone, so they could be scanned through the machine which was standard as those at any airport. When Madeley was happy, he beckoned Mickey through the scanner, recording no beeps or sirens as he passed through. As he collected his belongings, Madeley prevented Mickey from putting away his phone.

'Mr Ross, I am sorry but electronic devices with photographic applications are not permitted any further than this point. You can collect your phone on the way out.'

Mickey was about to protest, but remained silent and handed his phone over to the man at the controls of the x-ray machine.

The man in turn handed Madeley a bunch of keys much the same as the one that Mickey had. They both walked to the end of the corridor where Madeley typed a six-digit code into a keypad on the wall to the left of the door.

'Mr Ross, would you now please type in your six digits.'

Mickey reached into his coat and took out the box containing the key and the six-digit code. He re-checked the number and typed in the code. There was a long beep followed by three short ones, with the LED on the pad changing from red to green. Madeley swung the wheel to the right and the door began opening inwards under its own power. Within was a giant vault: letterbox-size drawers stacked six feet high covered three of the four walls, while off to the right was another short corridor containing several doors or cubicles such as those in a shop's changing room.

'Do you know your drawer number, Mr Ross?' Madeley asked.

'It's two six seven,' Mickey replied.

Madeley walked to a drawer on the far wall, about halfway down and just left of centre. He fumbled with his keys and searched for the correct one. On finding it he slotted the key into a round hole at the bottom left of the drawer and turned it a full three hundred and sixty degrees anti-clockwise.

'Now your key, Mr Ross,' Madeley said.

Mickey slotted his key into the hole at the bottom right of the drawer.

'Clockwise please, Mr Ross, one full turn.'

He did as Madeley said, and the key clicked as it turned to its limit.

Madeley, taking hold of the brass handle, removed from the wall a black rectangular drawer with its underside covered with green felt. He set the drawer down on a pine table in the centre of the room and removed his key from its front, followed by Mickey's, and handed it back to him.

'Cubicle three is available for you, Mr Ross,' Madeley said, pointing to the annexe off to the right.

'Thank you,' Mickey replied.

As he picked it up, Mickey was surprised by the weight of the drawer. Whatever it contained was quite light, as it weighed less than a bag of sugar. Cubicle three also required Mickey to enter his six-digit code into a panel on the door. The full-length door clicked open allowing him to pull it outwards. As he entered, a light flickered on; a small wooden table sat in the centre and a cushioned bench ran along the back wall. There was not much room for anything else as he pulled the door behind him, hearing it once more click as it shut. He then pushed the door to see if it would reopen, but it was secure. The carpeted cubicle was roughly six feet square. The walls and ceiling were painted white, but to Mickey it felt like a very small prison cell.

He set the drawer on the table along with the manila folder, sitting himself down on the bench and turning the drawer towards him. He tried to lift the lid off, but it wouldn't budge. He then pulled on the brass handle with the same result. He turned the drawer around in a full three hundred and sixty degree turn, looking for a button or latch, before picking it up and checking underneath but there was nothing. He set it down again, staring at it, thinking he'd been the butt of someone's joke, when he spotted a small round hole on the lid near to its rear left corner, a similar one to the two at the front. He inserted his key and tried to turn it clockwise, a natural reaction and one that most right-handed people would subconsciously make. The key moved and continued for a full turn; hearing it click, he removed the key and slid the lid of the drawer towards him.

Inside was a document containing eight pages. It was a company release of PetroUK, detailing current and future energy exploration with executive holdings, including Harrison's. The last two pages contained the most interesting information, referring to an area in the Caucasus, on the shore of the Caspian Sea in Azerbaijan known as Block 12, about sixty miles north of the capital Baku, close to the town of Siyazan. Controversy had arisen regarding PetroUK's proposed gas extraction by fracking. Preliminary findings were completed and drilling was due to commence by February of the following year.

Mickey had an idea what fracking entailed; he also knew it was banned in many countries, as accidents could lead to chemicals contaminating the ground water around the fracking site.

On the document's final page, he found details of future oil exploration in the southern African country of Namibia. PetroUK had secured a 30% stake, while the Namibian government held 55%, with the final 15% assigned to a company known as Black Castle.

'Black Castle?' he said, a little too loud. Flicking back through his notes, he now added Namibia to his list and remembered that Black Castle held 8% of PetroUK's stock. At the bottom of the page there were signatures belonging to three of PetroUK directors, the only missing name being that of

Harrison's, with the document dated 31 October, four days before Harrison's death.

Also in the drawer, he found a mobile phone, a small basic type without a camera. Pressing the power button, the keypad lit up, illuminating the screen with the maker's logo. It was on silent and Mickey was half expecting a dozen or so messages to appear, but nothing did. He highlighted the menu to read any saved messages, but again there was nothing. Mickey searched the contacts and found two listed: one for a minicab company and the other a number without a name. Cross-checking, he saw that the second number matched the one on Leila's business card. The call history showed that the minicab company was the last number dialled at 8.58 p.m., and before that Harrison made two previous calls, both to Leila, one just before six p.m. and the other at 6.38 p.m. He saw that the only number received was that of the minicab company, probably when Harrison failed to arrive at the meeting point.

His gaze landed on an A4 sheet of paper, secured by a paper clip to its top left corner, along with a passport-size photograph. The photograph was of an attractive woman in her thirties with blonde hair, and underneath a brief description of who she was. Her name was Carol Freeman, aged thirty-five, divorced with two teenage sons and employed by PetroUK for the previous nine years. Her job description read that she worked as a secretary and personal assistant to David Harrison. The detail also included an address for her in Enfield, North London.

There was a further item within the drawer, a brown padded A4 envelope, thick and bulging, and sealed with clear tape. On its front, also stuck down with tape, was a regular-sized white envelope, with the words, *Half now, the rest later. Lauren* along with a contact number. Mickey punctured the envelope with his pen, before sliding a finger along its edge to open it. He slipped in his hand and pulled out a wad of banknotes, sealed together with a narrow band of paper. As he flicked them, he saw that each note was a Bank of England fifty, and as he turned the envelope up on its edge a second bundle, similar to the first, tumbled out. Both bundles were marked 50x50, and as he did the maths, he totalled £2,500 in each, with a total of £5000 on the table and if this was half, Lauren was paying £10,000.

He broke open one of the bundles and picked out three random notes, holding them to the light, seeing their metallic watermark and hologram distinct throughout. Mickey switched off the phone and placed it back in the drawer. He counted off £2,000 in consecutive serial numbers of the new fifty-pound notes, putting the rest back into the envelope and setting it into the drawer. The information on Harrison's PA he shoved into his folder, along with the documentation on PetroUK. He slid the lid of the drawer back on, feeling it click in place and pulling at it to ensure it was secure. He picked up the drawer and the folder and walked to the door. The door release, like a panic button and red in colour, was set to the side. On pressing it, the door opened and as he walked out, the light within the cubicle flickered off. A few feet from Mickey and in the centre of the vault, Madeley was patiently waiting.

'Everything to your satisfaction, Mr Ross?' he asked.

'Yes, thank you,' Mickey replied, handing him back the drawer and watching carefully as he inserted it back into its slot in the wall. Mickey heard it click as it locked itself in place, while Madeley pulled on its handle to check that it was secure. Mickey collected his smart phone, before Madeley escorted him back to ground level. While they were in the lift, Mickey asked, 'Would anyone else have a key to the drawer?'

'Just you, Mr Ross, and ourselves, but we need both to unlock it from the wall,' he replied.

Madeley led him to the front of the shop and finished with, 'Good night, Mr Ross, and feel free to return at any time during our hours of business.'

'Thank you,' Mickey returned.

Madeley buzzed the inside door and Mickey walked into the short hallway. When it closed behind him, the outside door buzzed and Mickey, pulling it open, felt a blast of cold air as he stepped out onto the pavement.

Chapter 9

Monday morning arrived and at five forty-five, Mickey awoke quite refreshed and managed to waken before Lucy came bounding up the stairs to jump on the bed. It was a little over two hours before the markets opened and three before Harrison's holding would be sold. Through the blinds, he checked the weather outside. It was still the middle of the night and diagonal streaks of rain were trying to cut through the glass. The forecast the previous evening had given that the rain was due to clear from the west by mid-morning. He went downstairs, switching on lights. Lucy was still in her bed, but on hearing him, got up and stretched.

'Good morning, Lucy,' he said, ruffling her head. 'Looks like the outside toilet's a bit wet this morning.' When Mickey opened the patio doors, Lucy hesitated, but gathered enough courage to make a dash for it.

He switched on the television, tuning it to CNBC, the financial news channel, who were broadcasting from their studio in Singapore, with the time at the bottom of the screen telling him it was approaching one p.m. The female anchor presenter was talking to a reporter in Sydney.

'...This could be bad news for the Australian mining industry,' the reporter in Australia said.

Mickey glanced at the news ticker at the bottom of the screen and saw that Aussie stocks were down and its currency had plummeted against the Yen and the US$. He soon saw the reason. China was forecasting its economy to contract over the next quarter. The previous three months had shown a drop in growth from 1% to 0.2%. If China fell into recession, Australian exports would slow.

With his own financial knowledge, he knew that over a fifth of Australian exports were to China, consisting mostly of coal, iron ore and gold. If the Chinese figures were true, then the large mining regions across the country, especially in Western Australia, would suffer.

The scraping at the door brought him away from the television. Lucy was standing soaking wet and waiting to get in. He dried her off, gave her some breakfast and went for a shower.

At seven forty-five, he booted up his laptop, set it on the kitchen table and logged into Sharecom, an online stock portal, which allowed him to view and trade live prices on any company or commodity on the London Stock Exchange, Europe and Wall Street. Mickey also had access to a library of information, just as if he was one of the dealers three miles away on any of the trading floors. At eight a.m., the markets in London and across Europe opened. Their counterparts in the Far East and Australasia had now closed, deciphering the impact of China on the markets. The Aussie Dollar was down 5% on Sterling and the Australian Stock Exchange had slid over 700 points or 18%. San Roja, the British-Australian multinational mining company, the largest in the region, had lost a fifth of its value. At eight fifteen, London had not escaped. The top 100 shares were down 7%, and by eight thirty, it was clear the market was taking a pasting. It was a fire sale. Across all the boards, red was the colour, with the sellers out in force. When the volatility eventually eased, the market would recover, retracing in part some of its losses, before the city boys continued the massacre, shorting carefully selected stocks, companies that had much to lose if China went into recession.

The US light crude oil index had lost 6% while PetroUK's share price was 8% lower from its opening. As the top of the hour approached, Mickey sat glued, watching the five-minute chart and trades of PetroUK, as its share price continued to fluctuate. Since eight a.m., there had been sixty-seven trades, a few buyers, but mostly all sellers, with the company chart now entirely red.

With a couple of minutes before nine a.m., Mickey poured himself a cup of strong tea, piping hot and almost the colour of tar. He sat back down at his laptop and watched as the second hand of his Spurs wall clock ticked towards the hour.

At nine a.m., the top one hundred share index for companies in London was still falling, though now at a slower pace. Commodity prices including Oil had now steadied after the initial shock from the Far East, but were significantly lower from Friday's close. Gold, often seen as a safe haven in times of financial crisis, had spiked 4%. At 9.02 a.m. PetroUK had dropped another 2%. In one hour, the company had lost 10% of its value and up until then, private and institutional investors had sold forty-six million of PetroUK's shares, totalling a market value of over one hundred million pounds. At 9.04 a.m., Mickey was poised for Harrison's stock sale by Compton and Cook brokers. He sat pokerfaced studying the screen, as if at a card table as players laid down their hands.

At exactly 9.05 a.m., a sell trade appeared on PetroUK's trade chart. One hundred and sixteen million shares. Mickey stared at the figure for a few seconds, absorbing the size of the trade, as each share had sold at 232 pence, giving a total of almost £270 million pounds.

Mickey, though, was not the only person watching PetroUK's chart and trades. Four miles away in a first-floor office of a terrace block above an oriental supermarket in Chinatown, Lee Chiang sat patiently waiting. All the necessary statistics displayed on his laptop were in front of him. Chiang had used a different online broker to Mickey, but the real-time information was the same. In front of him sat a Gaiwan bowl of Chinese tea, made from Baihao Yinzhen leaves, the highest grade of white tea, from Fujian Province in southeast China. He gave a gentle nod and allowed himself a satisfying smile, as Harrison's PetroUK by Compton & Cook trade of one hundred and sixteen million shares appeared on his screen. He took a few seconds to digest the information before clicking on the blue buy link on the menu bar on the left-hand side of the page. The new page loaded almost immediately, as he was using a modem with an Ethernet cable. For something as important as this, he did not want to risk the possibility of a wireless signal dropping out. The cable had a second purpose, one that would be used shortly.

Chiang typed into the subject box the number of shares he wanted to purchase: one hundred and sixteen million. He carefully counted the zeros, then typed in his password and again clicked on the buy link. A second page loaded with a real-time price, along with a timer counting backwards from fifteen seconds to zero. This was the time permitted to accept the current price of 232 pence per share, before the page would once more refresh with a new price. Chiang watched as the timer counted backwards. He was a gambling man, and willing to bet that the price would pitch lower. He waited. Three, two, one, aware of the beads of sweat that now appeared on his brow. Zero. The page refreshed and the countdown began again. Chiang smiled once more: the price had dropped by two pence as he clicked the confirm trade, knowing that he had just saved himself three million pounds.

The information travelled from his laptop along the cable to the modem on his desk; it then continued out the rear of the modem, but before it reached the telephone line, it passed through a small black communication box, which contained a portable telephone scrambler, blocking out his IP address. With each email and item purchased online or a video uploaded, the Internet Service Provider pinpoints the user to an area within approximately one hundred yards. This was something Chiang wanted to avoid, as anonymity had been the key to his success over the years. As soon as Chiang confirmed the trade, his IP address bounced almost half way across the world, to an office on the twenty-second floor of a high rise in Wan Chai District on Hong Kong Island.

While Mickey was digesting Compton & Cook's placed trade, PetroUK slipped a few more pence. He was now watching for a buyer, a large player who would snap up Harrison's shares or maybe a few individual trades, each taking a large chunk. He didn't have long to wait; less than a minute, in fact. The full one hundred and sixteen million shares had been bought in one quick deal. Mickey clicked on the link to see who had made such a substantial purchase, only for it to show as unknown trader and unknown broker.

'Unknown my ass,' he said, picking up his phone and dialling a stored number, with it being answered on the second ring.

'Rocco Bennati,' came the reply.

'Rocky! It's Mickey Ross.'

'Mick-ee! How's life in the slow lane, mate?'

'A lot better than one of your dad's dinners.'

'Now, Mickey, you know my old man makes the best Carbonara this side of the river.'

'What's happening this morning, Rocky?'

'China's happening. Shit's hit the fan. Market's heading south. If you have any Aussie stock, ship it, mate. Anyway, what can I do for you?'

Rocky was a good friend of Mickey's; they had worked together at Lehman's. While Mickey got out, Rocky stayed in and got hired on by Morgan Stanley. He was third generation Italian, looked and dressed very much as a Versace model, but with a thick London accent.

'Rocky, PetroUK,' Mickey said.

'Yeah, what about them?' he asked.

'Someone's just bought one hundred and sixteen million of their stock and I want to know who it was.'

'Click on the link, mate; you haven't forgotten already, have you?'

'I did, Rocky, it's shown as unknown.'

'Unknown?'

'That's what I said.'

'Shit!'

Mickey could hear him typing on his keyboard.

'Bastards!' he exclaimed after a few seconds.

'What?'

'You'd think they would have learned by now, mate, after the banks went tits up a few years back. We don't do *unknown* anymore; it's supposed to be a new, all crystal clear world,' he said.

'Someone's not playing the game, Rocky. Can you find out?'

'You're damn right I can. What's this all about, mate?'

'A spot of PI, Rocky.'

'No worries, I'll call you back.'

While he waited, Mickey looked up Black Castle. They were, as Lauren said, a private equity firm with a registered address on Northumberland Avenue close to Trafalgar Square. He checked the building number and found it to be just a private mail drop point with a post office number.

An hour had almost passed by the time Rocky phoned back. 'Okay, Mickey, I've had a look and I know it's taken a while, but someone has made it their business to try and make sure this one stays hidden,' he said.

'What did you find?' Mickey asked.

'It's an eastern trade.'

'Russia?'

'Further than that, mate, an investment house called Tai Sing, on Hong Kong Island.'

'Never heard of them,' Mickey said.

'Neither had I, mate, so I looked them up on the Hong Kong registry. Oh, they exist all right, but it's owned by some Jiading Financial in Shanghai, so I looked Jiading up and guess what?'

'A ghost chase?'

'You got it. Someone else owns them.'

'Thanks, Rocky. Any chance you can find the happy ending?'

'It'll cost you a few pints, mate.'

'I wish Sophie had been that cheap,' he joked.

'Here, Mickey, that geezer Simon she's with got canned this morning.'

'Really?' Mickey asked, trying to feign surprise. He was shocked nonetheless, with Rocky confirming what Lauren had already told him on Saturday.

‘Yeah, poor bastard bet the house on that Viarad tech firm and lost three million quid.’

‘I read about them at the weekend,’ Mickey replied innocently.

‘Apparently, he arrived at his usual time this morning and found that his pass had been cancelled. Security escorted him to his desk to collect any personal stuff, before he met with his line manager, who then handed him an envelope containing his termination letter.’

‘Shit!’ Mickey said.

‘That three million could have gone towards another striker. Are you for the Lane on Wednesday night?’ Rocky asked.

‘When do I miss a home game, Rocky?’

‘I’ll meet you in the Bill Nick before kick-off, about six thirty, and I’ll give you the heads up.’

‘Thanks, Rocky, see you then.’

‘Ciao!’ he replied, and then he was gone.

Chapter 10

The rain had ceased, as Mickey parked his black cab at the multi-storey car park adjoining a supermarket in the centre of Enfield. A severe chill from a northerly wind blew through the suburban streets and with it remaining a dull overcast day; it made Enfield seem an even more depressing place than usual. The few shops that remained in the area had at least made the effort to bring a little Christmas cheer to the place, and in the square close to the town hall stood a solitary tree, decorated half-heartedly by a few council workers. Mickey had driven the seven miles across North London which had taken him just under an hour and now he was walking the final half mile.

Carol Freeman lived in The Ridings, a beautifully squared cobbled courtyard with an entrance archway, which backed onto a golf course. The courtyard was in a quiet residential area off Enfield High Street. The surrounding semi-detached houses had neat front lawns with short driveways, built in the 1950s post-war boom, at a time when Londoners were moving away from the city for cleaner air, escaping the poisonous smog that in winter would engulf the city. The Ridings contained a dozen relatively new two-storey houses, built using period brick and probably within the last five years. Each house had a different coloured solid front door and brass knocker, a few now adorned with Christmas wreaths. Black-painted Victorian lamps hung on the walls to the left of the doors and to the right were similarly painted brackets, which in summer would be occupied by hanging baskets. The windows were sash, keeping to the contemporary feel of the courtyard, along with four ornamental cast-iron street lamps, again painted Victorian black, equally positioned throughout, and except for the half a dozen or so parked cars, the place was more suited to the time of Dickens.

There was a good possibility she would not be at home and if this were the case then Mickey had an alternative in mind, so his afternoon would not be entirely wasted. He was looking for number seven and with the houses numbered consecutively he spotted it quite quickly, its bright red door tucked into the right-hand corner as he approached from the archway. Each house was allocated two parking spaces and a silver Mercedes two-door sport was parked nearest to Carol's door. Mickey glanced in as he passed, and laying on the passenger seat were two empty shopping bags with the brand of a large food retailer upon them, but apart from that, there was nothing to suggest the owner was male or female. He lifted the doorknocker, hitting it twice against its brass plate, and glancing around as the sound echoed across the courtyard. Now Mickey stood looking at the door, with the manila folder sitting uncomfortably under his arm. He adjusted it self-consciously, now unsure what to say if she answered. His mind went blank upon hearing the faint sound of footsteps, before the lock turned and she opened the door.

They stood looking at each other, probably for no more than a second or two, but to Mickey it felt like an eternity.

'Mrs Freeman?' he stammered.

'Ms,' she replied curtly.

She was wearing a peach-coloured hooded top, zipped three quarters of the way up, with a white tee-shirt underneath and casual navy bottoms. A pair of sandals with a toe post were on her feet, but most of all Mickey noticed how tired and weary she looked, and yet her beauty shone through this.

'Ms Freeman, my name is Michael Ross,' he said, handing her his card.

'Private Investigator?' She shrugged.

Mickey took a deep breath. 'Would it be correct to say that you currently work for PetroUK?'

'Actually, it would be wrong to assume that,' she replied frowning.

Mickey was taken aback and, seeing the expression on his face, she added, 'I used to work there, but I don't any more. I'm sorry, I can't help you,' she said, taking a step back to close the door.

'This is about David Harrison,' he said quickly.

She hesitated, but replied slowly, 'David is dead.'

'I know,' he whispered sympathetically. Mickey paused, glancing around before he continued, 'I think he was murdered.'

Her reaction was not one of surprise. She closed her eyes and dropped her head; when she lifted it again and looked at him her eyes were moist.

'You'd better come in,' she said, pulling the door open wide and allowing Mickey to step into the short narrow hall.

A canister of furniture polish sat beside a table lamp, which illuminated the hall with a soft inviting glow; he saw that she was holding a yellow duster in one hand and maybe this was the reason for the smell of citrus.

'I was dusting,' she said, 'but I'm going to make a coffee, if you would like one?'

'That would be nice, thank you,' he replied.

She led him into the kitchen. It was a standard room with a table and four chairs at one end. A large window looked out on to a small garden roughly twelve feet square that ended at a low wall made of brick, topped off with black railings and a matching gate, leading to a path which ran parallel with the rear of the houses. Beyond, was a hedge about five feet high that marked the perimeter of the golf course, with the greens sloping down and away from the houses. In the distance stood a clump of trees bare-leaved, with their branches spread like fingers on a hand pointing skywards and silhouetted against the grey sky.

'You can see the Natwest Tower and the Gherkin on a clear day,' she said.

'I'm sure it's a lovely view.'

'Milk and sugar?'

'A little milk, but no sugar, please,' he replied.

Mickey set down his folder and took a seat facing the window. Carol brought over two steaming mugs made of pottery, each producing a strong, pleasant aroma. She went back to the worktop and carried over a side plate of assorted biscuits, before sitting down facing him. She used both hands to cup her mug and lifted it to her lips without taking her eyes off him.

It was the cue for him to start talking, but Mickey was unsure how to begin, so he started with 'Ms…'

'Carol, please, Mr Ross,' she cut in.

He smiled. 'It's Mickey, then.'

She relaxed. Mickey noted she was of average weight, with her blonde hair tied into a tail, which enhanced her good jawline and high cheekbones. Her eyes when he looked into them were the colour of cobalt.

'How well did you know David?' he asked.

'I had been David's PA for roughly six years, having started with the company three years earlier. I handled any business or personal issues that David needed help with. I was also there during the time his wife died.' She stopped mid-flow before adding, 'Did you know about Natasha?'

Mickey nodded. 'It must have been an awful time for him.'

'It was, and he never got over her death. There were a few nights that we cried together in his office.'

He looked at her, contemplating his next question, but she was quick, reading his mind before he could open his mouth.

'And no, we were not lovers, if that's what you were thinking.'

Mickey raised both hands in a gesture to show that he believed her.

'It's not that I didn't find David attractive; he was a very handsome man, but David was first a boss and then a friend, though that didn't prevent him from sometimes being abrupt.'

'Can you take me through the last day you worked with David?' Mickey asked.

Before answering, she asked one of her own. 'Who sent you, Mickey?'

'It's a client that wishes for me to enquire into David's death, but first I need to get a picture of what happened. That's all I can say at this time, I'm sorry.'

'Okay,' she said with a shrug. 'It was a normal Friday morning. I gave David his diary for the day. As usual, it was quite full, but only until lunchtime. He listened as I read out his appointments while he made the coffee. This was a daily routine; there aren't too many company directors who make coffee for their secretaries!' she said sadly. 'We had what was known as a buzz session every morning, for about twenty minutes,' making a face as she gestured two inverted commas with her fingers. 'It was introduced by the company a few months previously, but David hated it, the term that is, not our one-to-one meetings, calling it unnecessary twenty-first century crap. He despised business clichés, such as thinking outside the box, team player, and go for low hanging fruit.'

Mickey smiled and raised his eyebrows at the last one.

She laughed. 'I'm serious. To David it was all bollocks; he would say God help us all if this is the road city business is going down. He preferred our unofficial half hour during the morning, and he often said that I knew more about the company than the rest of the board.'

'And did you?' Mickey asked.

'Damn right I did,' she replied, rolling her eyes. 'I could have run that company without the board. In fact, when David was taking care of Natasha's business after her death, the chairman Sir John Warricker asked me to sit in on board meetings in place of David.'

'How did that go down with the rest of the directors?'

'They weren't impressed, especially when Sir John, asked for my opinion.'

Mickey smiled. He was beginning to like Carol. He opened the folder and took out the dossier regarding fracking in Azerbaijan, sliding it across the table in front of her and watched for a reaction.

She frowned. 'Where did you get this?'

'From the same people who hired me,' he replied. 'Were you aware of the prospecting site?'

'No, I haven't seen this paper before and I wasn't aware of any prospective drilling site and certainly not one in the Caucasus. David was against fracking; he knew that there was a possibility of pollution if something went wrong.' She hesitated. 'Did David know about this?'

'Look at the last page,' Mickey said softly.

Carol turned to the page with the four signature lines. 'He didn't sign,' she gasped.

'David died on 4 November and the page is dated 31 October,' he said.

'I don't really understand this.'

'Do you think David knew about the deal?' he asked, taking a mouthful of coffee.

'It's possible; I don't know. I'm trying to think. I remember that after lunch David did appear to be quite upset. He had one of those business lunches with the other directors upstairs in the boardroom, but when he returned, he was irritable and distant,' she replied.

'Who was at the meeting?'

'The three directors Roger Mildenhall, Harold Goodwin, Geoffrey Burbridge, and a Mr Chiang.'

'Chiang?'

'Yes, he had sat in on a few meetings, previously, I remember,' she replied.

'Is Chiang a board member?' Mickey asked.

'No I didn't know who he represented, but David wasn't happy with him being there.'

'Did you ever sit in on the meetings again after David returned?'

She took a biscuit from the plate, dunking it twice into her coffee. 'I used to, until Mr Chiang arrived, then I was barred. Apparently, it's a Chinese thing; they don't accept women, especially secretaries or PAs, sitting in on all male board meetings.'

Mickey made a few notes and waited until she had finished chewing, before he asked, 'I wouldn't have thought Chiang had that much power?'

She dodged the question slightly. 'As I said, David didn't like it, but there was nothing he could do.'

'Why not?'

'Because the other three directors wanted Chiang to be there and outvoted David.'

'But what did…' he shuffled through his papers, 'John Warricker make of this? Surely he could have voted on the side of David, cancelling out the other three.'

'Sir John was recovering from his triple bypass and during that time he was either in hospital or in Tuscany; but my memory is a little vague on it now and I can't remember clearly,' she answered.

Mickey looked at his notes, while gently gnawing at the edge of his thumb, before asking, 'Have you ever heard of Black Castle?'

'No, but I see their name on the dossier.'

'They have a huge stake in Namibia,' he said.

She shrugged, dropping her lower lip.

'Would there still be papers in David's office?' Mickey asked.

'I shouldn't think so. They would have cleared everything from there,' she replied.

'When did you leave employment?'

Her voice got stern. 'Fired, you mean. I received a phone call from Harold Goodwin on the Sunday evening saying that David had suffered a heart attack on Friday night and sadly had not survived, and that I wasn't to return to work.'

'What did you do?'

'I was devastated. My boss had died two nights previously and I had just found out by a telephone call. I didn't sleep a wink that night and was convinced it was a mistake or some awful prank, so I waited until the next morning and phoned

Harold's PA. She confirmed it and said the whole company was in shock. Emily, David's sister, was arriving from Australia. I got the address of where she was staying in London and met up with her.'

'How did you get on with Emily?'

'I didn't know her that well, but I had met her a few times on previous occasions, and I got some comfort from her when she said that David had thought highly of me. Emily mentioned that she had been to David's house in St John's Wood and was convinced that someone had been in the house looking for something.'

'Had he been burgled?'

'No, that's not what she said. It was as if they had been searching for a specific item. Emily said that drawers and cupboards had been opened and not properly closed, throughout the house.'

'So the place hadn't been trashed?'

'No. After the funeral Emily stayed until the house went onto the market, and she mentioned nothing more about it.'

'Did Emily contact the police?'

'I suggested that to her, but as nothing seemed out of place, apart from the opened drawers, what could the police do?'

Mickey agreed.

A man walking his dog along the path at the rear of the house stopped, as the dog had a sniff outside the gate, before they both walked on, with the two of them disappearing from view.

'Did the company offer you any counselling?' Mickey asked.

'You're kidding! The day after the funeral, I received a letter stating that my services were no longer required and that

I would receive full compensation for my nine years with the company, which surprisingly they honoured.'

'That was it?' Mickey asked surprised.

'Pretty much, apart from, they never asked for my keys; they may not have known that I had a set. David got an extra set cut and warned me not to say a word to anyone.'

Mickey had a thought: it was a long shot, but maybe Carol would play along. 'Do you think we could go to your office and have a look around?'

'I'm not sure,' she mused. 'Do you want me to help?'

It wasn't a thought that had crossed Mickey's mind, but Carol was easy to talk to and her knowledge of the company was invaluable, so without another word he said, 'Yes.'

'Who is it that sent you, Mickey?' she asked again.

He hesitated before replying, 'Have you ever heard of an organisation called Chameleon?'

She made a face. 'Who? What are they?'

'I'm not entirely sure; I can't find any information on them.'

'Nothing online?' she asked.

'Not even a cached page and my only contact is a lady called Lauren.'

'Maybe she's a spook,' she laughed.

Mickey wasn't sure about Carol's humour, because she could have just hit the nail on its head.

Chapter 11

They jumped into the Mercedes Sport and Carol began navigating along the side streets of Enfield, before turning south towards the city. She was hard on the throttle and even harder on the brakes. Mickey glanced anxiously across to her, while keeping hold of the handle above the door.

'Relax, Mickey,' she said, 'I was a rally driver in a previous life.'

He laughed nervously.

'It's true. When you grow up in the country, without sisters, there isn't much to do during the long winter nights. My older brother had a mark one Ford Fiesta that my father bought for him; they put a V8 engine into it and most evenings, after finishing my homework, I would go into the barn and watch them tinkering with it. It was spine-chilling listening to the roar of the engine in an enclosed space.'

Mickey was experiencing his own spine chill as he watched Carol jump a red light.

'My brother started racing in amateur rallies around Norfolk where we lived and when I was tall enough to reach the pedals, I started racing too and, by the time I was eighteen, I had a cabinet full of trophies.'

'What happened?' Mickey asked.

'The little girl grew up, left for university, discovered boys and got pregnant.' She glanced across to Mickey, shrugging her shoulders, but he was keeping one eye on the road. 'There was a shotgun wedding before Matthew was born, then two years later Christopher arrived and not long after that the marriage crashed.'

'Where are the boys now?' Mickey asked.

'They're boarders at Stow School,' she replied. 'Their good father and his new infertile wife pay for their education.'

Mickey gave her a puzzled look.

'Sorry, I forgot to mention, their father is the son of the Earl of Blackthorn.'

'Really?' Mickey said in astonishment.

'I'm… I was, should I say, the embarrassing extra. The one who couldn't conform to the stay-at-home mummy style that his parents wanted. I'm now the ex-wife who's the secretary, or maybe I should say the ex-wife who's the ex-secretary,' she laughed.

Mickey smiled. He wanted to relax into his seat, but he couldn't. He was thinking that Carol was venting some of her frustration through driving. Though driving and venting at the same time was maybe not a good combination.

'I couldn't care less,' she added. 'I preferred to go out to work and not stay at home to bake cakes.'

It was raining again, and little pearl drops had begun to appear on the windscreen. With a slow flick, the long single wiper pushed the droplets across the glass, clearing the view.

'I got a house out of the divorce and three thousand pounds each month for the rest of my life, but he got custody of the boys.'

'I'm sorry,' he said.

'Not your fault, Mickey. It's a bit weird: my relationship with Edward, the boys' father, is reasonably good. I think we have matured with age. I see the boys whenever I want and Edward gives me plenty of notice if he plans on taking them out of the country.'

'What about Christmas?'

'The boys are skiing in St Moritz with Edward and Cassandra, Eddie's wife.'

'What does Cassandra work at?'

'Oh, she has a tough, busy time throwing parties, attending coffee mornings and shopping frequently in New Bond Street. Though being the only daughter of Carlton Havisham, the property magnet, who owns half of London's Docklands and the very foundations that Canary Wharf sits on, you don't need to work.'

Mickey gave a wry smile. 'Aren't you at all a little jealous?' he asked.

'Of course I bloody am, but I didn't want to turn into a soccer mom,' she replied, imitating an American accent. 'At least I have a pretty good CV and, unlike a lot of people, I actually enjoy working. It gives me a sense of purpose.'

The going was slow as the traffic increased the closer they got to central London. Carol turned left, as the high-rises of The Gherkin and Natwest Tower came into view. The little light that had been left of a dreary day had extinguished as they found a rare parking space within the Square Mile.

'Can I come with you?' she asked.

'Might be best if it was just me. There may be questions to answer, if you bump into someone you know,' he replied.

'Okay. The office is on the nineteenth floor of the Klondyke Building, and you'd better take this.' She handed him the keys and a stiffened A4 envelope with PetroUK written on it. 'It's empty, but it adds a touch of realism.' She smiled.

Clever lady Mickey thought, but he was beginning to feel guilty leaving out some of the detail on Harrison, the part that included Leila. 'Look, Carol, there's something I haven't told you about David.'

'What?' she asked.

'I know you said he was a great boss and you thought very highly of him.'

'I did.'

'The night that he died,' he said slowly, 'David may have just left the company of a female escort.'

She stared ahead out of the windscreen, as if the buildings around them were not there, as if she was focusing on a point not in the here and now but in the far-distant past.

The only sound Mickey could hear was of the wiper and the hum of the engine, as he took Leila's business card from his wallet, passing it to her.

She glanced at it. 'I had an idea,' she said distantly, her gaze returning to a point within the car. 'He would sometimes use a pool car,' she added, now turning to him. 'And you know what drivers are like,' she said, sounding more upbeat, 'they tend to talk, and I believe it's an area of expensive apartments. She's probably a high-class lady.'

'With airbrushing and Photoshop anyone can look good on a website.'

She sighed. 'He was a still a good man, Mickey; my opinion of him hasn't changed.'

He gave her a sympathetic smile. 'Okay. It looks as if we lost one of the good guys,' he said, opening the passenger door.

'Hold on,' she said suddenly, 'I remember now: he asked me if there were any cars available, just before I left that evening, but there weren't.'

With one foot on the road, Carol grabbed Mickey's arm.

'Wait, there's something else,' she said.

'What?'

'He said to me, something along the lines of, *Good night Carol and thank you for your loyalty to me and the company.*'

'What did he mean by that?'

'I don't know; it was the first time he had ever said anything like that to me.'

'Do you think he feared for his life?' Mickey asked.

'With hindsight now, it's possible.'

Through the oncoming headlights, Carol pointed out the building and said she would wait until he returned. Mickey, now out of the warmth of the car, immediately turned up the collar of his coat. The air mixed with rain was frigid. He crossed over the road and for some reason or another glanced at his watch: it was a little after four p.m. The Klondyke Building was up ahead, its copper plate on the wall outside announcing it as number thirty-seven Devonshire Square. An automatic rotating door began to move as he walked between two of its spokes. Inside, the atrium was high and wide and two lifts sat maybe thirty feet to his left. As he began walking towards them, an eagle-eyed security guard sitting behind reception spotted him.

'Can I help you, sir?'

No, piss off, Mickey wanted to say.

A young female receptionist decorating a Christmas tree looked up and smiled.

'I have an urgent package for PetroUK, which must be hand delivered,' Mickey replied.

'I'm afraid you're three days too late, chum,' the guard returned, rather too smugly.

'What do you mean?' Mickey stuttered.

'They've moved.'

'Moved?' Mickey asked, glancing at the floor plan on the wall behind reception, which read PetroUK, floors 17-20.

The guard, following his gaze, added, 'We're still waiting on maintenance to unscrew the plaque.'

Mickey looked at him, and asked, 'Did they leave a forwarding address?'

'Yeah, you can't miss it.'

'Tell me then.'

'It's the tallest building in London.'

What is this, a quiz?

'The Shard,' Mickey said.

'You got it!' the guard replied

Once outside, Mickey sprinted back to Carol's car.

'That was quick,' she said, once he was inside.

'They've gone,' he replied, catching his breath.

'What?'

'They've moved.'

'Where to?' she asked.

'To the Shard, apparently.'

'When?'

'The guy on reception said three days ago, so Friday must have been their last day, and the removal guys would have been in over the weekend,' Mickey added, his breath returning to normal.

'Did he tell you anything else?' she asked.

'That was pretty much all he said. I didn't know Petro were planning to move.'

'We… I mean they, were not supposed to move until January. We got word in August that the company had signed a lease with the Shard, but I don't know why they would have left before the New Year.'

'Maybe it had something to do with David or this bloke Chiang,' Mickey offered.

She made a face, as if working out a crossword puzzle, checking her mirrors as she did so, and then indicated, before moving out into the traffic.

'I rarely drove to work: couldn't stand the traffic and the train was more convenient, but I have the code for the car park. Let's see if it still works,' she said, inching along the road.

On the right-hand side about two hundred yards up was a roller shutter, marking the vehicular entrance to the building. She manoeuvred the Mercedes onto the lip of the ramp and switched her phone to Bluetooth. Once paired with the Klondyke Building, she typed a four-digit code into her car stereo. After a few seconds the shutter twitched and began to rise, squeaking and squealing as it fought against friction. Once it was two-thirds raised, Carol eased the car down the ramp into the poorly illuminated car park.

'This was another reason why I didn't like bringing my car,' she said. 'I'm not great in the dark, even more so, when, just like now, the car park is less than a quarter full.'

It was as quiet as the grave and large enough for two hundred cars. Carol picked a parking bay against one of the walls, number twenty-seven, in bold white paint.

'We had fifteen spaces, numbered twenty-two through to thirty-six inclusive. Obviously, the new tenant will take these when they move in. I don't think it will matter if we park here for a little while.'

They exited the car and walked a short distance to the stairwell. A keypad on the wall operated the automatic fire door. Carol used the same four-digit code to open the door. Once inside, Mickey started towards the lift, when she whispered, 'That will only take us to the ground floor, and then we'll have to transfer to the other lifts beside reception.'

'Okay,' he said.

'If we take the stairs to level one, it will bypass reception and the cameras. Then we can use the lift up to the nineteenth floor.'

Their feet echoed with every step on the concrete stairs. The handrail was of light steel, riveted at its joint and the colour of wet sand. High above, a door slammed as someone joined or exited the stairs. Condensation had formed on the casing of the wall lights and they could see their breath as they climbed. After four flights of stairs, Carol opened the door to the first floor, and, stepping into the corridor, they felt the temperature rise by about twenty degrees.

A multimedia and graphic design company occupied the first floor; the frosted glass on its office door announced the name as Bluecube. While in the stairwell, they had decided that, if the lift was occupied, Carol would get in and Mickey would take the stairs. Thankfully, on arrival it was empty. She pressed for the nineteenth floor. On the journey up, they both remained silent, though their eyes darted around as their breathing quickened, with nerves, or the two storey's they just climbed. The coldness that Mickey had felt earlier had worn off, but now his hands were clammy, with his back soaked in sweat.

When they arrived, the nineteenth floor was in darkness, apart from the emergency lighting. Carol froze to a spot inside the lift, while Mickey, finding a switch for the lights, flicked it. They stuttered on as Carol gingerly walked beside him.

'I haven't been here since…' she said, her voice dropping off.

'I know,' he said. 'If it's too much for you, we can leave.'

'I'll be fine. It's just so sad seeing it empty. Part of me is expecting David to appear from his office and ask me to type something up for him.'

Her desk had been cleared of any notable items, and only contained a few scraps of paper and the odd sweet wrapper. She checked the drawer and cupboard as she walked behind it, shaking her head in disbelief. 'Empty. It's as if I'd never been here,' she said.

Two other rooms on the floor had also been cleared, leaving nothing, not even a chair. Carol handed Mickey the key to Harrison's office, which he inserted into the lock, turning it anti-clockwise and hearing a dull click as the lock slid into the door. He pressed down on the handle, pushing it open. Despite it being so large, the door moved effortlessly across its arc. They were nineteen storeys high and only a faint glow of light from street level illuminated the room. He groped, feeling for the light switch, aware of Carol breathing heavily at his shoulder. Mickey felt his feet sink into the carpet as he entered the room, and in the centre of it, neatly positioned, was Harrison's desk.

'My God! They haven't taken it, that's David's desk,' she exclaimed, walking over and brushing her fingertips across the surface of the wood. 'The television's gone, though,' she added, glancing up at the far wall.

A second door off to the right led to a small, clean and empty bathroom. Mickey spotted an indent of carpet near to the window, which Carol confirmed as a space for a now long-departed filing cabinet. At Harrison's desk, they found both the drawer and cupboard locked.

'Do you know what he kept in here?' Mickey asked.

She shrugged. 'Could have been anything, work or personal belongings. I know he kept a photograph of Natasha on his desk.'

Mickey took out a set of keys from his pocket with a small penknife attached. He inserted the knife into the lock of the cupboard and jiggled it a few times before it turned, but on opening it he found the cupboard to be empty.

'Damn!' he said.

Carol sighed. 'Try the drawer.'

The drawer took slightly longer, but eventually the lock turned with Mickey pulling on its handle and again finding it empty.

'Shit,' she whispered.

The drawer sat deep into the desk and came out a little too smooth and fast, slipping off its rollers and thumping end down onto the floor. They both froze, thinking that someone would come running to investigate the noise. When they were happy nobody had heard them, Mickey fixed the drawer back onto its rollers and slid it into the desk.

Carol stood staring at the floor. 'Mickey, what's that beside your knee?'

He looked down and saw a small pink USB flash drive. Wondering where it had appeared from, he pulled the drawer out again, examining its edges, and found that on one side a slot had been chiselled out, which the little device now fitted snugly into. When he had dropped the drawer, it had dislodged itself.

'Do you think this is what the visitors to David's house were looking for?' she asked excitedly.

Mickey looked up at her, smiled and said, 'I don't know, but there's only one way to find out. Let's go!'

Chapter 12

Mickey asked Carol to drop him at the multi-storey in the centre of Enfield, so he could retrieve his cab.

'What do you drive, Mickey?' she asked.

'A black taxi,' he replied.

She gave him a puzzled look.

'I'll explain later.'

They agreed to meet in a Starbucks on the Pentonville Road at around eight p.m. so they could view Harrison's memory stick in a public place that also had Wi-Fi. Kings Cross and St Pancras stations were close by, which almost guaranteed that a large amount of people would be continually passing through. Carol offered to bring her laptop and suggested that Mickey should hold onto the flash drive until then.

Mickey dropped off his cab, took the tube and arrived early. He managed to get a table against a wall facing the door. Carol walked in a few minutes after eight, looking good. The ponytail from earlier was gone and her blonde hair sat just above her shoulders. She had used a little blusher on her cheeks, with the same amount of lipstick, and wore a chocolate-coloured corduroy wax jacket with matching belt and stone-coloured jeans that hugged her ass. She sat down facing him and apologised for being late. Mickey waved it away and got up to order the coffee.

Foreign students from the nearby English school half-filled the café, most of them deep in conversation regarding some subject or other and mixed with good-natured humour. Across from Mickey, an Asian couple were enjoying a coffee while their little boy sat in his pushchair playing with a straw. At another table, two men sat holding hands. Smiling, he thought this was a good mixture of London in one small place.

He inched in beside Carol with the two coffees as she powered up the laptop.

'Do you mind if I sit beside you?' he asked.

'Well, how else are you going to view the laptop, Mickey?' She smiled. 'Then again, it might be best if we both sat with the wall behind us, for it will stop any prying eyes that may be around.'

'Good idea,' he said.

They played musical chairs until they got comfortable, with the laptop centred between them.

'What's with the black taxi, Mickey?' she asked again.

'I use it for my cover and work as a cab driver from Euston Station,' he replied.

'You're a smart cookie,' she said.

He told her about his time at Cambridge, working as a trainee private investigator, before joining Lehman's, losing his job during the crash and applying for his taxi licence. He also dropped in the break-up with Sophie.

Carol nodded, said nothing and sipped her coffee. 'Where is Sophie now?' she asked, when Mickey had finished.

'With some Simon bloke in Chelsea.'

'I think you're better off without that one,' she winked.

As she slid the laptop closer to him, their knees touched, and he felt a spark of electricity run through him, as he inserted the drive.

The laptop contained a background picture of a beach with golden sand and clear blue water, and beyond it, a rocky headland with the sun low in the sky.

'Crete,' she said happily. 'I got up early one morning to catch the sunrise. A girlfriend and I went there in September. Have you been?'

Mickey had been to Paris, New York and Barcelona with Sophie, to visit an array of shops, and apart from a week in Benidorm and a long weekend in Ibiza, with a couple of mates from the city, that was the height of his culture. 'No, I haven't reached the Eastern Med yet,' he bluffed, 'but, it's a very beautiful picture.'

'Thanks.'

The memory stick loaded, with Mickey selecting all files. A password was then required for the encryption and he glanced at Carol for ideas.

'Try Natasha,' she said.

'Are you sure?'

'David hated passwords,' she replied. 'He couldn't remember them and always said what was the point if he had to write them down, so he kept them simple and used Natasha for his computer log-on and for ordering cars.'

Mickey was amazed that with the publicity around cybercrime, Harrison chose something as simple as his wife's name. 'Capital N?'

'Yes, and lower case for the rest.'

Four files appeared, with the first bomb hitting when they opened the first file named simply as, *letter*. It was from Harrison to the board of PetroUK.

Date -- -- ----

For the immediate attention of,

Directors PetroUK.

I, David Harrison, Director and major shareholder of PetroUK regretfully announce my resignation as a board member and as an employee of PetroUK. This is effective from the date above.

Yours sincerely,
David Harrison.

'He was going to resign,' Carol said, almost tearfully, 'and the bastards killed him!'

'Hold on, Carol,' Mickey whispered, looking around to make sure nobody had heard her. 'We don't know that for sure, and if you look closely, even though it states his resignation from the date above, he hasn't inserted one, nor does it contain David's signature.'

She made a face. 'Yeah, but maybe he was working on the letter and hadn't decided when to resign, but he was obviously considering it when they killed him.'

He pondered, thinking that she could be right, before he looked at her and said, 'You might be onto something, Carol, but let's not jump to conclusions, just yet.'

She nodded, but with tears in her eyes.

They closed the file and opened the second one. Named *Block 12*. It was a PDF file on Fracking in Azerbaijan. Harrison had been involved in discussions on the planning process but had not signed an execution order. The third file, labelled as *Sector 34*, detailed the site in Namibia, but again nothing new that Mickey hadn't already found out from his visit to Lansborough's. He again mentioned Black Castle to Carol, but she was still unaware of who they were.

The second bomb hit, when they opened the fourth and final file known as *Zone 7*. It was a new exploration, and initial testing suggested a potential hit of oil at 70/30 in favour.

'That's high,' she said, 'it's usually a ratio of 60/40 in favour, sometimes 50/50; it can even drop as low as 40/60 against a strike.'

They needed to scan through the complete document as it was difficult to pinpoint the location of *Zone 7*. Again, Black Castle came in as an investor. Except, this time, it was a lead partner and PetroUK was named as its subsidiary.

'Subsidiary?' she whispered. 'Maybe Petro didn't want to be known as the main investor,' she said, pointing at the screen. 'But look, PetroUK will fund 65% of the exploration, Black Castle 20% and the Iranian Government 15%.'

'Iran?' Mickey questioned. 'Do we not have a trade embargo against Iran. Their London embassy was closed a few years ago after the British one in Tehran was attacked.'

On the penultimate page, a map of *Zone 7* showed its location. It was an area in the Persian Gulf not far off the coast of the Iranian mainland and close to the island of Dehriz. Each of the directors' names, including Harrison's, appeared on the final page below four empty signature lines.

'It's strange that this *Zone 7* document hasn't been signed,' Mickey continued.

'Do you think it's been processed, now that David is dead?' Carol asked.

'We could find out.' He smiled.

'How?'

‘By getting access to their computers.’

‘That’s impossible, Mickey, they’re in the Shard now and we couldn’t get past security.’

‘You haven’t met Vinnie,’ he said.

‘Who’s Vinnie?’ she asked.

‘He’s my cousin.’

Chapter 13

Mickey's cousin Vinnie was a six-foot-five-inch tall Afro-Caribbean from the West Indian island of St Kitts and as far removed as a relative of Michael Ross as he could possibly be. Vinnie owned an electronics and surveillance shop on the Portobello Road. The electronics he advertised, the other stuff he didn't. Vinnie was also a huge reggae fan and any visitor to his shop in West London would hear the dulcet tones of Bob Marley, Freddie McGregor, Shaggy and many more.

Carol offered Mickey a lift home from the Starbucks, but as it was in the opposite direction to where she was going he declined; as well as that, the tube station was only a short distance away. Mickey promised to phone her once he made contact with Vinnie, then he informed her of another plan he had for the following evening; one for which he needed her help, if she agreed. She said yes, but not before raising a questioning eyebrow.

Next morning Mickey dialled the number for Vinnie's shop. A young lad, sounding half-asleep, answered the phone.

'Is Vinnie available?' Mickey asked.

'Who wants to know?' the young lad replied.

'It's Mickey Ross.'

'Sorry, Mickey, I didn't recognise your voice, it's Leroy. Hang on and I'll get him, he's in the back chipping phones.'

For roughly one hundred quid, Vinnie would chip or adapt your pay-as-you-go mobile phone, for endless usage without your operator billing you. He had regular customers and, due to the continued development and design of handsets, also an endless supply of income.

'Yo, Mickey! What's ticking?' Vinnie's deep voice came down the line.

'I need a scouting mission, mate.'

'Where for, man?'

'The Shard,' he replied, holding the phone away from his ear.

'What the fuck, man,' Vinnie said, disbelievingly.

'You heard.'

'What you gotten yourself into, Mickey?' he asked.

If only he knew, Mickey thought. 'Not over the phone, Vinnie.'

'No worries. I'm here until lunchtime, what time can you get here?'

'It's, what, nine now. I could be there for half eleven, if that's okay?'

'That'll do,' he replied, 'and hey, Mickey, bring your wallet, it's gonna cost ya, man!'

With that, Mickey heard his big laugh, as Vinnie put down the phone.

Portobello Road runs straight into the heart of Notting Hill. The same Notting Hill so famous they made a movie about it, but it was the antique shops, cafés, market stalls and second-hand bookshops that Mickey would come to this part of London for. That was how he found Vinnie.

Portobello Road was a multi-cultural mix that the United Nations would have been proud of. With black, white, Asian and Chinese businesses trading side by side. Vinnie's shop sat in between a Turkish barbers and one of those second-hand bookshops. A few years previously, Mickey decided to get rid of some books he had gathered from his university days. He had heard of a bookshop owned by a retired English tutor from Oxford who would buy them from you. Alfred Somersby, the proprietor, was a cunning old fox: yes, he would buy your books, but he did it in such a way not to give you any money. In fact, he had an unnatural way of selling you someone else's unwanted books. Stepping into his shop was a timeless wonder, the sounds of the road outside disappearing, as you were transported back to a world of ticking clocks, musty books and the sounds of Mozart, Strauss and Elgar drifting through the bookcases from stereo speakers on crackly twelve-inch records played at thirty-three and a third rpm.

Just after eleven a.m., Mickey exited Notting Hill tube station along with a dozen or so other people. It was another cold, crisp morning. The sun had returned and the cloudless sky seemed to have lifted everyone's spirits. He cut through a couple of upmarket residential streets until he came upon Portobello Road. The market was buzzing and the road as usual full of people's bobbing heads as far as the eye could see. The stalls with their covers and the pastel-painted shops made the mile-long road a mixture of colour and energy. Mickey, side-stepping people as he went, made his way down the centre of the road, until he heard his name called.

'Mickey!'

He looked around, trying to find where the voice had originated. He then spotted the mischievous boyhood grin standing beside a fruit and vegetable stall. The grin belonged to Tom Cheevers, a bloke he had worked with at Lehman's. His family had owned a stall on Portobello Road for generations. A decade previous, Tom left to seek his fortune in the City. Now he was back behind the stall with his father and sister.

'Tom, good to see you. How's it going?'

'Flat out, mate, still selling stock,' he laughed, biting into a pear. 'Are you wandering or buying?'

'I'm headed for Vinnie's,' Mickey answered.

'You still doing that private eye stuff?'

'Yeah, I'm enquiring into one for a client. I need Vinnie for some help though.'

'Okay, mate, if you're passing on the way back, stop and we'll grab a cuppa.'

'No worries, Tom, thanks.'

Mickey was walking away when Tom shouted, 'Oi, Mickey, catch!' He put out his hand and caught a shiny red apple. 'Just polished this morning, mate.'

'Cheers,' replied Mickey.

Tom disappeared behind the stall and Mickey walked on, chomping into his apple. Mickey initially missed Vinnie's shop, because of the number of people on the Portobello Road that morning. He doubled back, glancing in at Somersby's bookshop as he went by. Somersby was in there, somewhere, probably lost in some dusty piece of literature.

When he opened the door to Vinnie's shop, he saw a young lad he didn't recognise dressed in street gear behind the counter. The young lad pulled his head up in a greeting and spoke to him in urban language.

'Whatcha.'

'Is Vinnie around?' Mickey asked.

'Are you the Old Bill?'

'No, he's not the Old Bill,' said a voice from behind, giving the young lad a clip around the ear.

'Hello, Vinnie,' Mickey said.

'Yo, Mickey.' The big man smiled, showing him his shiny white teeth, putting a hand out for him to shake. He gripped Mickey's, squeezed it playfully and then let go. 'This is Theo, my youngest nephew. My sister asked if I could give him a job to keep him off the streets.'

Mickey followed Vinnie into his workshop and closed the door. Vinnie sat down in a swivel chair behind his desk and offered Mickey a seat. He nodded at Vinnie's brother Leroy, sitting at a wall bench removing a cover from a games console.

Vinnie wasn't into anything illegal, nor was he a wide boy or a spiv, though sometimes he did sail close to the wind; but Mickey found him trustworthy and considered him a friend.

'So, Mickey,' he asked, 'what do you need?'

'A recon of the Shard, the new offices of PetroUK.' Mickey passed him some information on the company, taken from their website. 'I also need access to one of the computers belonging to one of these three directors,' he added. Mickey laid a sheet of paper on his desk containing a list with the names of Mildenhall, Goodwin and Burbridge on it.

Vinnie sat with his hands clasped in front of him, nodding slightly and listening.

'There's also another fellow, goes by the name of Lee Chiang. He's not a director, but he may have an office or use of a computer,' Mickey finished.

'Okay, Mickey, I can have a go at that,' he said. 'The Shard, though, has all the latest security and firewalls; it also has the ability to block all wireless transmissions, if it believes it is being hacked.'

Vinnie went over to a wall cupboard and took out what to Mickey looked like a standard smart phone.

'This is the latest kit,' he said, 'it's called a VFW.'

Mickey looked at him dumbfounded.

'It stands for Virtual Firewall. In other words, with this device I can access their firewall codes and link into their computer diagnostics. In simple terms, if I want to take part in a Santa race, I put on a Santa suit and everyone thinks I'm one of them. It's the same principal: I get in, their system thinks I belong there and it will talk to me.' He stopped and looked at Mickey.

'I feel a but coming,' Mickey said.

He nodded. 'I need to have the correct codes within sixty seconds or everything shuts down.'

'You mean we're dead?'

'Pretty much; we get one shot at this.'

Mickey groaned and rubbed his eyes. 'Okay, let's give it a go.'

'Leroy and I will do the groundwork and we'll get back to you in a couple of days. When do you need to go on this, Mickey?'

'Just whenever you have the info, Vinnie. The next few days are fine, and then we'll take it from there,' he said, taking out his wallet, before Vinnie stopped him.

'Wait until it's complete, man. I know I'll get paid.'

'Thanks, mate.'

On his way back to the tube station, Mickey met up again with Tom Cheevers. They went to a greasy spoon, for a cuppa and a bacon sandwich.

'So, Mickey, who's the client this time?' Tom asked, as they found a seat beside the window. 'Is it some hot blonde whose husband is dipping his wick?' He chuckled.

Mickey smiled. 'Not this time, mate. A good-looking lady, but it's blue chip business.'

Tom raised his eyebrows. 'Blue chip, you say. Which company?'

'PetroUK.'

'And who's the good-looking bird?'

'A lady called Lauren King.'

Tom was munching on his sandwich, but his eyes narrowed.

'What?' Mickey asked.

'I've heard of her.'

'You couldn't have, mate.'

'No, Mickey. I'm sure I have. She'd be, maybe, mid to late thirties?'

'Yeah, that's about right,' Mickey replied eagerly.

'Before I went to Lehman's,' Tom said, taking a mouthful of tea, 'I worked for Barclays in the Wharf. There was this Lauren King who worked in fraud. She'd eavesdrop on our calls, made sure we weren't inside dealing; you know the kind of stuff they do.'

'Go on,' Mickey said.

'Then one day she left, no notice or nothing.'

'Did she get fired?'

'I was shagging one of the girls in fraud at the time.'

'I should have known, Tom,' smiled Mickey, shaking his head.

'Anyway, she told me that Lauren arrived for work one Monday morning, and everything was as usual as it should be. Then two official-looking men along with a woman turned up. They went into the office of Lauren's line manager, who then called Lauren in. Not long after, the line manager left, leaving Lauren alone with the three visitors, for around two hours. When they'd finished and got up to leave, Lauren went with them, collecting her bag along the way, not speaking to anyone as she left, but it was all quite formal.'

'Who were these people?' Mickey asked, shivering suddenly, as he recalled Carol's joke about spooks.

'No one really knew, but, apparently, she was headhunted?'

'Headhunted? By whom?'

Tom took another mouthful of tea, looked around, leaned in towards Mickey and whispered, 'By MI5.'

Chapter 14

As he was in West London, Mickey headed once more to Lansbourgh's and re-visited the safety deposit box. Madeley was again there to greet him, with Mickey beginning to think he lived in the place. After twenty minutes, Mickey left with a few more fifties in his wallet. He looked around for a quiet spot on the Brompton Road, eventually finding an entry which sat between two buildings with a car parked on one side and a couple of blue industrial bins filled above their rims on the other. A slight stench from the drains caught his nostrils, along with a waft of warm air from a generator room; but, more importantly, it was empty of people. He took out the little card and dialled the number upon it. The phone rang three, maybe four times and he was about to cancel the call when Leila answered.

'Hello, how may I help you,' she asked.

He caught his breath before he spoke. 'Hi, could I make an appointment for this evening, please?'

'At what time would you like?' she asked.

There was an accent, from where he did not know, but her English was excellent.

'Nine p.m., if possible,' he replied.

'Okay, it is £250 for one hour. Ring me thirty minutes before this to confirm, then I will give you directions. Is this clear?'

'Yes.'

'Good, see you then,' and then she hung up.

Mickey stared at his phone and mouthed, 'Wow!'

What a piece of work! Talk about straight to the point. He dialled Carol's number, told her about his visit with Vinnie and the appointment he had arranged with Leila for later that evening. She laughed and agreed to drive him.

'Do you want to meet for food first?' she asked.

'Sure,' he replied. 'Any ideas?'

'I know a great pub just off the Bayswater Road; it will be convenient for your Holland Park liaison,' she teased.

'Okay, what's it called?'

'The Jekyll and Hyde. It's across from Hyde Park.'

'Right. Is seven o'clock too early?' he said, feeling as if they were arranging a date.

'Seven works for me,' she said.

'Great,' he replied. 'See you then.'

Mickey headed home, before taking Lucy to the park and thought about Lauren. Why would an MI5 officer, if that's what she was, contact him to investigate PetroUK, and apart from the Iran business what else were they connected with, to attract the attention of the security services?

Looking down at Lucy, he asked, 'Any ideas, girl?'

'Gruff,' she replied.

'My thoughts entirely, Lucy.'

They spent an hour in the park and left when it began to get colder as the sun dipped towards the west.

When they got home, he powered up the laptop, and with the Stock Market in London closing within the next hour, Mickey checked in on the current day's trading, starting with the top one hundred share index, before moving to Wall Street, which had just opened, and then US crude oil. With his quick scan complete, he browsed over the share price of PetroUK, which was currently steady at 232p, up slightly on the day before, but had not moved since earlier that morning. Trades were reasonable, with roughly the same amount of buying as selling. As he was about to sign off Sharecom, an alert tone along with a little red flag appeared, drawing his attention to the top of the screen, informing him that a company he was following had made an announcement to the London Stock Exchange. Clicking on the link, he saw a statement from PetroUK, which read:

Announcement to the London Stock Exchange and shareholders of
PetroUK Limited.

Appointment of Director.

PetroUK is delighted to announce Lee Chiang's appointment as director of the company to replace David Harrison, whom, we are sad to announce, recently passed away. Lee has joined the company from Tai Sing in Hong Kong and will take up his new position with immediate effect.

Signed,

Roger Mildenhall
Harold Goodwin
Geoffrey Burbridge.

Mickey, checking the director holdings, found that, surprise, surprise, Lee Chiang now held one hundred and sixteen million shares. He now believed that Chiang was Tai Sing or Jiading and whatever other shit Rocky could dig up. He was hoping Rocky could provide a few more clues as to what the hell was going on, when they met the next evening before the football.

Mickey arrived early at the Jekyll and Hyde. It was a quaint and cosy place, with a real Christmas tree. Its white lights gently faded in and out, along with the smell of fresh pine, which stirred his senses as he walked in. He found a table close to a wall and ordered a pint of Coors from a waiter wearing a traditional bar apron with Guinness emblazoned on it. Mickey told him he was there for food, but was waiting on one more. Only a few of the tables were occupied with diners, although a small group of people stood at the bar, city types, enjoying a Christmas drink.

Carol arrived a few minutes later, wearing a short, red, double-breasted wool coat, with a tartan scarf and a dark, woollen mini skirt, with thick tights.

She took a seat opposite Mickey, smiled and said, 'Hi.'

'Would you like a drink?' he asked.

She removed her coat, exposing a short sleeve white cotton top. 'As I'm the nominated driver, I'll have fresh orange over ice, please,' she announced.

Mickey nodded at the waiter, who came and took the drink order, leaving two food menus.

'Is the beer a little Dutch courage for later?' she asked, with a smile.

'You could say that,' he replied, taking an envelope from his pocket. 'I appreciate your help, Carol, and I don't expect your time for free,' he said, sliding it across the table.

She opened it, leafing through the five hundred pounds in fifties, and then looked at him, a little startled, and said, 'I'm not doing this for money, Mickey. I'm doing this for David!'

She looked a little cross, but Mickey calmly added, 'I totally understand, Carol, but I want you to have it. Your support is invaluable.'

She relaxed. 'Thank you, you're very kind.'

The waiter returned with Carol's drink and took the food order.

'There's something else,' Mickey said, handing her a printout of PetroUK's announcement to the Stock Exchange.

She read over it, and in a low voice said, 'This is a conspiracy, Mickey. They needed David out of the way to push through the contracts and put Chiang on the board.'

'It's beginning to look that way,' he replied with a sympathetic smile.

'We should go to the police,' she whispered.

'No, Carol. There isn't enough evidence and we still can't link them to David's death or murder. If and when we do get the evidence, we can turn it over to Lauren and let her deal with it.'

'Okay,' she sighed.

'By the way, there's one more thing I found out today.' He smiled teasingly.

She took a sip of her drink, and looked at him. 'What is it?' she asked slowly.

'You were right about spooks.'

She raised an eyebrow. 'What, Lauren?'

'Yup, she's MI5.'

'Shit!' she whispered.

He told her about meeting Tom Cheevers, his time with Barclay's and Lauren working in the fraud department.

'Do you think it's the same person?' she asked.

'She seems to be, and this Chameleon group she represents could be a unit set up to investigate industrial espionage and her previous experience seems to fit the MI5 profile.'

'But why you?'

'I really don't know,' he replied, taking a mouthful of beer.

She shrugged, and asked, 'Anything from Vinnie?'

'No, it's too early yet. He'll case the area first and get back to me in a few days.'

The waiter brought the food, and they were ready for it, as they both said very little throughout the meal. They relaxed and chatted over coffee, and Mickey felt his heart skip a beat as their fingers brushed each other's when they both reached for the milk.

'I could sit here all night,' she eventually said. 'I'm really enjoying the conversation and the company.'

Mickey smiled. 'I'll phone Leila and cancel,' he said, getting out his phone.

'No you will not,' she said with a grin. 'This is the reason we're here; we wouldn't be in this pub if you hadn't made a date with Leila.' She winked.

'Oh, don't call it a date; I'd rather have the one we're…'

'Having?' she mused.

'Yes,' he replied, feeling his face flush slightly.

She moved her hand half way across the table, with Mickey meeting it with his own, feeling her warm, soft fingers, as he reached the palm of her hand.

'Thank you for a lovely evening,' she said, gazing into his eyes.

'It's a pity we have to leave shortly,' he replied, holding her gaze, searching for something appropriate to say.

'Well, you have another lady to meet, and I hope you don't make as good an impression on her as you have on me.' She smiled. 'Right,' she added, gathering herself, 'you'd better make that phone call, Mr Ross.'

He returned her smile, shaking his head, and dialled Leila's number, with her answering a lot quicker than previously.

'Hello,' she said.

'Hi, I'm confirming my nine p.m. appointment,' he returned, glancing at Carol, now looking at him through her fingers, trying not to laugh.

'Do you know Holland Park underground station?' Leila asked.

'Yes,' he replied.

'Cross at the pedestrian lights. Once over the road, turn left, then take the next right into Netherby Way. When you reach the gate of number eighty-seven phone me again.'

'Okay.'

'See you soon,' she said, and hung up.

'Well?' asked Carol.

'Number eight- seven Netherby Way,' he replied.

'Let's go then,' she said.

'Right behind you,' Mickey replied, somewhat reluctantly.

Carol dropped him at the tube station, near to a coffee bar, and said that she would wait for him there.

'As soon as you're out of there, phone me,' she said.

'Don't worry, I will,' he replied, opening the door. 'Hopefully, this will not take long.'

Mickey watched as she drove off, turning into a side street. He used the pedestrian crossing and thought about the night Harrison was here. Once on the other side, he looked across at the tube station and the row of shops. It would have been a

Friday evening, earlier than what it was now and with more people around. He turned into Netherby Way, as Harrison would have, and walked along the tree-lined street. The walled entrance to the park was across from him, with its gate bolted and padlocked.

At the corner of Holland Court, he briefly paused, picturing the taxi patiently waiting with its engine running, the driver stretching and maybe yawning in his seat, thankful for a few minutes' rest, and then Harrison, a few yards further along, on the ground with his life slowly ebbing away. He surveyed his surroundings. It was quiet and the only sounds were his footsteps and the distant rumble of traffic from the main road. A line of cars sat parked at the kerb and roughly, every one hundred feet, he caught the glow of a street lamp. The bare branches of the overhanging trees played tricks with the light, as they danced shadows along the pavement, while Mickey became suddenly overcome with a sense of loneliness. He wondered if that was what Harrison had felt, still grieving the death of his wife, but seeking solace and companionship from a somewhat professional woman.

Number eighty-seven wasn't any different to the other properties in the row. He found nothing unusual about it and nothing that seemed out of place. It was a normal residential building, in a normal residential street; granted, a very upmarket street. At the gate, he dialled the number, with Leila answering almost immediately.

'I'm outside number eighty-seven,' he said.

'Good. Walk to the door. On the keypad press the button for number five. When the door buzzes, push it open, walk up the stairs and gently knock on the door in front of you.'

'Okay,' he replied, 'number five.'

Mickey pushed open the gate, catching a sliver of light from a twitch in a curtain, before he reached the door. He pushed the fifth button and waited, glancing around and spotting a security camera staring down at him. The door buzzed and he pushed it open, walking inside, with the door closing gently behind him. The hallway was silent, totally without sound, and unnerving. The wooden staircase smelt of fresh wood, as it wound upwards and to the right, with only the emergency lighting illuminating his way. On reaching the upper floor, he saw the apartment directly in front of him. He stepped towards the door cautiously, before giving it a gentle knock.

She opened the door slowly, then further, revealing herself, wearing a white chemise with matching underwear.

'Hello,' she said.

'Hi,' replied Mickey, somewhat nervously.

'What is your name?' she asked.

'It's Michael.'

She gave a faint smile, inviting him in, beckoning him to follow, along the short hallway, with her dark hair fallen across her shoulders and her chocolate eyes full of seduction. To Mickey, she seemed to glide across the floor, as if on ice, in one smooth and graceful movement.

The room when he entered it contained expensive furniture and a double bed, with pleasant low lighting, which gave off a warm, welcoming and relaxed feel.

Turning to face him, she asked, 'Is it one hour you require?'

'It is.'

'Full service?'

Mickey had no idea what full service was, but he nodded politely.

'The price is two hundred and fifty pounds,' she said, standing, smiling and oozing sex appeal.

It hurt Mickey to hand over five of Lauren's fifty pound notes, but he hoped it would be worth the cost.

'Would you like a drink?' she asked, as he passed her the money, which she took elegantly, as if an illusionist demonstrating a sleight of hand card trick.

'Please. Water, sparkling with ice and lemon if possible.'

'I will return shortly. Please remove your clothes and make yourself comfortable.'

Mickey had no intention of removing his clothes although he did take off his coat. He sat down in a leather armchair and made himself comfortable, just as Leila suggested. As he looked around the room, he thought the expensively decorated apartment was excessive to the point of garish, with an Italian chestnut three-seat leather sofa, gold leaf-framed mirror and two crystal chandeliers.

Leila returned a few minutes later with a small bottle of carbonated water, a tumbler with ice, but absent of lemon. More noticeable was her lack of underwear. She saw that Mickey was still fully dressed and now displayed a perplexed look on her face.

'Is there anything wrong?' she asked, as she handed him his drink.

'Would you mind if I asked you a few questions?'

'Are you the police?'

'No, I am not the police,' Mickey replied, handing her his card.

She nodded, but said nothing.

Mickey had enlarged the still of Harrison walking along a street; he unrolled it and handed it to her. While studying the picture, Leila's body stiffened, ever so slightly, and just a flinch. If Mickey had not been watching her closely, he would have missed it. While she absorbed the photograph, Mickey poured a little water into the glass, before taking a mouthful.

'Do you know this man?' he asked.

'I don't think so, should I?' she replied.

'He may have been a client,' he added.

'No, I don't know him. I'm sorry, I can't help you,' Leila said.

'His name was David Harrison,' Mickey replied, locking onto her eyes, before adding, 'David is dead!'

Having time to compose herself, the reaction to the mention of David's name and death sent a shiver down Mickey's spine. Leila returned his stare with one as cold as winter wind. 'Again, I'm sorry, I cannot help you. I haven't met this man.'

Mickey took another mouthful of water, stood and put on his coat. He walked towards her and said, 'Thank you for your time. If anything comes to mind after I have gone, you can ring the number on the card, or leave a message.'

She said nothing as he left the room, standing arms folded, holding Mickey's card, as he let himself out.

With the apartment door closed behind him, he almost bolted down the stairs. Once outside, Mickey breathed the fresh cold air into his lungs, being relieved to be out of Leila's apartment. The way she turned from a warm almost caring host to someone as cold as steel had unnerved him. He took out his phone and dialled Carol, who answered almost immediately.

'I'm out and walking towards the main road,' he said.

'I'm on my way,' she replied.

He walked briskly along the pavement, listening for any footsteps apart from his own. His hair raised on the back of his neck as he passed the spot where Harrison fell. Glancing behind, the street remained empty. Parked cars looked as if they had been there for hours and he jumped slightly as a cat moved across his path about ten feet in front. He was so highly strung; his own shadow would have frightened him. After another hundred yards, he saw a car turn the corner with its headlights bouncing along the street and slowing as it approached. He squinted at the car's registration plate and, seeing it was Carol's, he moved towards the kerb, putting his arm out as if stopping a bus. She pulled parallel to the kerb and flung open the door.

'How was the hot date?' she asked.

Blowing out his cheeks, he replied, 'A very confident, sophisticated and affluent lady, but when you look through all the crap, she's as hard as nails.'

'Did she admit to knowing David?' she asked, passing him a polystyrene cup. 'I got you a coffee.'

'Thanks,' he replied, removing the lid and setting it on the dash.

She switched her headlights to park, but kept the engine running.

'To begin with, she was a very welcoming exotic host, dressed in expensive underwear.'

Carol's eyes widened. 'You weren't there to look at her body.'

'She offered me a drink, took the money and disappeared from the room. When she returned, her expression changed when she saw that I hadn't taken off my kit. Then, when I started asking about David, her exterior hardened and more so after I showed her David's photograph, but she denied ever knowing him.'

The steam from the coffee began to mist the windows. Switching on the Mercedes air con, Carol said, 'Maybe she didn't know him.'

Mickey reached for his cup, shaking his head. 'I don't believe her. There is something about Leila, but I don't know what it is.'

The mist cleared, with Carol staring out of the windscreen, before she asked, 'Is this where David died?'

'Somewhere between here and the bend in the road, I'm afraid.'

She nodded, and then asked, 'Is Leila as attractive as her photographs?'

'When she opened the door, I could understand why David had befriended her. She is a very beautiful woman, but also an actress. When I started digging her veil dropped.'

'So, Mr Ross, what's next?' she asked.

'I think we should tail her.'

'How do we do that?'

'I sit across the street and wait until she leaves the apartment, then follow her.'

Carol pondered slightly before she asked, 'Do you have another car, Mickey, apart from your black taxi?'

'No, why?'

'It's just that your black cab will, sort of, stick out a mile in this street.'

'I hadn't thought about that.'

She was silent for a few seconds and then, turning to him, she said, 'Tell you what.'

'What?'

'I'll do it.' She smiled.

'Are you sure?' he asked quizzically. 'It's not much fun, Carol.'

'Yes, I'll arm myself with a flask of coffee and my tablet. I've an idea how she looks and her height.'

'You'll have to follow her, if she leaves.'

'I know.'

Mickey took another mouthful of coffee, drumming his fingers on the side of the door. 'I'm not sure. It could be dangerous,' he said.

'I'll be fine. I promise I'll keep my distance,' she said, leaning in towards him.

'Do you really want to do this?' he asked, questioning her sanity.

'One hundred percent. When do you want me?'

Mickey looked at her. Her face was half in shadow, but he could see her features quite clearly. When do you want me? she had asked. How about right now? It had been quite a while since he had kissed a woman in a car. 'Would the day after tomorrow be too soon?' he finally asked.

'Perfect!' she replied. 'Where to now, Mickey?'

'You could drop me at the station.'

'Would you object to a lift home?' she asked, putting the car into drive.

Being driven home is generally a simple, straightforward question, thought Mickey, but being driven home by a woman you are becoming attracted to could raise complications. It had, though, began to rain again and the car was warm, the coffee good and the company great, so he replied, 'Thanks.'

Leila watched as Mickey exited the gate and began his walk along the street. Once he was out of sight, she went to her private bedroom and removed a mobile phone from a bedside drawer. The switched-on phone was set to silent, but she scrolled the contacts list until she found the name she wanted, before returning to the main room and again peering through the curtains, this time checking to be sure that no one was loitering below. Further along, a car had stopped with its parking lights on, possibly her visitor, then again possibly not. She dialled the number and waited.

'Yes,' the man said, when he answered.

'I've just had a visitor,' Leila replied.

'What did they want?'

'*He* was asking about David.'

The man paused. 'Do we know his name?'

'He left a card; his name is Michael Ross, a private investigator.'

'Do we have a face?' the man asked.

Leila moved towards the back of the room to her laptop and pressed a random key. The screen illuminated with a larger-than-life photograph of Mickey, looking full on into the security camera.

'Yes, we have a face,' she replied. 'Pity it's such a handsome face.'

Chapter 15

On the drive home, Mickey learned a few more things about Harrison. He once played amateur rugby in his younger days, union that was, not league, although Mickey didn't know the difference, he didn't ask.

'Mickey, did you ever play rugby?' Carol asked.

'No, footie's my game,' he replied. 'I'm for the Lane tomorrow night.'

'The Lane?' she questioned.

'White Hart Lane.'

'Spurs?'

'You got it.'

'I'm a Gooner,' she said.

Mickey looked at her, horrified. 'Arsenal! You are joking, aren't you?'

'Yeah, I just wanted to see the look on your face,' she replied laughing.

'Very funny,' he said, stretching out in his seat.

It was approaching ten p.m. and the rain turned to sleet as they slowly drifted in a northerly direction, passing through Marylebone. Central London remained heavy with traffic as they turned left before Euston, avoiding the escaping shoppers and skirting the fringes of Regents Park. Not long after, the traffic thinned out, and they quickly continued their journey.

'David must have been very fit,' Mickey said eventually.

'Do you think so?'

'He ran The Three Peaks, didn't he?'

'And this year's London Marathon, and all for charity,' she said proudly.

'Charity? Good for him,' he said.

'Every year, around this time, we would have a company lunch in some plush London hotel and David would announce to the board and the rest of us who next year's designated charity would be.'

'Who is it this year?'

'Medicines San Frontiers,' she replied, 'Doctors without borders. They are very much involved with the medical relief in Syria. David was disturbed about what was happening there and the refugees streaming into Europe.'

'Do you think they'll carry on the tradition?'

'I doubt it,' she said. 'It was all David's work. He would ask me to contact the charity and organise a meeting between himself and their UK chief executive, explaining how the charity would be promoted: such as sporting events, auctions and special lunches. The charity would also be carried on company material such as stationery, with coverage on the website and television commercials.'

'He sounded like a great boss and I'm genuinely sorry you lost him.'

'Thanks. He was, and I am,' she said sadly.

They travelled the rest of the way in silence, until close to Mickey's street.

'Turn left here,' he said. 'After the next corner turn right, then up to the end of the cul-de-sac. Then you'll see the house on the right, with the black taxi in the drive.'

'Very nice,' she said, after completing the directions.

'You think so. I got it second hand.'

'The house, Mickey, not the cab,' she laughed.

'Right.'

There was an awkward silence as they both undid their seatbelts, before looking at each other, smiling. Mickey leaned in towards her and Carol did the same, with their lips touching lightly before fully, as their tongues searched each other's mouths.

'Thank you,' she softly said, when they parted.

'You're probably sick of the sight of coffee, but do you fancy another?' he asked.

'Sure. I'll park behind your cab, if that's all right.'

They went inside, turning on lights as Lucy came to meet them.

'Lucy, this is Carol. Carol, meet Lucy.'

'Hello, Lucy.'

'I'd better let her out.' He opened the patio door, with Lucy bounding out into the garden.

'So, here you are, all on your own, in a three-bedroom semi,' she said.

'It wasn't supposed to be,' he replied, filling the kettle. 'Sophie upped sticks and left.'

'Where's the bathroom?' she asked.

'Upstairs, first door on the right,' he replied.

Lucy was at the door waiting to get in. 'Well, girl, what do you think?' he asked her. Wagging her tail, Lucy gave a quiet woof of approval, as Mickey heard Carol coming slowly down the stairs.

'Do you take sugar?' he asked, with his back to her.

'No, just a little milk,' she replied softly.

Turning around, he saw that she had a smile on her face, but it wasn't just her face he was looking at. She was walking towards him with just her top and underwear on, having removed her skirt and tights. 'Shall we skip the coffee?' she asked.

'We could,' he replied, as she got close enough for him to smell the faintness of her perfume.

They stood looking at each other for a few seconds, before slowly moving their heads in, their lips meeting again. Mickey put his hands on her waist and she gripped hers around his neck, as they stood locked together, not wanting to let go. When they did break, Carol took his hand and he led her upstairs.

In the bedroom, he slipped off her top, gently kissing her neck, before he reached around, unclipping her bra. She gave a gentle moan as his mouth and tongue moved down over her pert breasts and erect nipples. She undid the buttons on his shirt, sliding her fingers through the hairs of his chest, allowing the shirt to slip from his back, as he unbuttoned his trousers. They moved onto the bed, their arms and legs searching for each other, as he lowered his hand, slowly removing her underwear and gently stroking her soft flesh as their mouths and tongues entwined. She gave a sharp intake of breath as his finger searched inside her, with him kicking away his shorts as she fumbled with the waistband. Grabbing hold of him, she caressed his throbbing erection, as the moment arrived. Sliding underneath, she parted her legs as he moved on top. With her hand, she guided him down, and in one gentle movement he entered her, feeling a buzz of electricity run through him as he felt her body gyrate. A sheen of perspiration appeared on her body, while Mickey held the small of her back, with Carol wrapping her legs around him. Pushing deeper with each thrust, he found his animal instinct released, as he grew inside her. With his head buried in her chest, he held both breasts, sucking on each ripe nipple, as their breathing increased, heavy within their bodies. Mickey, unable to hold back any longer, released himself inside her. Carol squealed in delight, holding him, with her fingers digging into his back as their momentum gradually slowed, before coming to a stop. They stayed still for a time, not moving, just the two of them together as one. When she opened her eyes, she smiled and said, 'Thank you.'

Mickey rolled onto his side as Carol snuggled into his chest. Neither of them spoke as he stroked her hair, breathing her scent. The light from the landing was comfortable and soft. He heard the rain beating off the window and Carol's soft breathing as he realised she was drifting to sleep. Glancing at the bedside clock, he caught the time as it turned to 11.32 p.m. and, with a warm relaxed feeling, he closed his eyes and soon after he also was asleep.

When he awoke, he was alone, the room was in darkness, the door tightly closed and the only light was from the street lamps outside. He got up, slipped on his boxers and put on a T-shirt he found in a drawer. When he opened the door, the light from the landing was on and as he went downstairs, he found Carol in the kitchen, as she cooked breakfast.

'Good morning,' she said. 'Did you sleep well?'

'The best, and you?' he replied, noticing that she was wearing his shirt that he had worn the previous evening.

'Yes, like a log. I hope you don't mind,' she said, pointing at his shirt.

Shaking his head, he asked, 'Why did you get up so early?'

'Well, a certain little lady ran up the stairs and licked my face at six o'clock, hence the shirt,' she replied.

'Oops, I'm sorry,' he said, glancing at the clock for the first time since he got up. 'She was looking for me, but you were the first one she found.'

'I let her out and gave her some breakfast and now she's nibbling on a piece of bacon.'

'Looks like you've made a new friend, Lucy,' he said, rubbing her head. 'Where did you find the bacon?'

'Lost at the back of the freezer. There were even sausages hiding in there too,' she answered tongue in cheek.

'I forgot about them,' he said. 'I usually have porridge in the morning, but this smells really good.'

'Almost ready, if you want to make the coffee.'

'I'll have tea, but I'll make you coffee.'

'Tea will do me,' she said. 'Toast is on the table.'

'Great.'

He walked behind her, stopped and kissed the back of her neck.

'Hmm, thank you,' she said.

He thought she looked fabulous with just his shirt on. He wanted to take her back upstairs and take everything off her again, but, putting those lovely thoughts to one side, he asked, 'What are your plans for today?'

'I'm meeting a friend for lunch and then we're going Christmas shopping.'

'Bah humbug,' he said, taking a seat. 'Only joking. I quite enjoy Christmas.'

'Good, so do I, which makes me ask, where will you be at Christmas?'

He shrugged. 'I haven't really thought of it. I'll probably go back home to Cornwall; that's where I've gone for the last few years.'

'Is that what you and Sophie did?' she asked, sliding a plate of sausages, bacon and eggs in front of him.

'She was from Sevenoaks,' he said, buttering a slice of toast. 'So we would go to Sophie's parents for Christmas, then to mine for New Year, though each year we switched it about. I always found it stressful. I would have to put up with her parents and then my parents would have to put up with Sophie.'

'Sounds delightful,' she said, with a wink. 'And I bet you wound her up by calling it One-oak,' she added.

Mickey smiled. 'Would I ever? Anyway, what are you doing for Christmas?'

'The boys are going skiing, so I won't see them until after the New Year. I'll probably go back to Norfolk,' she replied sadly.

Mickey didn't say anything for a few seconds. He chewed on his food and then asked, 'Well, considering we just met two days ago, why don't we do Christmas?'

'You serious?'

'It's just a thought; have a think about it.'

'It's mad, isn't it? We hardly know each other and here we are discussing Christmas,' she said.

They had finished eating, and were enjoying a second mug of tea and each other's company, but as her cleavage was showing through his shirt, Mickey was beginning to have those lovely thoughts again, so he asked, 'What time are you meeting your friend?'

'Not until twelve,' she replied with a twinkle in her eye. 'Don't worry, Mickey, I'm not going anywhere without part two.'

Part two lasted just as long as part one, as they experimented with different positions. When they eventually prised themselves from the bed, it was shortly after nine a.m.

Carol used the shower first and through the sound of the water she shouted, 'Mickey, would you go out to my car and take out the sports bag from my boot, please.'

He found her keys and collected her bag. When he got back upstairs, she was sitting on the bed, with a towel wrapped around, drying off her hair.

'Thanks,' she said. 'Do you have an iron?'

'Of course. I'm not entirely undomesticated.'

She made a face, then opened her bag and took out a hair dryer and straighteners, some make-up and a change of clothes.

'Do you always carry these things in your car?' he asked.

'No,' she winked. 'Just last night.'

He laughed. 'You crafty devil.'

'Well, when we were having coffee in my kitchen the other day, I thought, he's a bit of all right.'

'Just as well,' he said, 'because I was thinking the same.'

She smiled. 'Well, I haven't time to get back into bed again, not that I wouldn't want to.'

Mickey pulled a face and asked, 'What else do you have in your bag?'

'Just my tablet,' she said, unrolling the hairdryer.

'Can I have a look?' he asked.

'Sure, but this is going to make a noise,' she said, pointing at the hairdryer. 'Anyway, I thought you were going for a shower?'

'I will in a minute. I'll give you the password for the Wi-Fi first,' he said.

'Thanks.'

The water in the shower was hot and the power massaged his back. When he was finished, he took a towel, dried himself and went back into the bedroom. Carol was dressed and sitting on the bed with the tablet on her lap.

'What was the address for Leila's website, Mickey?' she asked.

'Hold on and I'll find the card, it should be in the back of my trousers. Why?'

'Last night when you were with her…'

'Don't say it like that. It sounds as if I was a client.'

'Sorry. After I dropped you off, I brought up her website. Just for curiosity and to have a look at her.'

'And?'

'Well, this morning, I can't access it.'

Mickey frowned. 'That's strange. The address should be in your history, unless you deleted it.'

'I didn't delete the history; the website's not loading.'

He found the card and passed it to her. She typed the web address exactly as it appeared on the card. The tablet searched for the site and came back unavailable.

'You must have made an impression,' she mocked.

'Try another site,' he said.

Carol tried the BBC News website, which loaded almost immediately, and then a second site, which also loaded.

'Try Leila's again.'

Retyping the web address, the tablet searched again, but came back with the same result.

'What do you think?' she asked.

'Either she has deleted the website or the server has.'

'Maybe you hit a nerve when you mentioned David.'

'Where's your phone?' Mickey asked.

'It's in my coat, why?'

'I want to see if her number is still available.'

He dialled Leila's number, putting Carol's phone on speaker, but got a dead line.

'You've spooked her,' she said.

'Do you still want to do tomorrow's stake-out?' he asked.

'Do you think she'll still be there?'

'It would be a bit drastic if she moved out because of one visit from me. I believe she'll still be there, but Leila may be more aware of what's going on around her if she leaves the apartment. So, if you don't want to do this, it's okay.'

'Stop worrying, Mickey. I'll be there by six thirty in the morning,' she said. 'Which should be early enough, don't you think?'

He nodded and kissed her.

When they parted, she shook her head and said, 'I'd better go and put the kettle on, because we'll get nothing done today if we stay up here.'

Mickey got dressed, went downstairs and they both had coffee. They chatted about everything and nothing, before he reminded her about Rocky's search for the Tai Sing connection. Carol said she would phone the next morning when she was in place near Leila's apartment. Then it was time for her to go. They stood in the hall and kissed like teenagers, before he carried her bag to the car and they kissed again through the window. She started the engine, reversed down the drive, tooted her horn and, with a growl from the exhaust, she took off down the street like Lewis Hamilton.

Lucy was standing in the hall, wagging her tail.

'Don't worry, girl, Carol will be back,' he said.

Chapter 16

For the time of year, it was a reasonable morning. The rain from the night before had gone and although the sky above remained grey, there was little to suggest that anything else would fall from it.

'Let's go for a walk, Lucy,' he said, patting her on the head.

In the park, Mickey released Lucy from the lead, but she remained close. He walked slowly, thinking about the case and stepped aside as a couple of cyclists rode slowly towards him. He snapped the lead back onto Lucy when a long line of primary schoolchildren, wearing hi-vis vests, along with a few teachers, took a short cut through the park. As he stopped to let them past, he eyed three men entering the park, each of them carrying a coffee to go. They were clearly business types, with the man in the middle gesticulating with his free hand and, every so often, one of the other two men would nod or say something in return. It reminded Mickey of Harrison's photograph, the one given to him by Lauren, and ultimately he had shown to Leila. A captured moment in time. He had a thought, so he got out his phone and dialled Carol's number.

'Do you miss me already?' she answered.

'Yes, but that's not why I'm ringing,' he replied.

'Aww, and I thought you were being romantic.'

She was still driving, as he could hear the ticking indicator. 'Are you parked?' he asked.

'No, I'm sitting at the traffic lights waiting to turn.'

'Good, this won't take long,' he said.

'What do you need, Mickey?'

'Carol, which of the directors, if any, would you say was close to David. In other words, who was he friendliest with?'

'Let me think,' she replied. 'David couldn't stand Harold Goodwin: they had a personality clash. Harold is roughly ten years older than what David was, and when David first started at the company, Harold was his boss. So, when David got a board position, Harold claimed it was only because of who his father was.'

'And did you think this was true?'

'To a point yes, but David knew the firm inside out and he had been there most of his working life.'

'Okay, what about Mildenhall and Burbridge?'

'He had a good working relationship with Geoffrey Burbridge, but I would have to say that was all it was. They wouldn't have spent any social time together.'

'That leaves Mildenhall,' he said.

'It would have to be Roger. He supported David after Natasha's death. Now, when I think about it, he helped David sort out the legalities of selling his property on the South Downs.'

'Roger it is then, thanks,' he said.

'What did you want to know this for, Mickey?' she asked.

'It's an idea I have,' he said. 'You have a good afternoon shopping and lunching and whatever else you girlies get up to when you're together and forget all about this for the rest of the day.'

'Yes, sir,' she replied, sarcastically.

'Thanks for last night,' he said.

'And this morning,' she replied.

There was a short awkward silence as he heard her car slowing down and then the indicator blinking again.

'That's me home now, Mickey,' she said. 'I'll phone you tomorrow morning. I hope you enjoy the football tonight.'

'Thanks,' he replied.

He put away his phone and continued walking with Lucy. At the far end of the park, was a pond with a low rail, but high enough to prevent wandering toddlers from falling in. A few hardy ducks floated on top of its surface. As a young mother with a small child in a pushchair stopped to throw broken pieces of bread onto the water, the ducks quacked excitedly as they began homing in on the grub. Mickey held Lucy tight as she barked at the ducks. When they were almost home, Mickey felt the phone in his pocket vibrate; he checked the screen before he answered, and saw the private number, but took the call anyway.

'Hello, Michael,' she said.

'Lauren?'

'That's right. I'm ringing you for an update.'

Not wanting to sound silly, Mickey decided not to ask about MI5, so instead he said, 'I met with Harrison's PA, Carol Freeman.' He wasn't sure how much he should tell Lauren about Carol, but didn't think it mattered much, if she knew Carol was working with him.

'Was she helpful, Michael?'

'She is,' he said, smiling, as thoughts of the previous evening came to mind.

'Is she helping you with the case?' she asked.

'I find her input useful, Lauren.'

'Good.'

He told her about Chiang and the investment company known as Tai Sing, along with his visit to Leila and her subsequent denial of ever knowing Harrison.

'Hmm…' she said. 'I wasn't expecting that.'

Mickey was noncommittal.

'Do you think Leila's lying?' Lauren asked.

'I think she is, but I can't be entirely sure, Lauren,' he said.

'So, what's your next move?'

'Carol's going to tail Leila tomorrow; if she leaves the apartment, that is.'

'Do you think that's wise, Michael?'

'What, tailing or letting Carol do it?'

'Carol doesn't have any experience, and it could be dangerous.'

'Why would Carol be in danger?' he asked.

'I… who knows, Michael. Leila could have something to do with Harrison's death,' she replied, slightly flustered.

Mickey noticed the hesitancy in Lauren's voice. For the first time he had struck a nerve. 'I won't put Carol at risk,' he said.

'Anything else?' she asked, now having gathered herself.

He decided not to be entirely truthful with her and skipped over the flash drive they had found in Harrison's office.

'Nothing else at the moment,' he said.

'Good work, Michael, and it's only been a few days,' she said. 'If you find anything of urgency you can always contact me by telephone.'

'Thanks, I will,' he replied.

When he got home, Mickey had a quick look at the markets. It had been a quiet day all round, with the graph on PetroUK practically flat-lining, as were most of the commodities, including Oil and Gold, and with the Christmas holiday approaching more days of static trading were to be expected.

When Mickey exited Seven Sister's underground station on the Tottenham High Road, he saw a line of traffic, as far as the eye could see, sitting bumper to bumper, and inching forward ever so slowly. A car horn blasted as a driver pulled out of a side street blocking one of the lanes, and every few minutes a red London bus would crawl past, as slow as everything else. It was two hours before kick-off, but the match traffic mingled with the commuters in one monotonous slow progress through Tottenham.

Shops remained open whenever a match was on, the fast food takeaways full and, with Tottenham having a diverse multicultural population there were many varieties of food on offer. The area had received bad press, after the 2011 riots, but Mickey had been the token white man on the High Road many times late at night and hadn't ever encountered a problem. He often thought Tottenham was as cosmopolitan as many other parts of London, but he would admit that maybe it was a little rough around the edges.

It was a twenty-minute walk to the football stadium, with numerous pubs for supporters to quench their thirst along the way. Mickey was heading for The Bill Nick, named after Tottenham's most successful manager, Bill Nicholson. Nicholson had been responsible for bringing the glory days to White Hart Lane, when, in his first game in charge in October 1958, Tottenham beat Everton 10-4. A successful period for the club culminated with a league and cup double in 1961, retaining the FA Cup in 1962 and the following year becoming the first British side to win a European competition by defeating favourites Atletico Madrid 5-1 in the final in Rotterdam to win the now-defunct European Cup Winners Cup.

The Bill Nick pub was only five minutes from the ground and set in a three-storey art deco building which pre-dated the Second World War, with the inside probably remaining untouched since the builders left. Strands of fraying thread showed from the original cloth bench seats, which over the decades had been patched up. The lighting was dim and when empty it was a dark, depressing place with a dirty tiled floor, but on match day it morphed into a lively, boisterous boozer, full of Spurs fans.

Mickey got himself a pint and, for all its faults, The Bill Nick served good, cold beer, with plenty of bite. He nabbed the only available table, but soon realised why it was the solitary empty one. The table was soaked with spilt beer, with either the table base uneven or the floor it was resting on. He grabbed a pile of napkins from the bar counter, dried the surface, and had only just sat down when Rocky appeared with a pint in one hand and a couple of bags of nuts in the other.

'You doing a bit of housekeeping, Mickey?'

'Yeah, you could say that. How's it going, Rocky?'

'Ask me after the game, mate,' he said with a smile.

Spurs were at home to Sunderland, who were languishing very close to the relegation area; Tottenham again were pushing for a top-four position and Champions League, but if this season went to form, and it usually did, they would again finish fifth and miss out once more on that coveted fourth position. Every game was a must-win, and after Saturday's draw at Newcastle, three points were required.

'Relax, Rocky, we always beat Sunderland.' Winked Mickey.

'That's right, mate, you put the scud on us,' he said, throwing Mickey a bag of nuts.

Rocky made himself as comfortable as he could on a wooden stool, smoothing his hand across the table to ensure it was dry and free from any stickiness, before unrolling a couple of sheets of A4 paper.

'Right, Mickey, I did a lot of digging and I mean a lot. These people don't want to be found.'

'Did you hear about the new director at PetroUK?' Mickey asked, cutting in.

'It's all over the city, mate: Lee Chiang. I'll tell you more about him later.'

'I'm all ears,' Mickey replied, opening his bag of nuts.

'Right, let's start. I told you about Tai Sing, so we can tie this Chiang fellow to them,' Rocky said. 'They are a subsidiary of Jiading Financial in Shanghai; again, as you know.'

Mickey nodded, but remained silent.

Rocky turned the first sheet of paper towards Mickey, showing a chart, much like a family tree, connecting Tai Sing and Jiading.

'The trail moves to Jakarta in Indonesia, and a company called Nangapinoh, which deals in import and export.'

'What do they import?'

'Plastic.'

'What sort of plastic?'

'All types of plastic, anything from bottles to the plastic casings on electronic devices. It's a throwaway world, Mickey, we dump it and the Far East collects it.'

Mickey nodded.

'And then all that shit stays put in some warehouse in Jakarta, before it's exported to Sri Lanka, about three weeks later.'

'But what do they do with it, before it's shipped?' Mickey asked.

'Nothing,' he replied.

'Nothing? This is bollocks,' Mickey said, throwing up his hands.

'I know, but here's the best part: the authorities in Jakarta just turn a blind eye.'

'Yeah, unless they're on someone's payroll,' Mickey said. 'Okay, mate, I'm starting to feel like Thomas Cook. Who does the plastic get exported to… hold on, Rocky, who owns this Nanga… what the hell you called it?' he asked, taking a mouthful of beer.

'Nangapinoh, and it's our friends in Shanghai, Jiading Financial, who it's registered to.'

'Lee Chiang again,' Mickey said.

'You got it,' he answered. 'The plastic travels across the Indian Ocean to a container port in Colombo. From there it goes by road to an industrial estate in Padukka on the outskirts of Colombo. Here, the plastic is melted down in the Tatrun factory, and finally made back into consumer items for the European and UK market.'

'What type of products?'

'Toys, electronic devices, smart phones,' holding his phone up to show Mickey, 'and fleeces.'

'Fleeces?'

'Yeah, the fleece you zip up after a workout or while walking the dog comes from plastic bottles.'

'And who runs this Tatrun?'

'Nangapinoh.'

'Timeout, Rocky, I need another pint. Do you want one?'

'Sure.'

Mickey drained his glass and went to the bar for another two beers. The pub was filling up with supporters, and his head was thumping, craving for something much stronger than beer, but he still wanted to go to the game and if he appeared intoxicated he'd be denied entry. He came back with two pints and a couple of bags of crisps, passing one to Rocky.

'Thanks, Mickey, I'm starving. By the time I left the office, I didn't have time for food.'

'It's the least I could do,' he said. 'So, Rocky, what happens to these products after Sri Lanka?'

'Ceylon Operators, an independent Sri Lankan shipping company, sets sail with the containers, along with hundreds of others. They travel through Suez, and then offload at Limassol in Cyprus. The other containers are eventually picked up by various carriers and distributed across Europe, but the ones we are following sit for a week to ten days, before being put on board the *Saga Moon*.'

'*Saga Moon*?'

'It's a container ship that used to sail between Limassol and Tilbury Docks in East London, but since they opened the new London Gateway port in the estuary, it docks there now instead. It has a registration with a post office number in Larnaca, Cyprus, and is owned by a private equity company.'

'Private equity company?' Mickey asked, holding a large crisp mid-air.

Rocky ran his finger down the page. 'That's right, Mickey, the name's here somewhere,' he replied. 'Found it, it's called Black Castle.'

Mickey stared at him. 'Black Castle; you did say that, didn't you?'

'Yeah, what's up, mate?'

'Rocky, you're telling me there's a link from Black Castle to Jiading and ultimately Tai Sing.'

'That's right,' Rocky said, taking a sip of beer. 'There's something else bothering you, mate, yeah?'

'Rocky, we have Lee Chiang as Tai Sing and Jiading, then we track him with the scrap plastic to Sri Lanka, across the

Indian Ocean to the Med, with the cargo on board the *Saga Moon* registered to Black Castle.'

'Shit!' The penny finally dropping, Rocky looked at him open mouthed, before whispering, 'Chiang is Black Castle.'

'The boy's a genius,' Mickey replied sarcastically. 'Not only that, Rocky, Chiang owns 10% of PetroUK's stock and is installed as the new director. Black Castle owns 8% of PetroUK's stock; therefore, Chiang now has 18% as a director, trumping the other three's 10% each. Only Sir John Warricker, the chairman of the company, has an extra 2%.'

'Wow, Mickey! This is big shit, man, you need to be careful.'

'Why?'

'Remember I said I knew more about Chiang. Well, I have a contact in Hong Kong, Li Yung is her name, she works the trading floor on behalf of JP Morgan. Hot bit of gear she is; I'm waiting for a trip out to the Far East so I can hopefully nail her.'

'Typical, Rocky, always thinking about your dick.'

'After I phoned you back the other day, I rang Li for some lowdown on this Lee Chiang fellow. She knew of his name, but she also did a lot of detective work to confirm it was the same bloke.'

'Go on.'

'It appears Lee Chiang is a nasty piece of work, with connections in racketeering, money laundering, drug smuggling and prostitution in Hong Kong. Chiang, according to Li, is head of a Chinese Triad family.'

When he said that, Mickey almost choked on his pint.

'You okay, mate?'

'I was, until a few moments ago.'

‘I’m warning you, Mickey,’ he said. ‘Be careful. Whatever you’re doing, don’t risk your life for an extra few quid. These Triads don’t piss about.’

‘Yeah, I know,’ he said.

Mickey’s concern was Chiang’s prostitution link and maybe Leila, which meant Carol, could be at risk.

It was a half an hour before kick-off. Mickey and Rocky finished their pints and left the pub. Police on horseback co-ordinated crowd control, with the traffic on the High Road now static, as a crescendo of Yid Army erupted from Spurs’ large Jewish following as they walked towards the entrance on Park Lane.

They got into the stadium and took their seats, with a section of Sunderland fans to their left creating plenty of noise, and at five minutes to eight, the referee led the two teams onto the pitch.

‘I can’t believe what I just saw,’ said Rocky, as they were leaving the stadium.

Mickey was having difficulty believing what he’d just seen as well.

‘The biggest piece of shit, they are,’ continued Rocky.

Tottenham had failed to score. For ninety minutes, they watched as Sunderland parked the team coach in front of their own goal. Hardly an opposition player had crossed the halfway line all evening, until the second minute of stoppage time. Spurs surged forward and then Sunderland caught them on the break. A counter-attack, with their striker picking up the ball just inside his own half. Tottenham’s back four were caught out of position and with the goalkeeper rushing out, the ball was hooked over him, with everyone watching as it rolled almost apologetically into the empty net: 1-0 to Sunderland.

Stunned silence around the ground, apart from the few hundred hardened away fans, who cheered and sang for the final sixty seconds of the game.

'What was it you said, Mickey? We never lose to Sunderland.'

'I didn't pick the team, Rocky, they rode their luck.'

'Yeah, but Sunderland.'

Rocky wasn't just annoyed about the result. Mickey knew that when Rocky returned to work the following day he was going to get it in the neck. On either side of him sat two other football-mad supporters, one an Arsenal fan, the other Chelsea.

'Never mind, mate,' Mickey said. 'I'm hungry, let's get a kebab, I'm buying.'

Rocky nodded, stuck his hands in his pockets and the two of them joined the rest of the despondent home fans and trudged down the High Road.

They took a seat in a kebab shop as Mickey felt his phone vibrate. He took it from his pocket and saw it was a message from Carol.

'*How was the football?*'

'*We lost 1-0, gutted,*' he replied.

She typed a sad face, then added, '*Maybe tomorrow night I could cheer you up,*' and ended it with a wink.

'*I look forward to it,*' he replied, with a smiley.

Rocky must have seen the look on Mickey's face, because he asked, 'You got a new bird, or something?'

'Possibly.'

'Who is she?'

'David Harrison's former PA.'

'Harrison?' Rocky thought for a second, trying to make the connection. 'That dead bloke from PetroUK. His secretary?'

'That's the one.'

'How?' Rocky was trying to swallow and talk at the same time.

'I called at her house to ask a few questions and then she offered to help.'

'Nice one,' he said. 'Have you shagged her yet?' he added, a little too loud.

A few heads at the counter turned in their direction, while one of the young girls behind it smiled and giggled.

Realising his indiscretion, Rocky offered a whispered, 'Sorry!'

Chapter 17

Carol parked her Mercedes in a side street that ran at ninety degrees to Leila's. She chose her parking space carefully to ensure she had an uninterrupted view of the apartment, and to avoid inconveniencing residents by parking close to a gate or driveway; but, more importantly, she didn't want to draw any unnecessary attention to herself. She parked near to the trunk of a large ash tree, with its roots rippling the pavement around its base, reminding her of a pebble when thrown into still water. A heavy frost had descended and the light from the street lamps glistened the road like little fragments of broken glass.

It was just before six thirty in the morning, and Carol had the heat at full blast, with the outside temperature a few degrees below freezing. She was wearing a pink scarf with a black puffed North Face jacket, blue jeans and a pair of short flat-healed furry boots to keep her feet warm and comfortable if she needed to walk. She sipped on a plastic flask cup filled with hot coffee and nibbled on a cereal bar, feeling a warm glow inside and not just from the coffee, smiling to herself with thoughts turning to Mickey. She was relaxed in his company and the lovemaking was special too, as she thought back to the morning before and began to feel aroused.

'Pull yourself together, girl,' she said aloud, to no one but herself.

The car radio, tuned to a local station, gave a traffic report of a shed-load from a heavy goods vehicle on the North

Circular road close to the Redbridge flyover, closing the southbound lanes.

She sent Mickey a message and told him she was in place. Not long after, he phoned.

'Good morning, Mickey,' she said.

'How are you this morning?' he asked.

'Slightly tired, but I have my coffee and a bar to chew on. How long do you want me to stay?'

'How good is your bladder?'

She laughed. 'What a question! If you must know, I peed as much as I could before I left.'

'Good. Give it a few hours; if you think it's a waste of time, then leave.'

'Okay.'

'Carol, if you do need to follow Leila, please be careful.'

'Why, what's up?' she asked.

'It's Chiang, he may have Triad links,' he replied.

She was quiet for a second. 'Okay, go on.'

'From what Rocky told me last night, Chiang could be involved with drugs, money laundering and prostitution.'

'Prostitution? Do you think there's something between him and Leila?' she asked.

'David's the common denominator, so it's possible,' he replied.

A car drove slowly along the street, its headlights reflected in Carol's rear-view mirror, dazzling her eyes.

'It's okay if you want to go home,' he said. 'I wouldn't put you in any danger.'

She thought for a moment. 'No, Mickey, I'll stay, I'll be fine,' she said, before adding, 'will I see you tonight?'

'That was my next question.'

'What?'

‘Do you like stir-fry?’ he asked.

‘Yes.’

‘Good, because I’m making one for tea, if you fancy joining me.’

‘I’d love to,’ she said.

‘Great! Will you keep me up to date with Leila?’

‘I will. See you soon,’ she replied.

A chink of daylight appeared in the sky to the east, nautical twilight it was called. Something she had remembered from her school days, all those years ago. Nautical twilight began when the centre of the sun was geometrically twelve degrees below the earth’s horizon, and ended in the evening when it was not any longer possible to navigate at sea via the horizon.

The morning was cold and clear, and around her the street had begun to awaken. Lights appeared in upstairs and downstairs rooms, with gates creaking as the early risers started their cars and headed off for another day’s work. It was bin day and numerous black objects began appearing on the pavement. A trickle of people began walking along the street making their way to the underground station or bus stops, each of them muffled with overcoats, hats, scarves and gloves. Some walked gingerly along the frosty pavement, others preferring the quiet road.

By 7.20 a.m., the dark shadows had all but departed, the street lights blinked off and she was able to pick out proper shapes. More traffic appeared on the street, with one vehicle roughly every minute. A few dog walkers braved the cold; one man, with a large dog, walked slowly by her car, crossed over the road and disappeared, only to reappear ten minutes later with a newspaper under his arm. Carol heard a sound in the distance growing closer: it was the bin lorry beginning to make its round. She heard the engine strain as its rear mechanism lifted the bins and then the thump as they emptied and the rattle as they were trailed back to their gateways.

As Carol continued to keep warm and sip on her coffee, a few streets away, Benjamin Levy sat on a high stool at the breakfast bar in the kitchen of his home in Notting Hill. He had just finished his breakfast of hot porridge, which to him was an acquired taste. The porridge reminded him of Kasha, made from buckwheat, barley and oats, that had provided him with warmth on the snow-capped Mount Hermon in the Golan Heights, during those winter months whilst on Israeli national service.

He poured a second cup of coffee whilst reading an online news item from the *Jerusalem Post*, as tensions increased in the Persian Gulf, with Iran attempting to impound an oil tanker bound for the Jewish state. The Israeli Navy had sunk a gunboat containing members of the Iranian Republican Guard, while the United States and Russia mediated with both sides to diffuse the situation, whilst asking for safe passage of all vessels through the region.

Aged thirty-eight, Benjamin led the UK business of the Israeli electronic company Syscom, which developed microwave data link communications, transmitters, receivers and antennae systems for the military. He and his family had been in London for three years, and his wife Deena, an accountant, had secured a job with a large accountancy firm in the city, while their five-year-old daughter Sarai had recently started school, making new friends, as well as Joshua, a boy in her class who wanted to be her boyfriend.

Benjamin looked at his watch: it was seven thirty and he had a nine a.m. conference at his office in central London, but first he had the daily task of the school run. If he left the house before seven forty-five the journey would take around ten minutes; any later and it could take up to half an hour. He went into the hall.

'Sarai, we're going to be late, darling,' Benjamin called.

'Coming, daddy,' returned the muffled voice somewhere upstairs.

Deena appeared at the top of the staircase in her dressing gown.

'What's she doing?' Benjamin asked.

'Looking for teddy,' Deena replied, walking down the stairs suppressing a yawn. She had dark hair, now curly after a night's sleep. She kissed him on the cheek and straightened his tie. 'Hunky as ever,' she winked.

'There's coffee on the go,' he smiled. 'Arabic?'

'I know, sorry, it was Sarai. We were at the checkout before I realised; she liked the picture on the package, and said it reminded her of Grandma's house.'

'Well, Arabic or not, it's damn good coffee,' he said, kissing her on the forehead.

Sarai was standing at the top of the stairs with her coat on, Peppa Pig school bag in one hand and teddy in the other. Benjamin looked up at her: she was a miniature of her mother, with her hair a thicket of black curls. She still walked downstairs backwards, and always wanted Daddy at the foot of the stairs in case she fell.

When she reached the bottom, he picked her up, kissed her and asked, 'Ready, princess?'

'Yes, Daddy.'

'Bye, darling. I'll pick you up after school at Tiny Feet,' Deena said, kissing her on the cheek.

'Yes, Mummy, bye,' replied the little girl.

Benjamin picked up his briefcase and opened the front door, with Sarai running to the car.

'See you tonight,' he said.

She yawned.

'You should go back to bed for an hour.'

'I'm supposed to be working from home today,' she replied wearily.

'Holidays in a few weeks.' He smiled.

'I'm counting the days,' she sighed.

Benjamin kissed his wife and using the key fob turned to unlock the Jaguar XF. The car hadn't been his first choice, as he secretly admired the BMW 7 series, a notion he had shared with Deena, but to drive a German car among the Jewish community in London was out of the question.

For such a central location, the detached house had enough room to easily park two cars. It had a small piece of grass with a narrow border around it and a cherry blossom in the corner, which gave a rural feel in an urban area.

Walking across the gravel, he glanced briefly at a mark on the wall close to the gatepost as he dialled the code to open the electronic gates. After strapping Sarai into her booster seat, he went around to the driver's side and climbed in, inserting the key into the ignition slot as the doors automatically locked.

'Are you okay, princess?' he asked.

'Yes, Daddy,' she replied. 'Teddy is strapped in too.'

As he turned the key, Benjamin heard the engine as it tried to start. The force of the explosion shattered the glass as it ripped through the chassis under his seat, taking off both of his legs. The driver's seat now sheared from its mountings, shot upwards and back against the ceiling, snapping his neck, killing him instantly. The little girl in the back was knocked unconscious, receiving lacerations to her face and neck, while her mother, dazed and concussed after being thrown backwards into the hall by the force of the blast, managed to get to her feet, screaming hysterically when confronted with the carnage.

Carol jumped when she heard the explosion, but thought it was the bin lorry as it pulled parallel with her car. Two men wearing hi-visibility jackets and heavy-duty gloves dragged the bins to the rear of lorry, with a third driving. They were in festive spirit, with the three of them wearing Santa hats, while one whistled a Christmas tune. Tinsel had been wrapped around the aerial of the lorry and a little Christmas tree sat on the dash. She admired their enthusiasm as their job could be dirty and dangerous, but as the lorry moved slowly forward, a thought suddenly struck Carol, one she hadn't been prepared for. With the bin lorry now in the line of sight of Leila's apartment, she couldn't see the door, and if anyone left the building, they would be beyond the street corner before Carol saw them. She cursed herself for the oversight. Starting the car, she swung it around and almost collided with a motorcycle as she tore down the street. At the junction, two cars sat in front of her waiting to turn left, with her needing to go right, which would bring her past the underground station and the bus stop.

But what if Leila drove or was picked up? 'Shit,' she said, this wasn't as easy as she thought.

She sat at the give-way line, with the four-lane road in front of her filling with traffic. Across the road, a delivery truck was unloading, the driver using its tail-lift with a cage full of goods balancing precariously upon it. She heard an emergency vehicle in the distance, coming closer, before its siren faded, and then another, before that also faded. The traffic was flowing freely, but the gaps were not enough even for a champion rally driver like Carol.

'Come on, people,' she yelled.

Further along the road to her left, a bus had pulled into a stop, creating a gap. She looked right, and with the road clear, eased onto it, crossing over and slowing at the pedestrian lights by the tube station as they turned to red. She studied the people crossing: none of them resembled the photograph of Leila she had on the passenger seat beside her. Carol breathed out and relaxed; it had only been two minutes since she turned the car and she couldn't believe that if Leila had left the apartment, she would have missed her. Unless she had gone the other way, which was possible, but unlikely, she hoped. Leila was probably still at home having breakfast, or in bed asleep, where she herself should be. Then again the apartment could be empty.

She turned the car into Netherby Way and spotted the bin lorry a hundred yards or so further along the street, moving slowly towards her. Reversing into a space between an Audi and a battered Golf, she spotted a woman, a little further up the street, walking along the pavement towards her. Carol was unsure where she had appeared from, having glanced down at the car's transmission as she was parking. The bin men were ogling her, as Carol reached up and removed a pair of shades from the flip pocket in the car's ceiling, sliding them on.

The woman was closer now, wearing a Shearling Russian hat and a pink double-breasted woollen coat. Her eyes were covered with dark shades, even though the sun had yet to rise to cause dazzle. She walked with confidence, in a pair of low-heel knee-high boots. Carol played with her phone, while keeping her eyes on the woman, noticing her black leather gloves and Radley shoulder bag. Classy lady with expensive tastes, thought Carol, but was it Leila? As the woman passed by the car, her height, olive skin and long hair convinced Carol it was Leila. She disappeared into the blind spot of the car, and by the time she reappeared in the rear-view mirror Carol was on the phone to Mickey.

'I think she's just left, wearing a hat and shades, but I'm sure it's her.'

'Is she on foot?' Mickey asked.

'Yes.'

'Good, keep a safe distance. If you think she knows you're following, then drift away.'

'I will,' she replied.

Carol grabbed her bag and climbed out of the car, pressing the key fob and locking the Mercedes. She pressed the fob once more and the hazards flashed, arming the vehicle. Leila had crossed to the other side and was making for the corner on the main road. As she disappeared around it, Carol quickened her pace, reaching the same corner as Leila crossed at the pedestrian lights. Carol groaned as the lights changed to green, with Leila on the other side about to vanish into the underground station before she was able to cross.

But Leila didn't enter the station; she continued past to the bus stop, and stood with several other people. As Carol pressed the pedestrian lights, a red London bus approached from her left. Willing the lights to change, she glanced over at the bus stop as people gathered themselves to board. The bus slowed when it was twenty yards away from the lights, but sailed through to the stop as the lights changed from green to amber. Carol watched as Leila, in a short queue of people, moved towards the kerb. On red, Carol didn't wait for the green man; with the traffic stopped, she practically ran diagonally across the road. With one foot on the step and then the other, Leila was soon aboard. Carol heard the bus airbrakes release as it prepared to move off. It jolted forward and stopped suddenly, as a man running towards the front of the bus held his hand in the air. Carol silently thanked him, as the bus driver's hesitation was all she needed, reaching the stop before the driver could close the doors again.

Trying to compose herself, she fumbled in her bag for her Oyster card, thanking the driver as she swiped it. She walked up the bus, quickly scanning the passengers, with her brain programmed for a black hat and a pink coat. Initially, she didn't see anyone and began to think Leila had gone to the upper deck, but staring out of the window, a woman in a pink coat, that Carol was convinced was Leila, having removed her hat and shades. Carol glanced casually at her as she looked for somewhere to sit, now seeing her profile quite clearly. As the bus moved off she found a seat three rows behind, almost falling into the lap of a young black lad with earplugs sitting at the window, who looked at her in terror.

'Sorry,' she mouthed.

Contented with that, he went back to concentrating on his music.

Out of breath and beginning to perspire, she felt her face flush. Silently she told herself to calm down and breathe in deep and slow. As her heart rate returned to normal, she felt her body relax, before she messaged Mickey.

'*On bus, Leila three rows in front.*'

'*Good, which number*?'

'Shit,' she whispered. Apart from the bus travelling towards central London, she didn't know.

'*Don't know, going towards central London*,' she replied.

'*Okay*,' he sent, with a smiley, and added, '*Be careful.*'

'*I will*,' she returned.

As the bus continued its journey, it was standing room only on the lower deck. The young man beside Carol got up from his seat a few stops further along. Carol slid across to the window and got a better view of Leila, and watched as she took a mobile phone from her handbag and put it to her ear. Carol couldn't make out if she was talking or listening, but after a minute or so, the call finished and she put the phone back into her handbag.

The bus continued along the Bayswater Road, running parallel with Hyde Park, and by the time it reached Marble Arch, Leila began to move. She replaced her hat and pressed the stop bell, before standing. The bus stop was a few hundred yards into Oxford Street, a busy shopping area. Although many of the shops and businesses were still closed at this hour of the morning, the area was packed with taxis, buses and delivery trucks.

With a queue forming behind Leila as she waited at the door, Carol fell in behind an overweight woman who was almost as wide as she was tall. When the bus stopped, Leila got off, turned right and again used her shades to cover her eyes.

Carol took her time, allowing Leila to move a few paces in front. Walking briskly, Leila led Carol along Oxford Street with its department stores, smaller retail units and coffee bars. Carol slowed and looked in a shop window, using its reflection, while Leila stopped at a set of pedestrian lights. She watched as Leila crossed over the road and continued walking. Carol remained on her side, following again, but keeping Leila just in view.

A few minutes later Leila stopped in a doorway, one which was set between a sports and menswear shop. She pressed the buzzer and after a few seconds spoke into the intercom, before pushing open the door and going inside.

Now what, thought Carol, looking around, seeing her breath in the morning air. It was too cold to remain outside, and she would arouse suspicion if she stayed standing in one place for any length of time. Nearby was a hot food bar. She was freezing and hungry, so she went inside and ordered a large Americano along with a warm croissant, and took a seat by the window.

She studied the building across from her. It was late nineteenth or early twentieth century, within a continuous block and five storeys high, with rows and rows of small rectangular sash windows. In between the two shops, the door, dark in colour, was itself quite unremarkable looking, as if it shouldn't be there at all and not unlike a front door of any standard house.

When the waitress brought her coffee and croissant, Carol asked, 'Do you know anything about that building across the road, the one with the door between the two shops?'

The waitress looked and had a think. 'I've seen a few people come and go, but I don't really pay much attention, I'm usually too busy, but I think there are offices in there,' she replied.

'Okay, thanks,' said Carol, cutting into the croissant.

'No worries,' the waitress smiled, as she walked over to a young couple who had just taken a seat.

Carol opened a small plastic carton of strawberry jam, spreading its contents over each part of the croissant. Clasping both hands around her coffee she brought it to her lips, blowing on it slightly and taking a sip. It was hot, with a pleasant aroma and taste, but, more importantly, it warmed her insides. She wanted to text Mickey, but her tummy was screaming for priority.

Half an hour went by and with Carol on her second coffee, she was beginning to think if Leila remained across the road much longer, the extra caffeine would make her highly strung for the rest of the day. She decided to message Mickey, '*Sorry, can't ring, in coffee shop, Leila got off bus and entered building in Oxford Street.'*

'*An office block?'* he replied.

'*A door between 2 shops, used buzzer to enter.*'

'*Did she go in alone?'*

'*Yes, 30 mins ago'*.

Suddenly, the door across the road opened and Leila, with hat and shades, stepped back onto the pavement and continued her walk.

'Bugger,' she whispered to herself. '*Gotta go, she's on the move,'* Carol sent to Mickey.

Carol quickly grabbed her bag, threw down a few coins to cover breakfast and ran out on to the pavement. She crossed over the road and again began to follow Leila. She was grateful that the shopping area was returning to life, and with more people around Carol felt able to blend easily into the street. The overhead Christmas lights, which earlier had been lit, were now switched off as daylight returned.

Leila stopped and crossed a side street. Carol walked slowly behind, close enough not to lose her, but far enough not to give herself away. Leila, walking briskly and with purpose, ignored everything and everyone around her. Her entire focus was on where she was going. Where that was, remained a mystery to Carol.

In the distance, she saw a sign for the underground, with Leila plum in line for it. Carol sighed, as she watched Leila descend the steps of Bond Street station. Carol followed, again using her Oyster card, as Leila disappeared down the escalator. Carol picked up her pace but lost sight of Leila, as there were just too many people in the station.

Damn, she thought, where the hell is she?

Halfway down, she spotted a figure in a pink coat, with a hat, getting off the escalator and walking towards the Jubilee Line.

By the time Carol had cleared the escalator, Leila was on the northbound platform. Carol inched along the platform packed with people and spotted the pink coat and long dark hair. Leila was staring across the track to the far wall at an advertisement for a bank. It showed a smiling mother and father holding the hands of a little girl, as they walked happily along a beach. Leila's eyes appeared transfixed on the advertisement, but it was as if her mind was elsewhere, in a different time and place and not within the present here and now.

Leila was a very attractive woman with high cheekbones and virtually a perfect complexion. Carol now understood why David had been attracted to her and wondered if their relationship had been more than an escort service. A sound in the distance brought Carol back to the present. Leila turned slightly towards the sound, with Carol thinking she looked sad and almost detached. The warm air preceding the train blew along the platform as Leila took a step forward towards its edge. Carol's heart skipped a beat, as she watched, and for a moment thought Leila was going to fall in front of the approaching train, but instead, she took a step back as it entered the station.

It was standing room only as they boarded. Carol allowed Leila to take the lead and choose a carriage. Leila stood with her back to Carol, holding onto a central pole. Carol, meanwhile, stood facing the door, once again using the glass reflection. As the train travelled north from central London it began to empty. With Leila eventually taking a seat, whereas Carol continued to stand, but as the carriage emptied, she was beginning to attract attention. A man in a business suit looked up from his *Financial Times* and down his glasses in her direction. Feeling self-conscious, she took a seat adjacent to Leila, separated by the sliding exit doors, and studied the route map, having no idea which station they had just left, only that they were travelling north.

The remaining passengers either read or listened to music, but Leila's reflection showed that she sat with her bag and hands on her lap, without a book, newspaper or magazine and certainly absent of ear plugs, staring straight ahead in front of her, as if picking a spot on the wall of the carriage and refusing to divert her eyes from it.

The train rattled along the track and soon the outside darkness turned to light as the train surfaced above the ground, and when the train eased into Kilburn, Leila got up from her seat.

With Kilburn being an over-ground station, sitting on the corner of two main roads, the escalator ride was downward and short, and half the distance compared to the underground stations in central London. Carol used the buffer of two young people as she left the train and now willed them to go the same direction as Leila, but once outside the station, the couple hesitated before going a different way.

Carol followed Leila under the railway bridge, keeping a greater distance as the pavement was less busy. The narrow walkway between the road, its railing, and the bridge wall allowed single file only. As Leila cleared the underpass, a woman with a pram and a little boy beside her approached from the other side. Carol allowed the woman, who had a firm grip on the little boy, to pass. As the woman thanked her, there was an explosion of noise as a train passed overhead; the sound, amplified within the enclosed space, startled Carol, and with a heavy goods vehicle passing under the bridge simultaneously, it made the sound almost unbearable, as she put her fingers to her ears in an attempt to block most of it out. Fifty yards ahead, she watched as Leila disappeared around the corner into a side street.

The area was residential and quieter now. It was just the two of them, with parked cars lining either side, along with a row of post-war terrace houses with short front gardens.

Carol began to feel exposed; if Leila stopped to turn around, she would be seen. Leila could quite possibly make the connection from the bus to the tube or even from the very beginning while she had been in her car. Carol crossed over the road, using the cars opposite as cover. On a lamppost, a triangular sign informed road users they were approaching a school two hundred yards ahead. Carol walked slower now, keeping her head straight, but every few feet she glanced across to Leila. She could hear noise growing louder with every step. It was the innocent sound of children playing. Up ahead, a car stopped and a little boy aged around six got out with the help of his mother or nanny, wearing a cap, navy blazer and black trousers. Leila stopped a few feet from the school gate, waved and smiled at the little boy. Across the road and from behind, Carol heard the sound of running feet; she looked across and saw a little girl similarly dressed and around the same age as the young boy running towards Leila.

'Leila!' the girl shouted.

Leila turned around, bending slightly at the knee, laughing, and caught the little girl in her arms.

Carol leaned on a parked car and with her smart phone discretely snapped a few photographs of Leila. She watched as Leila walked in through the school gates with the little girl skipping beside her. A sign with a blue background stood just inside the school railings and upon it a small six-pointed star, which had writing in a language that Carol did not recognise. Near to the top of the sign appeared the translation in English, which read, The Star of David, a school for Jewish Children.

Chapter 18

The sun had gone by the time she reached Mickey's house. Carol had hailed a cab from Kilburn to collect her car and went home for a hot bath. They were sitting in his kitchen and had just finished eating, with her complimenting him on his stir-fry. Food first, talk later, Mickey had said. During coffee, he gave her an update from Rocky the night before, then Carol told him about her freezing morning tailing Leila, the building she entered in Oxford Street, before finally ending up at the school and with Leila hugging the child.

'She must work at the school,' Mickey said.

'Yeah, but don't you think it's a bit strange, Leila the escort working in a primary school. I don't think her fellow teachers would be impressed if they knew,' Carol replied.

Mickey thought about what she just said, before adding, 'Maybe she's not a teacher and was just visiting someone.'

'But the child called her by her name, Mickey, and something else is bothering me.'

'What?' he asked.

'How many escorts would use their real name?' Carol quizzed.

He shrugged.

'Unless Leila isn't her real name and if that's the case, why is she using a false name at the school?' she asked.

'She is a riddle wrapped up in a mystery inside an enigma,' Mickey said, getting up with the empty cups. 'More coffee?' he offered.

'Sure,' she replied. 'Who said that?'

'What?'

'The riddle thing you just mentioned.'

'Winston Churchill, many years ago, while describing Russia in a radio broadcast,' he answered, pouring the coffee.

'He was spot on there,' she laughed.

'What do you think about Leila?' he asked, sitting down again.

'I'm not sure,' she answered, before asking, 'Is Leila a Jewish name?'

'I think it originates from that region,' he replied.

Carol puffed out her cheeks. 'There's something not right here, Mickey,' she said. 'Can we check out that building in Oxford Street?'

'Sure.'

On the laptop Mickey loaded a street view map of Oxford Street, travelling the same direction that Carol had earlier in the day.

'How far along do you think it is?' he asked.

'Not much further; it was on the right, between a menswear and a sports shop,' she replied.

He moved the camera along; it had been photographed on a summer's day, with the trees in full bloom and pedestrians in short sleeves.

'Stop!' she said.

Mickey swung the camera around ninety degrees, centring it on a doorway between the two shops. There was a brass plate to the left of the door, containing a number. He zoomed in to read it, but zoomed too far, pixelating the picture. As he panned out, Carol read the number.

'One three nine,' she said.

Using Google, they searched the Oxford Street number and found the building contained serviced offices, where people and small companies could lease office space, with short-term rental agreements.

'Find out who's in there, Mickey,' she said.

He found a dozen or so businesses that all appeared quite innocent. There were two technology companies, one specialising in green energy, the other in business management software, along with a couple of charities that used the building as an administration office. There were also three consulting firms and a healthcare company.

'Maybe Leila was using a consultant,' she said, as she scrolled down the page.

Mickey was taking a mouthful of coffee, when his cup froze in mid-air as he stared at the computer screen.

'Stop! Go back up,' he said.

'What?' she asked.

'Move the side bar up, slowly.'

Using the mouse, she slowly scrolled back up the page.

'Got you!' he said, touching the screen.

Carol looked at where Mickey was pointing and saw that located at one three nine Oxford Street, was a company known as Black Castle.

The ringing was in his head; well, he thought it was. It was distant, like in a fog. With his eyes still shut he searched for the alarm, feeling the warmth of Carol's naked body curled into the small of his back. His senses were slowly becoming clearer: it wasn't the alarm, but his phone. He reached for it and it slid onto the floor, still ringing.

'Shit.' he said, as Carol stirred slightly. He fished for it with the tips of his fingers, the muscles in his back cramping slightly as he strained, not bothering to look at the caller ID.

'Hello,' he said, surprised at how hoarse his voice sounded.

'You still in bed, Mickey?'

'Who is this?'

'It's Vinnie, man.'

'What time is it, Vinnie?'

'Time you were up, brother. I've completed the recce of the Shard.'

'You have?'

'I have, man. What time can you be here?'

Mickey was still half asleep. 'What day is it?'

'Saturday, man. Have you been drinking?'

'No, Vinnie, just a late night.'

'Can you be here for eleven?' he asked.

Mickey looked at the clock: 9.02, and the room was very dark.

'How about twelve, Vinnie?'

He'd remembered getting up to let Lucy out at six o'clock and it was raining, then he'd gone back to bed after her trip to the toilet. Mickey once read that on average it rained in London about ninety days per year, but at that moment it seemed to be each time he needed to go out.

'Twelve is good for me, bro,' replied Vinnie.

'Good. See you then.'

Carol had been exhausted from the experience of following Leila, so they sat and watched a DVD. Of course, after it was over Mickey couldn't resist another look at Rocky's papers and stayed up until one a.m., then he had gone to bed with a thumping headache and none the wiser. Meeting Vinnie at twelve would give him time to waken, shower and have breakfast. Carol opened her eyes and stretched her arms above her head, yawning.

'Who was on the phone?' she asked sleepily.

'It was Vinnie; he's cased the Shard.'

'Really?' she said, leaning up on one elbow, with the bed sheet slipping, revealing a firm breast and erect nipple.

Mickey found himself beginning to waken. 'He wants us to call later.'

'Okay, what time?'

'I told him around noon.'

Carol looked at the clock, and smiled. 'We've loads of time,' she said, reaching down to feel if his little chum was awake.

She giggled as she lay down, while he pulled the sheet around them and buried his face in her chest. He licked and sucked on her previously exposed nipple as she moaned in delight. She led him on top, holding him as he hovered above, before he gently pushed against her, easing effortlessly inside. She moaned with pleasure as their bodies slid together gently in tandem. He moved his face up from her breast, reaching her face, while their tongues explored each other's mouths. He was hungry for her and moved a little faster, as her body twitched and pulsed while he moved closer to the point of no return.

'Not yet,' she whispered, 'I want to be on top.'

She slid him underneath and sat astride, guiding him between her legs, slowly sliding down, as he felt her warm insides enveloping him. He caressed the contours of her body, slowly moving both hands onto her breasts, squeezing them gently and lightly pinching each hardened nipple. Carol closed her eyes, threw back her head, as her body goose-pimpled and nerve endings tingled as the effect of the orgasm rushed through her. She relaxed and their bodies again began a slow rhythmic motion. Her eyes open again and with her face flush, they made soft sounds as their bodies moved together. Their rhythm quickened, slowly at first and then faster, he slipping the fingers of both hands in between hers as they pushed against each other, their breathing matching the movement of their bodies. He felt himself growing inside her and at the same time squeezing her fingers while looking deep into her eyes as he suddenly released himself. She squealed with pleasure, gripping his hands while holding herself rigid, before slowly relaxing as both their breathing gradually returned to normal.

They remained still for a while, her head on his chest while he stroked her hair in a comfortable silence, still inside her. He drew an invisible line with his finger down her face and onto her lips, where she opened her mouth and sucked on the tip of it. Mickey closed his eyes and felt himself beginning to drift, but forced them open and found Carol smiling at him.

'Thank you,' she said. 'That was lovely.'

He smiled in return, contented, and would have been quite happy to go back to sleep.

Glancing at the clock, she said, 'We should shower.'

'Well, I'm in a delicate place, so I can't move until you do,' he laughed.

She smiled, kissed him and eased herself off the bed. 'I'll go first,' she said. 'You can put the kettle on.'

Mickey yawned and stretched before slowly extracting himself from the bed.

Once showered, they breakfasted on cereal, toast and a large hot pot of tea and, as it was still raining, Carol drove to the tube station.

'What's Vinnie like?' she asked, as they hurtled down the street.

'Erm,' he replied, holding on tight while watching the road. 'He's a tall, broad, friendly guy from St Kitts, as black as your boot, with a full set of white teeth.'

'Does my driving make you nervous, Mickey?' she asked.

'No, it's just I wouldn't drive so fast along a residential street.'

'You're too used to driving that taxi of yours,' she said with a smile.

'Maybe I am.'

'Anything else on Vinnie?'

'He would do a great job chipping your phone.'

'Really?' She smiled.

'And he's mad on Eddie Grant.'

'Reggae?'

'Well, he is from the West Indies.'

It was the penultimate Saturday before Christmas, with the park-and-ride almost full; but Carol still managed to find a parking space, one that looked only wide enough for a child's buggy, and just like a contortionist, she managed to manoeuvre the Mercedes safely into it.

'Plenty of room,' she finally said.

'Yeah, on your side. There's a wall on mine,' Mickey moaned.

'I'm sure you could shimmy across to the driver's seat,' she laughed.

Carol got out and reached into the back for a golf umbrella while Mickey clambered across. Unfurling it, she handed the umbrella to him.

'HSBC,' he said.

'That's who I bank with.'

'My bank didn't give me an umbrella.'

'Did you ask?'

'No.'

'I did.' She smiled.

He shook his head, held the umbrella above them both and with the patter of raindrops on the nylon they walked into the station.

At 10.47 they boarded the almost empty Central Line train travelling towards Ealing Broadway, easily finding two seats together.

'Déjà vu,' Mickey said quietly to himself.

'What did you say?' Carol asked, half turning in her seat.

'Déjà vu. Last Saturday I travelled this train to meet Lauren.'

'Little did you know; you'd be travelling it again this week and with me?'

'I didn't know you last week.'

'We didn't know each other until last Monday.'

'Well, we know quite a lot about each other now,' he added, squeezing her hand.

She kissed him on the cheek, and looked as if she was about to say something, but stopped.

'What?' he asked.

She hesitated, before she spoke. 'Matthew and Christopher finish school on Thursday.'

'For Christmas?' he enquired.

'Yes,' she replied. 'I was thinking of picking them up and taking them to my parents for the weekend, since they will be away with Eddie and Cassie next week.'

'That will be nice for you and them.'

'I'll be back again Monday night,' she said.

Carol was about to say something else, but paused before she added, 'I told them about us; well, I actually told them I have a male friend.'

'Right, and what did they say?' Mickey asked.

'They were happy for me and would like to come and visit after they are home from skiing.'

'Seriously?' He smiled.

'Yes.' Then she laughed. 'But I think it's Lucy they want to come and see. I told them you have a West Highland Terrier and they can't wait to see her.'

Mickey thought for a second. 'It's Thursday you're going, isn't it?'

'That's right.'

'Why don't you take Lucy with you?'

'I couldn't, Mickey. What if she misses you?'

'What? The way she ran to you this morning. I think I'll miss her before she does me.'

'You're not jealous, are you?' she teased.

He made a face, and said, 'Yeah, just a bit.'

'I'll look after her,' she said, sympathetically, 'you do know that.'

He smiled and winked at her.

The train pulled into Liverpool Street, and Carol said, 'This is where David would have got on.'

'Central Line, all the way to Holland Park,' he replied.

'I wonder why he didn't use a taxi,' she mused.

'Did you order one for him?'

'I offered, but he said he would hail one in the street.'

'That's why he got the tube. Friday evening and if it was raining, he'd have had no chance of a cab.'

'I remember now. It was raining and because David had been distracted by the meeting earlier in the afternoon, he'd forgotten to ask me to order him a car.'

'That explains it then.'

Mickey looked around the carriage, and then whispered to Carol, 'If David had pissed off Chiang that much, do you think he would have had David followed?'

'That's a bit James Bond, Mickey,' she replied.

'Think about, Carol,' he said in a low voice. 'There would have been many people around, especially on a Friday evening. It wouldn't have taken much effort to follow David onto a train.'

Mickey looked up at the map of the Central Line and leaned in towards Carol and said, 'David would have got off at Holland Park, the stop after Notting Hill, where we're getting off.'

He closed his eyes and tried to picture the scene on that Friday evening in early November. A busy train with seats full and people standing. Busy train, lots of people. People Harrison wouldn't notice. He opened his eyes again. If Harrison was attacked after leaving Leila's, it would have been planned. That's it, he thought. An attack such as that wasn't something somebody pulled off in a few minutes or randomly. Taking out his notebook, he flicked through to his meeting with Lauren.

'What is it?' Carol asked.

'I'm checking something,' he said. 'Lauren mentioned that David was hit on the back of his legs, making him fall. He was a large man, former rugby player, isn't that right?'

'Yes,' she said.

'So, he would be able to handle himself on a one-to-one.'

'Probably,' she nodded.

'But what if there were more than one. The first one hits him, David falls, then he, along with another, holds him down, while a third…' Mickey stopped and looked at her, realising that he hadn't told Carol about the poison.

She was staring back at him.

Mickey glanced around the carriage, but everyone seemed absorbed in their own conversations. 'Carol, there is something I haven't told you about David. In fact, I'd forgotten about it until now.'

'What is it?' she asked hesitantly.

'David was poisoned.'

'What?' she whispered.

'He was injected with a chemical liquid called Halothane, which brings on a cardiac arrest.'

'Oh my God,' she murmured.

'I'm trying to piece it together, but I'm beginning to think that at least three people took David down,' he replied sympathetically.

'I didn't want to believe it after we saw David's resignation letter. He was such a gentle soul, it's hard to believe anyone would want to kill him,' she said, looking up at Mickey, with tears in her eyes.

Mickey saw the sadness in her face, and he thought back to when she first opened the door of her house to him, five days previously, when she was sad on that day also. He put a comforting arm around her, gently squeezing her side.

'I think David was watched and then followed from somewhere near his office,' he said softly.

'By Chiang?' she asked, looking up at him quizzically.

‘Or people belonging to him,’ he replied.
‘Triads,’ she said distantly.
Mickey did not reply, but grimly agreed with her.

Chapter 19

The rain had once again eased by the time they exited Notting Hill station, making their way towards the Portobello Road. The thoroughfare was once again crammed full of people.

'I don't believe I've ever seen this road empty,' Mickey said.

As time marched on towards noon and the middle of the day, a blanket of grey cloud sat above their heads. The dark day grew atmospheric as many of the stalls strung lights from their roof bars, some multi-coloured, while others slowly twinkled like fairy lights. A large man with rosy cheeks, dressed in whites, served fish from behind a stall. He was wearing a Santa hat while at the same time wrapping a fillet in brown paper. Mickey couldn't make out if his white beard was real or not.

'This is wonderful,' said Carol, 'I haven't been here before.'

'You're kidding!' Mickey replied.

'Honestly, I would have gone to Camden Lock, or to Petticoat Lane on a Sunday, but I hadn't any reason until now to come this far west.'

Mickey pointed out Tom Cheevers, busy serving behind his father's fruit and veg stall.

'I knew of Portobello Road and of course everyone's seen the movie, *Notting Hill*, but I didn't think it would be like this,' she said.

When they found Vinnie's, the Turkish barbers on one side had standing room only. A few young Asian men were outside, speaking in their native tongue, laughing and high-fiving.

'Oh, a second-hand bookshop,' Carol said excitedly, stopping at the window of Sommersby's shop. 'We'll have to go in when we're finished with Vinnie.'

Mickey smiled, but said nothing.

When they entered Vinnie's, he was behind the counter on the telephone and gave them a friendly wave and a big smile. They hovered around the shop until he was finished. Vinnie stocked a large selection of computer accessories, cables and connectors, many household gadgets and CCTV equipment.

'Mickey! My man,' Vinnie said, as he replaced the handset. 'Good to see you again.'

'And you, Vinnie,' he replied.

'Introduce me to your friend,' he said, producing his large smile and shiny white teeth for Carol.

Mickey made the appropriate introductions and Carol informed Vinnie that she had previously worked at PetroUK before they moved to the Shard.

'Excellent,' he said. 'You may find some of the information I've discovered interesting. We're just waiting on my nephew Theo and then we can make a start.'

'How is he progressing?' Mickey asked.

'Like pushing water uphill with a rake,' Vinnie answered, rolling his eyes. 'He minds the shop when I'm busy at the back, but I usually send him on errands to get him out of the way.'

Carol was giving them both puzzled looks.

'Theo, thought I was the police when I was here earlier in the week,' Mickey said.

'Old Bill was what he said,' added Vinnie.

Carol laughed. 'I bet he did.'

When Theo returned, Vinnie led them into the back of the shop where he had set up a laptop with a cable running from it to an overhead projector. He pulled a couple of chairs from the side of the room and invited them to sit down. They accepted Vinnie's offer of coffee and he handed them two polystyrene cups and a small chocolate bar each.

'Sorry about the cups, I keep these for visitors, more hygienic.'

'No worries, Vinnie,' Mickey said.

Leroy appeared, and again Mickey made the introductions, as Vinnie dimmed the lights, before taking a position beside the laptop with an infrared remote.

'I took photos of the inside of the Shard; the first few are of its outside concourse and inside to the atrium, reception, security area, the cafe and mezzanine. I'll not dwell too long on these as there are more important issues to cover,' he said.

Mickey had driven past the Shard many times, but he had yet to view it up close. From Vinnie's first few slides, taken on a bright sunny day, the Shard's square area seemed immense. The ground floor and first few upper floors were the size of a football pitch. Inside, the atrium was spacious, bright and modern. The café had a large seated area, with a separate juice bar and the mezzanine above provided a good view of the entrance and reception area. The reception itself and security desk were parallel to the entrance doors, meaning whoever was behind the desk would spot any visitors passing through, unless, of course, distracted. The desk stretched for approximately twenty feet and appeared to be about four feet high, with either a marble or a polished granite top. It reminded Mickey of a long bar counter, minus the bar taps. The wall behind did not contain spirits or bizarrely shaped named liqueurs, but it did have a mirror, running the full length, and incorporated into it were six clocks, each displaying different time zones: New York, London, Berlin, Moscow, Beijing and Sydney. Embossed in each clock was a five-pointed gold crown where the number twelve would have appeared and underneath in large gold letters the name Rolex.

'How did you take these, Vinnie?' Mickey asked.

'I was dressed business style, with a tie bar containing a pinhole lens and a shutter delay that can be adjusted, which, on this occasion, took a high-definition photograph every five seconds. I then downloaded the pictures, edited them and saved them onto the disc we're using now.'

'Amazing,' added Carol.

To the right of the café and juice bar stood the lift.

'The elevator is for public use,' continued Vinnie, 'and rises to the three restaurant floors on levels thirty-one, thirty-two and thirty-three. It also takes visitors to the three viewing floors on sixty-eight, sixty-nine and seventy-two. You can't, however, access the offices from this elevator; you need a security pass to enter through the doors further to the right. Once you pass through those doors, you can access every floor, if your pass allows it.' Vinnie pointed to a pair of double doors ninety degrees to the first lift. They appeared heavy-set, with an identical strip of glass running the length of each. Against the wall to the left was an access pad, the colour of pitch and roughly the size of a beer mat and not much thicker.

'The shot doesn't pick out the little red LED, but when you touch a security pass against it, the light turns to green, then you hear a dull thud as the door unlocks, before you pull the left one towards you,' Vinnie added.

'Were you able to get a pass, Vinnie?' Mickey asked.

Leroy spoke for the first time since the introductions. 'I've a mate whose mother works for some industrial cleaners contracted to clean the building. He borrowed it one day when she wasn't working, brought it here and we cloned it.'

'This is one of three copies we made,' Vinnie said, holding up the white piece of plastic, the size of a credit card, with the word *contractor* on the front and a black metallic strip on its rear.

'But if I gain access using one of those cards, will the woman's name not appear somewhere on a computer screen at the security desk?' Mickey asked.

'It would,' Vinnie said, 'but on this occasion, we have given you a pseudonym.'

'You have? What name did you give me?' Mickey asked cautiously.

Vinnie and Leroy exchanged a sideways glance. Mickey had a feeling it wasn't going to be some glamorous Hollywood movie star name.

'We wanted to keep it simple, Mickey, so we chose Harry Brown, a good English name,' said Leroy.

'We needed something common, that wouldn't stand out too much,' added Vinnie.

'Good idea, mate,' Mickey said.

'As Harry Brown the IT engineer, you will have access to all areas,' continued Vinnie.

'What about security cameras?' Mickey asked.

'There are dome cameras everywhere. I counted twenty in my head as I walked through the atrium.'

'Dome?' Carol asked.

'Yes, they look like upside down ornamental snowstorms.'

'Without the snow,' added Leroy.

'Okay. Got that,' she said.

'But don't worry about the cameras, I can take care of them,' added Vinnie.

Mickey nodded, while Carol glanced at him, raising her eyebrows as he winked back at her.

Vinnie continued with the overhead and pointed out the next set of slides.

'Once you go through the double doors, you will see another set of elevators; again, you will need your pass to call them. Once it arrives, get in and press for the forty-third floor,' he said.

'Forty-third floor?' Mickey quizzed.

'Yes, my friend, PetroUK is based on the forty-third floor. If you're the only person riding, then the journey should take less than a minute.'

'And if I'm not?'

Vinnie shrugged. 'Maybe two, three minutes or as long as five.'

'Okay, Vinnie, I reach the forty-third floor, the lift door opens and I step out; what happens next?'

He smiled, clicked the overhead through to the next slide and said, 'Meet the Rottweiler.'

The photograph was of a plump, middle-aged but smartly dressed woman, looking over the top of her glasses at the covert photographer.

'That's not a Rottweiler,' laughed Carol. 'That's Valerie. Her bark is worse than her bite.'

'That may be the case, but nothing or nobody gets past her. I spun her a story that I was writing an article about UK energy companies and asked if I could have fifteen minutes of someone's time. I wanted to check the layout of the floor and offices for the quickest entry and exit for Mickey, but she wasn't having any of it. She told me if I didn't have an appointment, then I would need to contact the company's press office to arrange one.'

'They didn't have a press office when I was there!' Carol exclaimed. 'In fact, I was the press office,' she added.

'Right,' Vinnie continued. 'So, I hacked into their pass card records and since they moved to the Shard this Valerie woman arrives for work at eight thirty every morning and doesn't leave until five p.m. She doesn't even check out for lunch.'

'Okay, what about D'Artagnan and our three musketeers?' Mickey asked.

'Oh, they're very different,' Vinnie smiled. 'You could set your watch by them, except Chiang.'

Vinnie brought up on the overhead. separate photographs of the four men. It was obvious that the photographs had been taken by something other than Vinnie's tie bar.

'Leroy took these, using a 135mm lens,' Vinnie said. 'Are any of these men familiar to you, Carol?' he asked.

'Oh yes,' she said. 'Top left going clockwise is Harold Goodwin, Geoffrey Burbridge, Roger Mildenhall and finally Lee Chiang.'

The four had been photographed at different locations, oblivious to the attention they were attracting. Goodwin had been snapped while buying a newspaper from a street vendor. Burbridge was also in the street talking on his mobile phone, while Mildenhall had visited a coffee bar and carrying a polystyrene cup as he walked. All three were in business suits or overcoats: they could have been on their lunch or arriving for work. The fourth photograph was of Lee Chiang and his pose was more formal: he had just gotten out of a dark stretch vehicle, smartly dressed in a dark possibly black suit. Chiang was not tall and a lot shorter than the two Oriental men standing behind him. The two men in the background were dressed similarly to Chiang. Both men had taken a stance as if discreetly checking the immediate vicinity, paying attention to their surroundings, as if on close protection, with Chiang as their principal.

Mickey was wondering if the two stooges were Triads.

'What's the story on all four, Vinnie,' Mickey enquired.

'I'll leave Chiang to the last,' he said, before continuing, 'Goodwin, Burbridge and Mildenhall, all arrive before nine thirty. If they don't come in by this time, then it is unlikely they will put in an appearance all day. They usually stay until one p.m., and then the three of them trickle away for lunch, sometimes together, sometimes in a pair, or they depart individually and don't return until after two p.m.'

'So that would give us approximately one hour, Vinnie?' Mickey asked.

'Yes, except Chiang is irregular.'

'How irregular?'

'He doesn't have a routine; he comes and goes frequently. He could arrive at nine a.m., disappear at noon, come back at one p.m. and go again at three p.m. Another day he arrives at eleven a.m. and stays until five p.m.' Vinnie paused, before he continued, 'By the way, Chiang has been a permanent fixture since PetroUK moved to the Shard, and not since becoming a director.'

'Interesting,' Mickey said.

Carol added, 'Chiang only appeared at director meetings when David was alive. David didn't even want him in the building, because he didn't trust Chiang.'

Vinnie continued, 'There's something else that I didn't know until I started playing around with the Shard's computer systems.'

‘What’s that?’ Mickey asked.

‘When someone enters or leaves the building from the front door or underground car park, the microchip within the pass registers with an infrared beam within the door frame. The pass emits a strong enough signal, regardless whether the pass is inside a coat pocket or at the bottom of a handbag.’

‘George Orwell wasn’t wrong: Big Brother is here,’ Carol said.

‘It’s been here a while,’ Leroy replied, before adding, ‘Take your mobile phone, for example, it sends intermittent signals to receivers to pinpoint your location; the only way you can’t be tracked is if you leave your phone at home or switch it off.’

They were drifting off at a tangent, so Mickey butted in, ‘Are there any other people who work in Petro’s offices?’

‘Around two dozen or so,’ Vinnie replied.

‘What do they do?’ he asked.

‘Probably administration, accounts, operation services, human resources and this newly formed press office,’ Carol added.

‘So, if I enter Chiang’s office as Harry the IT guy, nobody apart from Valerie will raise an eyebrow.’

‘Chiang’s office?’ Carol asked surprised.

‘He seems to be King Rat.’

Vinnie said, ‘It could be a problem, but I don’t really see it as one. They will be so wrapped up in their work that, as long as you are wearing your contractor’s pass, they shouldn’t give you a second thought.’

‘I’d like to eliminate any doubt, but this Valerie woman is a problem. Any ideas about getting around this?’ Mickey asked, looking around for suggestions.

‘We could put something in her coffee,’ suggested Leroy.

Carol and Mickey both laughed, but Vinnie and Leroy were poker-faced.

'You're not serious, are you?' Carol asked, self-consciously staring into her own cup.

Vinnie opened the door that led to the shop. 'Theo,' he shouted. 'Lock the shop door for five minutes and come into the back when you're done.'

Theo appeared within a minute, before Vinnie prompted him, 'Theo, tell our visitors about your friend who works as a porter at St Jude's Hospital.'

'I have a mate who is a porter at the day procedure unit,' Theo said.

Leaning forward, Mickey asked, 'Which sort of procedure?'

'Colonoscopy.'

'Colonoscopy?' Mickey frowned.

'Yeah, it's when they shove a camera up your ass.'

'Theo!' scolded Vinnie, glancing at Carol.

Carol laughed, and said, 'It's okay. I've heard a lot worse.'

'Sorry,' said Theo, sheepishly, before he continued, 'They have a miniature camera on a thin cable that gets put into your ass, sorry, rear end, which is used to inspect the colon and intestine for signs of cancer.'

'Go on,' Mickey said.

'But before they can do the test, the patient's bowel needs to be cleansed and they also can't eat for twenty-four hours.'

'So they need to fast, is that right?' Carol asked.

'Yeah, something like that,' replied Theo. 'They need to take something to make them shit, I mean poo.'

'A laxative,' suggested Carol.

'That's it,' remembered Theo.

From his pocket, he took a small opaque plastic medicine bottle and handed it to Mickey. It contained 80ml of a clear liquid called Omniclear. The instructions on the back of the bottle suggested measuring out half of the liquid and mixing it in a glass of water. Then four hours later mix the second half. It contained sodium and other unpronounceable chemicals that would help the patient shit.

'Does it work?' he asked, passing the bottle to Carol.

'Sure does,' said Theo, and while glancing at Vinnie said, 'Apparently, the shit doesn't hit the sides of the toilet, it goes straight down, like something out of NASA!'

'How long before it takes effect.'

'Within fifteen minutes, the user begins to feel uncomfortable, but you could use slightly more than half, because you don't have an extra four hours,' added Theo, sounding very knowledgeable now.

Mickey got up from his chair and walked behind it, leaning on its back. He thought for a moment and then suggested, 'If Carol arranges to call and see Valerie and brings her a coffee. I'm assuming she drinks coffee or tea?'

Carol nodded.

'We could pour the laxative into the cup, mix it and hopefully she'll drink it.' He paused.

'What about the sodium? It will have a salty taste, will it not?' Carol asked.

'I was thinking the same thing,' Mickey replied.

Theo added, 'You could put a sweetener in it, and just hope she doesn't suspect anything.'

'I think we'll be OK. Valerie takes two sugars in her coffee, so a little more won't matter,' Carol said, and then added, 'Poor Valerie.'

Mickey looked at Vinnie. 'So, when do we do this?'

‘It’s up to you, mate. The comms. can be in place within a couple of hours; just give me a few days’ notice,’ replied Vinnie.

Carol was contemplating something.

‘What is it?’ Mickey asked.

‘I got an email last week from HR about the Christmas staff lunch. They send the email by block and obviously, they still have my details in the company address book.

‘Okay, when is it?’

‘It’s on my phone.’ She fumbled in her bag.

‘Can I hold on to this bottle?’ Mickey asked Theo.

‘Yeah, sure, no worries, man, I don’t need it back.’

‘Good work, Theo,’ Mickey said.

Feeling proud of himself, Theo looked at his big uncle, who winked at him and then nodded for him to get back to the shop.

‘It’s one thirty p.m. this Wednesday in Zuplas at St Katharine Docks,’ Carol said, showing Mickey the email, along with the list of attendees, which included Mildenhall, Goodwin, Burbridge and Chiang. He also scanned another twenty or so names, but Valerie wasn’t on the list.

‘Valerie isn’t on it,’ he said.

‘I told you, she doesn’t attend anything during working hours. She stays and minds the shop,’ Vinnie said.

Mickey puffed out his cheeks and asked, ‘Does Wednesday suit everyone?’ He looked around the room; Carol nodded, then Vinnie and finally Leroy.

‘Let’s say we meet here in the shop at nine a.m.,’ said Vinnie, ‘then we can go over the layout of the building.’

Leroy added, ‘I’ll need to mike everyone up and ensure it works, so we can communicate with one another.’

Mickey took out an envelope from his pocket and handed it to Vinnie, who raised an eyebrow. 'Down payment,' he said.

Vinnie nodded. 'Thanks, Mickey.'

Once Mickey and Carol were outside, he asked, 'Fancy some lunch?'

'You bet.'

'I know a great greasy spoon.'

She looked at him.

'Joke!'

'Just as well,' she said, 'because I want a burger and a pint.'

He was happy with that, and happy that she had forgotten about Sommersby's bookshop next door.

Chapter 20

It had been a week since Mickey had last driven his cab and, feeling it needed a charge, he left the house early. He was hoping to time it just right and, driving into central London, he skipped past the rank at Euston and drove slowly further west, through Notting Hill and onward towards Holland Park, before turning left into Netherby Way.

Carol had reckoned it was just before seven thirty a.m. that Leila had appeared, and even though dawn hadn't long broken on an overcast morning, he still slipped on a pair of shades. The street was empty as he edged along at walking pace, easing off the throttle and allowing the black cab to cruise along under its own power, as if he was searching for a number, which in fact he was; the one he had visited a few nights previously. The street looked different in daylight, and not as menacing, though now, with hindsight, that night he had allowed his imagination to run riot.

He approached number eighty-seven at an angle and was surprised at the size of the property: an extension had been added to its rear to accommodate the apartments, practically doubling its depth, something he hadn't noticed in the dark. Mickey studied the front of the house as he passed, but saw no movement from its entrance. He continued on for a short distance and then stopped, keeping his eyes firmly on the rear-view mirror.

It was then she appeared. Was she late? She was walking fast, close to running. Mickey waited until she was out of sight, giving her an extra few seconds, before he turned the cab and drove to the end of the street. She had crossed over the road, but was running to the stop as her bus approached, reaching it just in time. Mickey took a note of the bus and its vehicle number, before driving to the beginning of Oxford Street and parking his cab in an empty taxi rank.

He waited ten minutes. Numerous buses passed, but none were Leila's. A short time later, he spotted another, further along the road. Squinting as it approached, Mickey matched the numbers with the ones he'd written down, just as Leila hopped off at a stop along with other passengers. There was an old newspaper in the door pocket of the cab, so he opened it and pretended to read as she walked by him. Leila was only one of the many commuters, who joined the passengers from the bus as they began their working day. She stopped at a set of pedestrian lights, before crossing over on red. Mickey watched as she pressed the intercom of 139 Oxford Street, waiting only a few seconds before she pushed open the door. He sat with the cab's heater burning and after a few minutes felt his eyes beginning to close. He climbed out and found a coffee bar, probably the one Carol had used a few mornings before, and ordered an Americano while sitting at the window watching the world go by, but at the same time keeping an eye on the door opposite.

Mickey was enjoying people watching rather too much, when his eye caught Leila stepping out onto the street and turning towards the tube station. He was about to jump up when he spotted a heavy-set, Middle Eastern man in a dark grey overcoat walk out behind her. He appeared to call out to Leila, because she stopped, turned around and walked back to him. The man handed her something, a letter or a small package, which Leila put into her handbag before again turning and walking away.

It occurred to Mickey the absence of any pleasantries between the two of them. Unlike a business transaction, there was nothing friendly about the exchange, not a kiss or a hug, and neither a handshake nor a smile as they parted. It was as if the man was giving Leila an order or a command.

The man moved towards the edge of the kerb, looking in Mickey's direction, or was it at his cab. Mickey, quick thinking, nonchalantly walked out of the café and jumped into the cab. The man waved over at him and Mickey did a U-turn out of the rank and pulled up alongside him, dropping the passenger window.

'Edgware Road,' the man said, in accented English.

Mickey gestured for him to get in. 'Which part of Edgware Road?' he asked.

'After the railway bridge, beyond the tube station,' the man replied.

It was only a fifteen minute drive, but his mannerism was abrupt to the point of rudeness, and then the man's phone rang, playing a bizarre tune, with Mickey imagining a group of women in a harem in some desert country.

The man spoke in a foreign language, softly at first, then he became more animated and louder, before shouting. He continued for a few minutes and then hung up, putting the phone back into his pocket, and for the rest of the journey sat in silence, staring out of the window.

Mickey stopped just beyond the tube station on Edgware Road, pulling in at the side of the road, with the man getting out and paying him. He watched as the man walked along the road for a hundred yards or so before turning left and disappearing around the corner of a one-way street. Mickey slipped on a beanie hat, zipped up his coat and jumped out of the cab.

The one-way street was narrow and cobbled, with cars parked on one side. The man was standing halfway along, talking to a second man with a similar complexion to his own. Mickey walked, pretending to be just another guy going about his business, while they in turn were too engrossed in conversation to notice him. Mickey continued past the two men before counting off thirty seconds in his head. He then stopped, looked around as if lost and turned, retracing his steps.

The two rows of three-storey buildings on either side filled the length of the street. The nineteenth century design suggested that in a previous life they had been built for use as warehouses. The ground floor of one had been converted to a car repair garage, with a car protruding beyond the garage entrance and another on a ramp inside. A radio was playing and Roy Orbison could clearly be heard as Mickey passed. Further along, a hairdressing salon had its window decorated with fake snow and a young woman stood inside styling the hair of an older woman. A dance studio occupied another, and a small quaint restaurant offering French cuisine with a Christmas menu was preparing to open. Mickey crossed the cobbles to where the two Asian men were standing, just as they walked through a doorway, pulling a jailer's gate behind them. As Mickey got closer, he saw that twelve inches beyond the gate stood a solid green door with a worn aluminium kick-plate a third of the way up. At eye level a brass plaque had been riveted to the door, telling Mickey that the building was the Islamic Community Centre for Paddington, North London.

Mickey got back into his cab and phoned Carol. She didn't answer, but returned his call a few minutes later.

'Hi, where are you?' Mickey asked.

'I'm at the London Library,' she replied. 'I've nipped outside to call you back.'

'Found anything?' he asked.

'I've had a few hits,' she replied. 'Where are you?'

'Edgware Road.'

'What are you doing there?'

'Long story,' he replied. 'Are you going to be there for a while, at the library?'

'Yes, it's got a lovely coffee bar.'

'Great, I'm on my way.'

'Are you a member?' she asked.

'What, of the library?'

'Yes,' she answered.

'No, is that important?' Mickey asked, slightly puzzled.

She laughed. 'You'll not get in. I'll wait for you at the entrance, and you can gain access on my ticket.'

'I didn't know it was that type of place. I've a ticket for my local library, if that's any use.'

'It's not that kind of library, Mickey,' she replied.

The London Library was situated in a seventeenth century building on a tree-lined square, just off Pall Mall and only a stone's throw from St James's Palace, with its entrance tucked into a corner next to the Cypriot Embassy. When Mickey arrived, Carol was waiting for him at the bottom of the stone steps.

'This is a bit posh,' Mickey smiled.

'It's a terrific place,' she said. 'When I come here, I could stay for days, never mind hours. I feel that the books in here have some greater unknown power. As if you can gain knowledge without even opening a book.'

The two of them walked through the entrance and the daytime noise from outside disappeared, into a world of silence. Carol handed her card to the lady on reception, who got Mickey to sign in before handing him a visitor pass. In front of them stood a set of old wooden double doors with opaque glass half the way up. With a swoosh both doors opened automatically and a man with a trolley full of books exited. Mickey caught a view of the room beyond. It appeared circular with rows of book stands, and more against the wall rising almost to the ceiling, along with many ladders, attached in a track, which could be wheeled around the room's circumference, and upon request a staff member would climb and collect a book for a member.

'That's the reading room,' Carol whispered, following his gaze.

'There must be tens of thousands of books in there,' he replied with amazement.

'The café is on the first floor; we can take the stairs, much nicer than the lift,' she said, in a low voice.

She was right. The corridor from the entrance hall led to a giant double marble staircase. From both sides, they could climb and reach the same landing as it swept up and along the side of each wall, while a claret and gold starburst carpet runner would muffle their footsteps. Adorning the walls were portraits of famous library members, past and present, including TS Elliot, who was once President; as were William Thackeray and Charles Dickens, who were founding members, while the Queen and the Duchess of Cornwall were Patron and Vice-Patron respectively.

'Not your typical library, then,' Mickey whispered into Carol's ear as they climbed.

'No, Mickey, I don't think you could nip in here and pick up a Mills and Boon.'

The café was situated in an extension over a covered courtyard, bright and airy, with floor-to-ceiling windows and an angular glass roof. They collected their coffee and took a seat beside the window, with views of the square and its leafless trees.

'Bliss, don't you think, Mickey?' She smiled.

'It's like stepping back into Victorian times,' he replied.

'Maybe it was more simple back then, before computers, internet, mobile phones and the like.'

'You don't have to go back that far,' he said. 'Thirty years ago, there were just four television channels and the radio for entertainment.'

'And books,' she said.

'Of course, books.' He smiled.

She took a sip of her coffee and asked, 'So, Mr Ross, what were you doing on the Edgware Road?'

Mickey told her about how he followed Leila to the same building in Oxford Street, and of the Middle Eastern man she spoke with outside, before accounting the trip to the Islamic centre off the Edgware Road.

Carol thought for a moment before she spoke. 'Why would a Jewish woman speak or interact with a Muslim man?'

'There wasn't much interaction when the two of them spoke,' Mickey recalled.

'Yes, but you understand my point, don't you?'

'Maybe she's not Jewish,' answered Mickey, taking a mouthful from his cup.

'Then surely she wouldn't be working in the primary school,' Carol returned.

Mickey rubbed his eyes.

'You're right, Carol. Leila doesn't add up, there has to be more to her.'

'But I think we can link Leila and this Muslim man to Chiang, Mickey.'

'Coincidence, do you think?' he asked.

'I don't do coincidence,' she said. 'Leila, Black Castle and Chiang in the same office building, I don't think so.'

Mickey nodded and looked around the café. 'You're obviously not here in the library to browse over the books,' he said to Carol.

'No,' she smiled, 'I came here to use one of those electronic thingy's called computers.'

'What's wrong with your own?' he asked.

'Nothing,' she replied, leaning across the table. 'But, because I am a paying member of the London Library, I can access the details of all the UK companies registered at Company House for free.' She winked.

Mickey returned with a curious smile, and said, 'Good thinking.'

'I had a look at Black Castle, and they are, as you say, an import and export company,' she said.

'Right, that backs up what Rocky told me,' he said. 'Anything on what they actually import?'

'Nothing, they've only been registered in the UK since 12 September this year.'

'So no financial figures, of course.'

'You got it, Mickey.'

'Convenient.'

'But Lee Chiang is a director and some other guy.' She smiled.

Mickey looked at her. 'Go on,' he said.

'The other director is a Mohammed Shakiba.'

‘A new name,’ he replied. ‘Any other info on him?’

‘No, just that he is a named director of Black Castle,’ she replied.

‘It could be the same guy I picked up this morning in Oxford Street.’

‘So what is Leila, who makes us believe she is Jewish, doing with an Arab?’ she queried, before answering her own question. ‘Maybe she services him, before going to school,’ she joked.

‘It’s not a pleasant thought, because Shakiba wouldn’t win any beauty contests. Anyway, there wasn’t anything warm about their exchange,’ he replied.

She fiddled with her cup and hesitated before she spoke. ‘It’s probably nothing, Mickey, but I caught the front page of the *Metro* this morning on the tube. Last week, when I was waiting on Leila, there was a bin lorry behind me. I heard a loud noise like an explosion, but thought it was the bin men and thought nothing of it. Later, I heard a police or ambulance siren, but again discounted it, but…’

From her handbag, she took out a folded copy of the *Metro*, a free daily newspaper for London commuters. On the front page Mickey saw the banner headline: “*Notting Hill Explosion Was Bomb*.” He read that an Israeli national called Benjamin Levy had been killed by a booby trap bomb placed under his car. His young daughter, who had been in the rear of the vehicle, escaped with cuts and was not seriously injured. Mickey read more on Levy’s employers, an Israeli software company that supplied the military.

‘What do you think?’ Carol asked, when he’d finished reading.

‘Coincidence?’

‘I don’t do coincidence, remember?’ she replied.

‘Neither do I, but who would be behind it?’ he asked.

She shrugged.

As Carol finished her coffee, Mickey stared out of the window, wondering if the car bomb had been a coincidence, or had someone suddenly just raised the stakes.

Chapter 21

Most people were breaking for lunch as Carol entered the Shard and approached the security desk. She gave her name to the guy standing behind the desk, who ran his finger along a visitors' list attached to a clipboard. With an orange highlighter, he marked off her name, before typing on his keyboard. From the desk drawer, he took out a visitor pass and scanned the metallic strip on its other side with an infra-red hand-held device before once more typing on his keyboard. He scanned the pass a second time and connected a red *The Shard*, lanyard to it, before handing it to Carol.

'You must wear this at all times, Ms Freeman,' he grunted, in broken English.

'Thank you, I will,' she replied.

Going by his nametag, the guy was called Dariuz and looked as if he had gone AWOL from the Russian army.

He informed Carol, 'This provides you access to the public areas and restaurants on floors thirty-one, thirty-two and thirty-three; also, the viewing floors on sixty-eight, sixty-nine and seventy-two, and the business floor of PetroUK.'

'Thank you again,' returned Carol.

She turned and walked through the atrium to the coffee bar and got herself a latte, taking a seat at the far end of the café, at an empty table that provided an unobstructed view of the atrium and the set of double doors.

She took a sip of her coffee and spoke softly. 'In position.'

‘Roger that,’ responded Vinnie, who was sitting at a table on the mezzanine level with his laptop open. He was smartly dressed in an open-neck shirt, suit jacket and trousers, portraying very much the business person.

Mickey sat in the passenger seat of a silver Ford Transit Connect van, parked two streets away. The van had a short wheel-base and was easy to park as it was shorter in length than an estate car.

The miniature device in Mickey’s ear crackled once more.

‘Leroy, are you in position?’ Vinnie asked.

‘That’s a Roger,’ he replied.

Leroy had drawn the short straw, standing on the concourse, wrapped up in layers of clothing, selling London’s homeless magazine, the *Big Issue*.

Mickey couldn’t see what was going on; he could only hear the brief chatter of the other three on the two-way communications. He drummed his fingers on the door panel with a slight hint of impatience, or was it boredom? He stopped drumming, as in the distance from around the corner to the right appeared a dark limousine. The limo, with its running lights on, a strip of bright white LEDs below both headlights, glided down the road towards him. Mickey sank lower into his seat as it passed. Half a minute later, a second limo appeared and then a third.

‘Three limos approaching,’ Mickey said.

‘Roger that,’ came back Vinnie.

Mickey soon heard Leroy’s voice.

‘Limos in view, approaching turning circle and front entrance,’ he said.

As it was lunchtime, the Shard’s café and mezzanine were beginning to fill with office workers. Carol was trying to drink her coffee slowly, while pretending to read some paperwork she had brought with her. The double doors across from her suddenly opened and a small group of people exited, an excitable bunch laughing, and joking with one another.

'That's them,' she said, covering part of her face with a hand.

'Are you sure?' asked Vinnie.

'Definitely. I recognise almost every one of them. I used to work there, don't forget.' There was sadness in her voice along with a little anger, as if she should be with them, attending a Christmas lunch as an employee. Another group walked through the doors, much the same size as the previous lot. Then a trickle of ones and twos. 'I think that's the last of them,' she added. 'Just the directors to come, but they'll travel in a different vehicle; that's in my experience anyway.'

A minute later, Leroy confirmed, 'Carol's right, the three limos have just departed with their passengers.'

Ten minutes went by, as they waited for Chiang, Mildenhall, Goodwin and Burbridge to make an entrance.

Carol was beginning to get impatient and eventually broke the silence with a frustrated, 'Where are they?'

'Relax,' calmed Vinnie, 'they'll show,' before adding under his breath, 'I hope.'

They waited a few minutes longer, and Mickey, still in the van, was becoming agitated.

'Vinnie, how much longer do you think we should give?' he asked.

'It's one ten now and lunch is at one thirty. I wouldn't like to think they'll be much longer,' he replied.

Vinnie was right. They didn't need to wait much longer than it took him to finish his sentence, as a dark SUV appeared from the same direction and from the same turning as the limos had. It eased effortlessly along the road, the large wheels and strong suspension supporting its huge bulk. It passed Mickey with little sound and only a low hum from its turbo-injected engine.

'Chauffeur-driven dark Land Rover Sport with tinted rear windows approaching,' he said, speaking into the pin-head of a microphone inserted into the collar of his coat.

'Roger,' said Vinnie. 'Leroy, let me know when you eyeball it,' he continued.

'Roger that,' came back Leroy.

Half a minute passed.

'Eyeball on Land Rover, registration, Charlie, Victor, one, six, Bravo, Foxtrot, Zebra, beginning to slow at entrance doors.'

Carol heard Leroy confirm the Land Rover arriving at the front entrance. She looked to her right, but couldn't see the vehicle or the turning circle. As she drained the dregs of her coffee, the double doors opposite opened and out strode three tall suited men. Her heart skipped a beat as the white-haired Mildenhall looked straight at her as he walked with Harold Goodwin. Thankfully her cup was to her mouth and his gaze didn't settle. The shorter Lee Chiang had paired himself with the other director Geoffrey Burbridge and the four men walked purposefully across the floor to the exit. Carol, with her head down, spoke into her hand. 'Directors on the move.'

'Got them,' Vinnie replied. 'Should be with you, Leroy, in thirty seconds.'

'Roger that,' Leroy said.

It was one fifteen, Mickey checking the time on his watch against the three hours remaining on the parking ticket. Sufficient time, he thought, unless something went wrong.

'Subjects in vehicle,' Leroy announced, and then a few seconds later, 'Vehicle clearing the area.... Vehicle clear.'

As soon as Carol heard Leroy call clear, she got up from her seat and returned to the coffee bar and ordered two lattes to go. Her stomach was in knots as the reality of what she was doing finally hit her, and found her hand shaking as she counted out the money to pay the Barista. Taking both cups, she carried them to a couple of empty stools at the wall counter, glancing around quickly to be sure she wasn't being observed, and with a black biro marked one of the cups with a small asterisk.

Vinnie's voice sounded in her ear with a reassuring tone. 'Relax, Carol, you're sitting nicely in a camera blind spot.'

'Thanks,' she replied. She removed the lid of the second coffee and from her pocket, took out the small plastic bottle containing the laxative. Unscrewing the top and picking off the waterproof seal, she poured a little more than half of its contents into the unmarked latte and with a wooden muddler stirred in the liquid before sipping it. She could taste a slight saltiness, so she added a packet of brown sugar and tasted it again. It was perfect and the coffee hot.

'It's ready,' she said, as she placed both coffees in a cardboard carrier and made her way to the double doors, where she whispered, 'I hope this works.'

'Roger,' Vinnie replied.

Mickey said nothing, but crossed his fingers.

Mickey waited for a few minutes before getting out of the van. He locked it and quickly scanned the area, thankful that no one was paying him attention. He wore a dark waterproof fleeced coat which acted as a good windbreak and was suitable for winter hill walking. It fitted well with his navy cargo pants, which had multiple pockets, as he wanted to look every inch an IT engineer. As he turned the corner of the street, the mighty glass and steel monolith of the Shard rose in front of him. He spotted Leroy a hundred feet away moving in a large slow anti-clockwise loop, trying to keep warm, and wearing a thick puffed jacket with a heavy beanie on his head and a pair of fingerless gloves.

Leroy looked in Mickey's direction as he approached, winked and pitched, *'Big Issue!'* to anyone and everyone in the vicinity.

The Shard's outer sliding doors parted as Mickey reached its entrance. The inner doors were already open as people passed him on their way out. He glanced in the direction of the reception and security desk with its many clocks behind, while a small queue of people gathered, as the guy at security typed furiously on his keyboard. Mickey was now aware that his pass had probably pinged a computer somewhere in the building, informing any watcher that Harry Brown, contractor, had entered the building. An extremely tall Christmas tree stood to the left of reception, with all the trimmings of lights and baubles, appearing taller than the tree in Trafalgar Square and the tallest Mickey had ever seen indoors.

He spotted Vinnie sitting at his laptop on the mezzanine fifty feet away, and with Mickey in full view of the cameras, Vinnie lifted his head, resting it on his hands, before he said, 'Carol is in the elevator. I'm watching for her exiting on the forty-third floor.'

'Roger, Vinnie,' he replied, trying not to move his lips.

Mickey carried a black computer bag containing Carol's tablet, a few cables and connectors, a packet of plastic tie wraps and an engineer's manual, all to add a touch of authenticity for any inquisitive security person. He bought a regular Americano from the coffee bar and took a seat, preparing to wait, but at the same time hoping Valerie would drink her coffee quickly and allow nature to take care of the rest.

The lift had a carrying capacity of twenty people, although another half dozen on top of the current seven including herself would be capacity enough for Carol. She wasn't particularly good with enclosed spaces or lifts, not since her first year at university when she became stranded alone and in the dark for three hours in the student halls after a few older male students thought it would be funny to tape a box of fireworks to the main power unit in the basement before lighting the fuse. The resulting explosion blacked out everything in the complex, including the lift Carol was riding in, leaving her suspended between floors four and five.

When the lift stopped at one of the restaurant floors, everyone got out, apart from Carol and a young Oriental man in his early twenties, wearing a visitor's pass similar to her own. He was fidgeting with a folder and appeared uncomfortable with his collar and tie, while furiously flicking his hair with his free hand.

Carol smiled and he returned it somewhat nervously.

'Interview?' she asked.

'Is it that obvious,' he replied.

'The terror in your eyes gives it away.' She smiled.

'Sorry.'

'Just try to be yourself. If you mess up no one is going to kill you.'

'Thanks.'

'Which company is it?' Carol asked curiously.

'PetroUK.'

'Really?' She asked, and thought, on the other hand, someone might kill you. She felt her eyes widening, before she added, 'That's where I'm going.'

'Do you work there?' the young man asked, now becoming interested.

'Yes… No… Well, I used to.'

The young man looked at her as if she was nuts.

'I'm visiting a friend,' Carol managed to say, before enquiring, 'What time is your interview?'

'Two-thirty,' the young man replied.

She glanced up at the clock above the lift door, its large red digits displaying the time as 13:21.

The young man, reading Carol's mind, said, 'I've a ticket for the viewing floors. I thought I should have a look while I'm here.'

'Good idea.' She smiled, and then asked, 'Do you know who is going to be interviewing you?'

'It's Mr Chiang.'

Carol thought she had misheard. 'Sorry, who did you say?'

'Mr Chiang, he is interviewing me,' the young man said again.

'Right,' she managed to reply, her stomach now doing somersaults. 'I think I saw Mr Chiang leaving for lunch as I came in.'

'That's right, but he'll be back for two thirty.'

Oh shit! Carol said to herself. 'You seem to know a lot about Mr Chiang,' she managed to say, her mouth momentarily becoming dry.

'Yes, he is a friend of my uncle.'

Is he indeed. She was almost at her floor and just had enough time to ask one final question, 'Which position are you applying for?'

‘It’s a personal assistant to Mr Chiang,’ the young man declared proudly.

‘Well, good luck with that,’ she said. ‘Maybe I’ll see you around.’

‘Thank you,’ he said.

When the lift doors opened, Carol hurried out feeling somewhat light-headed. Chiang was hiring one of his own.

Attached to the wall a Perspex sign told Carol that PetroUK’s offices were to her left, but as she was alone in the corridor she spoke softly into her free hand.

‘We have a problem!’

‘What?’ Mickey and Vinnie asked in unison.

‘I met a young Chinese lad in the lift and guess what, he’s only coming here for an interview at two thirty.’

‘We’ll work around it,’ Mickey said confidently.

‘That’s not the worst of it. Chiang’s conducting the interview.’

Silence. Mickey put his head in his hands before looking up at Vinnie, who shrugged his shoulders.

‘Right, we need to move quickly. Tell me this is good stuff, Leroy,’ Mickey asked.

‘It is, Mickey, we researched it. When Valerie’s finished her coffee, she’ll begin to feel uncomfortable within ten to fifteen minutes.’

‘Okay, we’ll continue. Are you fine with this, Carol?’ Mickey asked.

She hesitated. ‘Yes, but my stomach’s in knots.’

‘Relax you’re doing fine,’ he replied, but at the same time thinking it was all beginning to unravel.

Carol puffed out her cheeks and walked to the door of PetroUK. She touched her pass against the key pad and the door unlocked. She then pulled the door towards her and walked into a large open-plan office.

Chapter 22

Mickey entered the men's rest room on the ground floor: it was a large, spotlessly clean bright block with a tiled floor, six circular ceramic counter basins with brass taps and the same numbered toilet cubicles. He took the one furthest from the door, locked it, flushed the toilet and sat down. Removing his right shoe, he cut a slit into the heel with a small penknife, and from his pocket he took out a small polythene jewellery bag containing a large but slim watch battery and inserted it into a similar sized plastic device that Vinnie had given him. He then slid the device into the heel of his shoe, and sealed it with a line of superglue.

'Okay, Mickey, I have a signal: sixth toilet booth from the door,' whispered Vinnie.

'Hundred percent, mate,' he replied. Mickey flushed the toilet again, washed his hands and left.

Carol saw that Valerie was on a call. She looked up, smiled and waved, then gestured that she wouldn't be long. Carol set Valerie's coffee down on the counter in front of her and walked around the office. The layout was similar to a call centre. Rows of back-to-back partitioned cubicles, with keyboards, monitors and empty swivel chairs. At the far end stood four smaller offices, each with individual doors and windows with a view onto the floor, along with wooden Venetian blinds for added privacy. At ninety degrees to the offices was a meeting or board room, and taking centre stage in the middle was a polished oblong table and chairs, with six upturned gleaming highball glasses on white coasters. A large flat-screen television was bolted to a wall not far from a white-board and beside that a branded water cooler. On a smaller sideboard were two coffee machines, one with tall latte glasses and smaller espresso cups, the other containing larger cups for instant coffee or tea. It was a fresh and bright environment to work in and a world away from the Klondyke Building, but to Carol it felt clinical and without warmth, an appearance of strict authoritarianism, influenced possibly by Chiang.

What couldn't fail to impress her was when she walked to the window and looked out and down over central London: the view was stunning. Below, the city was a miniature world, with the Thames cutting a slice through its middle. It twisted and turned on its eastwardly journey, from its narrow western banks at Henley to its North Sea estuary far beyond the high-rises of Canary Wharf, which she could clearly see in the distance. Beneath and to the north stood the Gherkin, the NatWest Tower and the rest of the buildings in the Square Mile, and onward through the haze she could just make out Hampstead Heath.

'Impressive, isn't it?' Valerie said, suddenly appearing behind her.

'Breath taking,' replied Carol, turning around.

'I just love the view, when the day is as clear as it is now,' she said. Valerie smiled, but then it faded as she added, 'How are you, Carol? I haven't seen you since...'

'David's funeral?' Carol suggested.

Valerie nodded.

'I'm doing okay. I do miss you all, but I have to get on with it,' she replied sadly.

'Have you found any work?'

'No, I'm going to wait until after the New Year.'

Changing the subject, Valerie said, 'You look great!'

'And you look as if you've lost some weight,' Carol replied.

'Just under a half stone since we moved here. I've stopped nibbling, cut out chocolate and caffeine.'

'Caffeine?' Carol enquired, feeling the blood draining from her face while stealing a glance at Valerie's coffee sitting at reception.

'Oh, Carol, that coffee isn't for me, is it?'

'I'm afraid so,' she replied awkwardly, before quickly recovering. 'So, what do you drink now?' she asked.

'Oh, it's a mango and passion fruit smoothie, over ice, through a straw. I've a regular order at the juice bar in the foyer.' She checked her watch. 'In fact, it should almost be ready to collect, but they usually send someone up with it.'

Carol felt ill. 'Excuse me, but can I use the ladies?'

'Sure,' she said, as she pointed Carol to the door across from reception.

Checking that the three cubicles were empty and that she was alone, Carol spoke into her sleeve. 'Houston, we still have a problem.'

'What is it now?' Mickey asked disbelievingly.

'She's stopped drinking coffee.'

'You're kidding,' he sighed.

Vinnie and Leroy groaned.

'No joke! She has a regular order for a mango and passion fruit smoothie from the juice bar; they should be preparing it now.'

Mickey looked across to the juice bar. A young lady was pouring an orange and reddish mixture from an aluminium drinks mixer into a clear plastic cup before fitting a dome-shaped clear lid along with a straw on to it.

'Carol, is there any laxative left?' he asked.

'Yes, but just under half.'

'Okay, I'm going for the juice bar.'

Mickey strode over to the counter and asked if the smoothie for Valerie in PetroUK was ready.

'That's it over there,' the girl replied.

'Can I pay for it, please?'

'It's charged to their account.'

'Great.'

'I don't know you,' the girl said.

'It's okay, I'm her brother.'

'Yeah, so you say. How do I know you're not going to slip something into it?'

There was a queue growing behind Mickey, so he bluffed, 'Fine, send someone up with it then.'

The girl, realising she was going to be too busy, conceded. 'Go on then, you can take it.'

There were around eight people waiting for the lift when it arrived. Mickey got in and stood close to the floor panel. Four more joined behind him and as the doors closed he did a brief headcount. Unlucky for me, thirteen, including himself. Most of the occupants pressed for a floor. Mickey watched as the panel lit up like a bingo board. As nobody was exiting on the forty-third, he reached across and lit the number. *House!* he said to himself, glancing up at the camera, knowing that Vinnie was out there watching.

After pulling herself together, Carol had gone back into reception to find Valerie behind the counter eating yoghurt.

'You're really taking this seriously, aren't you?' Carol smiled.

‘I was at a christening a few weeks ago and when I saw the photographs, I looked the fattest person in the room.’

‘You’re not fat.’

Valerie made a face.

‘All right, maybe a few pounds over.’

‘Twenty-one to be precise. I want to lose a stone and a half by Valentine’s Day.’

‘Why, are you looking for a hot date?’

‘Possibly,’ she giggled.

‘Tell me more.’ Carol smiled.

‘I took out a membership to the gym on the sixtieth floor and kept bumping into this guy on a regular basis. He’s in his early fifties and divorced. We met for a drink one evening in the swanky coffee bar, just for a chat while admiring the view.’

‘Wonderful,’ Carol said.

‘How about you, Carol, any men on the horizon?’

Carol smiled. Little do you know, Valerie, he is a lot closer than the horizon. But before she could answer, the phone rang and Carol’s ear crackled at the same time.

It was Vinnie. ‘Carol, that’s me phoning Petro’s switchboard. Mickey will be at your floor in less than two minutes.’

‘Okay,’ she said, and almost kicked herself.

Valerie looked up and mouthed, ‘What?’

Carol made hand gestures about her drink arriving and walked towards the door. Once outside, she breathed out. ‘What the hell am I doing? I’m sorry, Vinnie.’

‘Relax, Carol. Did she get suspicious?’

‘No. Thankfully she was concentrating on the telephone.’

‘No harm done then. Mickey is about ten floors below you.’

In fact, he was on the thirty-fifth floor, eight below, with the doors closing and the only person remaining in the lift. Although not for long. Two floors later, four middle-aged men got in, travelling to one of the floors above Petro. They were discussing some financial contract or other, and to a former city analyst such as Mickey, he found the conversation enlightening, but as the lift arrived at the forty-third floor he bade his fellow occupants a good afternoon.

He found Carol standing halfway between the lift and Petro's offices. She looked stressed, but managed a weak smile.

'How are you doing?' he asked.

'I need a glass of wine, or maybe something stronger!'

'You're doing fine.'

She offered another smile and handed him the remainder of the laxative, which he poured into the smoothie.

'We're cutting it fine, Mickey. It's less than an hour now,' she said, with a look of panic.

'That's if Chiang turns up and on time; if he does, then we'll abort and think of something else.' He stirred the smoothie and handed it back to her. 'Hopefully, that is enough to do the trick,' he said.

She sipped it and smiled more confidently. 'Can't taste it.'

'Good.'

She was more relaxed now. 'Are you staying here, Mickey?'

'No, I'm going to the floor above; it's empty and Vinnie's got control of the cameras. When the shit starts, I can run down the stairs.'

She gave a nervous laugh. 'This is awful and none of it is Valerie's fault.'

'She'll be fine by tomorrow; she'll just have a sore ass tonight.'

Carol shook her head and turned towards the door. Mickey made his way to the stairwell and went up the stairs two at a time.

Carol took another deep breath as she pulled open the door, and saw that Valerie was on another call, and this one seemed more business like. Valerie eyed the smoothie, smiled and mouthed thank you, as Carol walked behind reception setting it down beside her, and saw the minutes on the small digital clock on the telephone console wink as it changed to 1:39 p.m.

She was figuring how she could get Valerie to drink the smoothie quickly, as she could talk for England, and any further delay would put them out of time.

Finishing the call, Valerie said, 'Now, where were we?'

'Why don't we swap seats and you can drink your smoothie while I operate the switchboard?' Carol quickly interrupted. 'You can keep an eye on me, ensure that I'm doing everything correctly.'

'Great idea,' she agreed.

They switched places and Carol sat in front of the monitor and keyboard. Any incoming calls she would hear through the headset attached to the telephone, but transfers could be done by a click of a mouse. She was hoping the telephone would ring so that Valerie would concentrate on her drink, but she needn't have worried, because, turning around, she saw Valerie slurping eagerly through the straw. She didn't want to ask her if it was good, for it would have been an excuse for Valerie to start talking again.

'Would you like a taste?' Valerie eventually asked.

'No, you seem to be enjoying it.'

'It's very good, although it tastes slightly different today, a bit tangy.'

Carol said nothing, and then she heard Mickey in her ear.

'Cough once for yes and twice for no. Is she drinking?'

Carol put a hand over her mouth and gave a gentle cough.

'Good. Hopefully she will feel the effect soon.'

She cleared her throat.

'Are you okay?' Valerie asked.

'Yes, I'm fine. I had a scone earlier downstairs and it must be a crumb that has stuck.'

Carol took a drink of her coffee and, between sentences, the contents of Valerie's smoothie slowly disappeared.

The telephone displayed 1:52 p.m. as Valerie's straw sucked air, reaching the bottom of the cup. The telephone rang a few times in between and Carol either took a message or transferred the call. With the smoothie now finished, it became a waiting game, though Carol hoped the wait wouldn't be much longer. At 2:03 p.m., Valerie was still chatting and Carol excused herself once more for the ladies.

'How much longer will this take?' she asked, panic rising in her voice.

Vinnie's reassuring voice came back to her. 'Carol, it shouldn't be much longer than fifteen minutes.'

She looked at her watch: twelve had passed and it seemed forever. 'It's like watching water boil.'

'As soon as she begins to feel unwell, that will be the signal to send Mickey down. Time is against us now if Chiang returns at two thirty, but it will only take five minutes to download the files.'

Valerie had switched seats again, as Carol returned to reception and was typing away on her keyboard.

'How are your boys?' Valerie enquired.

'Matthew and Christopher are doing well. They're going away for Christmas with Eddie and Cassie...' She stopped, because Valerie made a face, an uncomfortable grimace, while putting her hand across her tummy.

'What's wrong?' she asked.

'I don't know, my tummy feels kind of strange…' She lurched forward off her seat. 'I'm sorry, Carol, I'm afraid I need to use the ladies.'

Valerie disappeared through the toilet door and Carol waited for a few seconds until she heard the cubicle door lock, then she spoke into her hand.

'Okay, Mickey, you're clear.'

Mickey checked his watch: 2.08 p.m. They had twenty-two minutes, but was it enough time to download and get the hell out? He bounded down the stairs and Carol was there to release the door.

'I think that's Chiang's office straight ahead,' she said.

He handed Carol her tablet, jogged to Chiang's office and tried the door; unsurprisingly it was locked, with a key pad sitting to its left. Mickey, with another of Vinnie's tiny Wi-Fi devices stuck it magnetically to the pad and once it was in place a little light blinked red, waiting for the code.

'Okay, Vinnie, it's in place.'

Vinnie typed away on his laptop; a million binary combinations flashed by on his screen, until each of the four empty boxes at the bottom was filled.

'Four, seven, six, two,' he announced.

It was a random number. When Mickey typed it in and the lock clicked, he removed the magnetic device and opened the door.

Mickey found Chiang's laptop sitting on his desk, where the only other items of note were a couple of chairs, one behind the desk, a small coffee table, a filing cabinet and the faint ticking of a wall clock. Absent was the widescreen television with the latest stock prices which now appeared in many directors' offices and neither were there any wall photographs of Chiang shaking hands with the great and the good.

The coffee table sat against an internal wall and upon it was a large glass jug half-filled with water, along with one upturned glass. After finding the filing cabinet empty, Mickey turned his attention to the desk and walked over to Chiang's open laptop with its power cable attached, running through a hole in the desk to a socket beneath. The desk top was bare of any other items, not even a portrait photograph of a girlfriend, wife, child or dog. Chiang appeared to be a man with little time for sentiment; he obviously didn't spend much time in his office, nor did it seem he was planning on staying long with PetroUK.

'Vinnie, I'm in, and his laptop is here,' he said, sounding breathless.

'Mickey, is the computer switched on?'

Mickey moved his finger along the mouse pad and the screen lit up, displaying a screensaver of the company logo floating across the screen. It reinvented itself as it twisted and turned, morphing itself back into a readable word. He tapped the mouse pad again and this time the screen cleared, displaying a password window.

'Password protected, Vinnie.'

'Okay, insert the black USB memory stick,' Vinnie told him.

A blue light appeared from the USB stick as he inserted it into the port at the side of the laptop.

Vinnie was scanning Chiang's passwords, looking for a word or combination of letters and numbers used every day or a few times per day and not long after the laptop had been booted up.

'He must like his racehorses, Mickey.'

'Why?'

'Imperial Commander. A Gold Cup winner a few years back. It's used every morning after the boot up and each time after a period of inactivity,' Vinnie said.

The screen cleared after Mickey typed in the horse's name, only for a second password request to appear when he clicked on the document's icon.

'Shit.'

'What is it, mate?' asked Vinnie.

'Another password.'

'Give me a minute.'

The minutes were disappearing, as the clock's second hand reached half way between 2.12 and 2.13.

Vinnie crackled in Mickey's ear again. 'Try Sea the Stars, that's sea as in the North Sea. It won the Prix de l'Arc de Triomphe.'

He typed in the words and pressed enter, only for Access Denied to pop up in front of him.

'Wrong one Vinnie and it's informed me I have two attempts remaining.'

Vinnie searched again. 'Green Moon. It won the Melbourne Cup in 2012,' he said.

'How do you know this shit?' Mickey asked, as a few beads of sweat appeared on his brow.

Again, he entered the words and again his access was denied.

'Strike two, Vinnie, last chance saloon, give it your best shot, mate.'

The room was silent apart from the fan from the laptop and the ticking of the clock, which appeared to sound louder after every minute. He heard a noise outside in reception and between the slats in the blinds he could make out a young Oriental male standing in the empty reception.

Chapter 23

Carol had been checking on Valerie. She felt guilty that her friend was having an uncomfortable time in the ladies.

'Sometimes if you drink too many of those smoothies it plays havoc with your bowel,' she offered.

'Maybe I should…' Valerie said, before letting out another groan.

'I'll check on reception,' Carol replied.

She had forgotten about the young interviewee and she was almost as surprised to see him as he was to see her.

'Hello again,' she said.

'Hello, I thought…' the young man replied.

'It's the receptionist, she's feeling poorly,' said Carol pointing to the door.

The young man understood and said nothing else.

'Please take a seat. Mr Chiang should be here shortly,' although Carol was hoping something would delay Chiang, preferably indefinitely.

Vinnie took his time with the third password attempt. He knew it would be the last, but time was ticking away.

'Mickey, I'm afraid it's a bit like the red or green wire and not really knowing which one to cut,' he finally said.

'What do you have?'

'Two more horses.'

'Which two?'

'Animal Kingdom and Snow Fairy.'

'What did they win?'

'Animal Kingdom won the Dubai World Cup and Snow Fairy the Hong Kong Cup.'

'Which one is used more often?'

'Snow Fairy, but it hasn't been used today.'

'Shit! Sorry, Vinnie, I hate to put this on you, but you choose.'

'Thanks, mate.'

Mickey heard him deliberating, so he asked, 'Which horse won Hong Kong?'

'Snow Fairy in 2010.'

'Okay, we'll go with that one.'

'Why?' Vinnie asked.

'Hong Kong is close to home. The heart of the beast?'

'Your call, Mickey, good luck.'

He typed Snow Fairy into the password window, closed his eyes and pictured it running along the track, on a warm humid evening, under floodlights, with its hooves cutting through the dirt. There was silence in his ear. Vinnie would be sitting, staring at the screen, his hands clasped, looking pensive. Leroy, far below, was probably at this very moment staring up at the glass building. 'With you, Mickey,' he heard him say. Mickey glanced up, through the blinds and across the floor, meeting Carol's eyes, which contained a mixture of anxiety and terror. Puffing out his cheeks and with his index finger hovering over the key, he finally pressed enter.

For a second or two nothing happened. The screen turned to black and then it cleared, showing a list of files, each with individual names.

'Home run, we're in,' he said.

A relieved Vinnie replied, 'Mickey, use the second USB stick. Insert it into the other slot and download the files to F.'

Clicking back to the original folder, Mickey inserted the memory stick and selected Save. A second window opened to inform him it was downloading, with the approximate download time of just under eight minutes. It was 2.21 p.m.

'Seven minutes forty-five, Vinnie.'

'Shit, man. That stick is supposed to be superfast.'

Leroy's voice sounded urgent. 'We've got trouble. eyeball on black Land Rover, same registration, slowing at doors.'

Vinnie cursed and Mickey heard Carol whisper, 'Oh no.'

'I can't see who got out, but I'm convinced it's one of our guys,' continued Leroy.

Vinnie received a ping from Chiang's pass, five seconds before he saw him.

'It's Chiang,' he said.

Vinnie watched as he strode across the atrium towards the coffee bar.

'It looks as if he's going for coffee.'

Chiang then stopped, hesitated, glanced at his watch and then took a step to his right, putting him in line with the double doors.

'Shit, he's changed his mind, he's going for the elevators. How long do you need, Mickey?'

The download bar was inching along and the countdown clock turned to under five minutes.

'Four minutes fifty,' he said, but it would take another minute to get Carol and himself out.

As soon as Chiang entered the lift, Vinnie pressed a few keys and brought up a blueprint of the Shard's internal electrical system. He watched as Chiang's lift slowly rose and, once it was between the tenth and eleventh floors, he typed in a three-digit code and the lift suddenly stopped.

‘What’s that noise?’ Mickey asked, hearing a distant ringing.

‘That’s the elevator alarm. I cut the power to Chiang’s ride. It should buy you a little extra time before the manual override kicks in.’

‘Three minutes forty-two, Vinnie.’ Maybe a minute before the lift starts again, Mickey thought, and maybe another two before Chiang got here. It was going to be tight.

Two minutes twenty-five, was all that remained on the download when Vinnie’s voice sounded again, this time with a lot more urgency. ‘You better get out of there, mate, the elevator is moving again and Chiang’s the only passenger.’

Carol was close to having a coronary, and her nerves were in meltdown as she listened to Mickey and Vinnie’s conversation.

Fifty-eight seconds remained on the download.

‘He’s getting out of the lift. Get the hell out of there, Mickey,’ Vinnie said, the panic clear in his voice.

Lee Chiang opened the door to PetroUK’s offices on the forty-third floor of the Shard, and was surprised to see a former employee standing behind reception.

‘Good afternoon, Ms….’ he said.

‘Freeman,’ Carol smiled.

‘Where is the lady?’ Chiang enquired.

‘Valerie is feeling unwell and is using the restroom.’

‘Is it serious?’ Chiang’s English was good, but he had difficulty with his R’s.

What Carol wanted to say was: she’s got the two-bob bits, you bastard, but forever the diplomat she replied, ‘It’s a woman thing, Mr Chiang.’

Happy with this, Chiang nodded and looked in the direction of the young man. He spoke to him in Mandarin, and the young man replied with a nervous laugh.

Chiang then took a step towards his office. 'Thank you, Ms. Freeman, it is once more good to see you,' he said, beckoning the young man to follow.

Carol, forcing a smile, gave him the finger under the counter, but she was on the verge of panic as Chiang typed in the code to open his office door.

Both he and the young man entered and Chiang sat down behind his desk.

'Carol, where's Chiang?' Vinnie whispered softly into her ear.

'He's in his office,' she stuttered.

'Get out of there now.'

'What about Mickey?' she asked, almost tearfully.

'He's clear.'

'What? How?'

'He'll explain later. You did a great job, now make your way to the rendezvous point.'

As the USB was downloading, and two minutes before Chiang entered the offices of PetroUK, Mickey was unscrewing the cover to an air vent. The vent was a few inches above the skirting, and Mickey calculated that he could fit through without too much trouble. When the download completed, a few seconds after Chiang walked into reception, his conversation with Carol delayed him enough for Mickey to plan his escape. Removing both memory sticks from the laptop, he set the screensaver to thirty seconds and logged off. He crawled backwards into the air duct and replaced the cover by setting it in place with a piece of chewing gum.

On Vinnie's computer, Mickey appeared as a red dot, being directed backwards on his stomach through the air flow duct on the forty-third floor. At a juncture in the aluminium shaft, Mickey turned around and faced frontward.

'About twenty feet ahead it should start to rise,' announced Vinnie. 'Hopefully your hands and feet should provide enough of a grip to pull you up the incline.'

Mickey reached another crossway and saw light ahead as the shaft rose slightly above him. It was a narrow enclosed space and it made the incline feel steeper than it truly was. He almost laughed at the absurdity of it all and at one point thought of humming the tune to *The Great Escape*, as if he was one of the seventy-six Allied servicemen escaping from Stalag Luft III.

Near to the top of the shaft he spotted dust, as it caught the sun's rays, drifting through the vent on the empty upper floor. He once more swung himself around at another juncture, approaching the cover feet first and lightly touching it with his foot, before pushing himself up with both hands whilst pressing against the walls of the shaft. Mickey raised his right knee and with as much force as possible kicked forward at the vent cover. The screws screeched and moved half an inch. He kicked once more and the metal grill swung open like a stable door and a gateway to freedom.

They were sitting in the rear of Vinnie's shop, having made it back safely after going their separate ways. Leroy had hopped onto the number forty bus towards the Elephant and Castle and then used the tube for the remainder of his journey. Vinnie hightailed it out of the mezzanine and hailed a cab. Whereas Mickey had found Carol in a wine bar on Union Street, with her second glass of wine, one hundred yards from where the van had been parked. They were all high on adrenaline and greeted each other smiling with high fives and hugs, after Mickey had replayed the great escape to Carol in the van.

'I thought you were done for. I didn't hear you and Vinnie talking, as I was somewhat occupied by a certain Lee Chiang at the time,' she said relieved.

When they were settled, Vinnie brought out a six pack of bottled beer.

'Right, folks,' he said, flipping the lid off a bottle, 'the moment of truth; shall we see what's on the files?'

He inserted the USB memory stick from Chiang's computer and uploaded its contents, scanning each file individually. The first three recorded information on Black Castle and the future fracking of the area known as Block 12 in Azerbaijan. The February date had been put back until April, or as Chiang had noted in the file, until after the start of the new UK tax year. There was also reference to Zone Seven, the area in the Persian Gulf where a deal had been struck with the Iranian Government, but again, nothing they didn't already know. The drilling for oil in Namibia was also nothing of significance in the second file, nor the shipment of goods from Sri Lanka in file three.

'This is looking like a waste of time,' Mickey said, taking a mouthful of beer.

'There are still two more files to go, Mickey, keep the faith,' Carol said, patting his thigh.

Mickey passed the mouse to Vinnie and sat back as Vinnie opened the fourth file.

'What's this?' Carol asked.

The file introduced a new company known as Qom Pipe Supplies (QPS) of Iran. Tai Sing of Hong Kong had a trade agreement with QPS for supplying pipe material, and the named managing director of QPS was a man called Mohammed Shakiba.

'Shakiba,' Mickey and Carol both said in unison.

'You know him?' Vinnie asked.

'He's a director of Black Castle, along with Chiang, and Mickey thinks it's the same guy he picked up in his cab outside Black Castle's offices in Oxford Street,' Carol replied.

Vinnie used a search engine and found more information on Qom Pipe Supplies, detailing the production of parts for the oil and gas industry.

'Pipe supplies,' Mickey said. 'It looks as if PetroUK are buying from an Iranian company, somewhat indirectly though.'

'What do you mean?' Vinnie asked, sitting back in his chair.

'Black Castle, with Chiang as a director, own a large chunk of Petro shares, and are registered to a company known as Jia Ding and then onto Tai Sing.'

'It's a tax dodge,' offered Leroy.

'It could be a lot more sinister than that, but it's something we don't yet know,' Carol replied.

'Let's open the remaining file,' Mickey said.

Vinnie clicked on the fifth and final file. It took a few seconds to load while it converted to PDF. When it eventually opened, they all stared open mouthed at it.

The file contained a bank credit transfer statement for a transaction of $30 million US dollars, divided into three accounts of $10 million each, which had been deposited with Banque Cantonale de Geneve, in Switzerland. The three accounts were opened in the names of Roger Mildenhall, Harold Goodwin and Geoffrey Burbridge.

‘Wow,’ Carol said, ‘that’s about £6.5 million each, in a Swiss bank account, and look at the date of the transaction. It’s the day after Chiang joined the board.’

‘And our old friends Tai Sing in Hong Kong deposited it,’ added Mickey.

‘Maybe you should give this up, mate, for your own good,’ advised Vinnie. ‘This looks way too big, man.’

Mickey didn’t reply: he was staring at the computer screen contemplating his next move.

Chapter 24

The man appeared relaxed as he walked casually across the concourse, tall and with a full head of silver hair; he was dressed for the business day, wearing a red tie and black overcoat for extra warmth, and under one arm he carried a broadsheet newspaper, which was quite possibly the *Guardian* or the *Daily Telegraph*. He paused at the portable coffee bar: it was an odd design, in the shape of an old steam railway engine. Its sides opened outwards and up, to protect its customers from the rain, not that it was required this morning, as the weather gave the impression of an early spring day and not one just a week before Christmas.

The sun had risen a few minutes earlier and on the opposite side of the river its rays were beginning to clip the tops of the high rises before reflecting off the glass and creating a corridor of light at street level. A sharp breeze suddenly blew up from the Thames and across the concourse, with the man pulling up the collar of his coat as he waited in line. Exchanging pleasantries with the young man serving, he turned with coffee in hand and walked towards the entrance of the Shard.

'Mr Mildenhall?' Mickey called out to the man.

'Yes?' he replied, suddenly pausing, displaying a friendly expression, but quizzical at the sheer mention of his name.

'Mr Mildenhall, would you mind if I asked you a few questions regarding the operations of PetroUK?'

'Young man, if you are a journalist, you will need to make an appointment with our media department,' Mildenhall replied, as he again turned and this time quickening his pace.

Mickey skipped a few paces to keep up.

'Mr Mildenhall, I would prefer to keep this away from the media department if at all possible,' he said.

Mildenhall slowed, looking at Mickey, considering his reply, before he again picked up his pace and said, 'I'm sorry, but all correspondence must now be directed through…'

Mickey cut him off and before he got any closer to the Shard's entrance. 'I know about the money in the Swiss bank accounts,' he said.

Mildenhall stopped dead, as if the power had been cut from a children's fun ride. He turned to look at Mickey, his smile vanishing. Mickey took a step back, allowing his words to sink in. Mildenhall was at least an inch taller, and a frown now wrinkled his tanned forehead, where before there had been a smile. Around the edges of his steely blue eyes a few lines could clearly be seen, but his face and chin were absent of fat, instead rugged, as if carved from granite. Mickey slipped a card into Mildenhall's free hand, he took it, looked at it and then nodded.

'I understand, Mr Ross. I must attend a meeting now, but I will contact you later this morning,' he said.

Mildenhall turned and walked away, Mickey noticing his pace now slower, with his shoulders slumped, as if right now he carried the weight of the world upon them.

The call came at seven minutes past the hour. Mickey was drinking coffee at a street cafe on the north side of the Thames, overlooking London Bridge, beside Monument and Pudding Lane, where the Great Fire of London had started three hundred and fifty years previously. The winter sun was warm on his face as he sat shaded from the onshore breeze. He was down-wind of Big Ben and had heard the clock tower as it counted off the last few chimes of eleven a.m., when his silenced phone buzzed, vibrating on the glass table top as the blocked number appeared on its screen. Mickey picked it up and answered.

'Mr Ross, it's Roger Mildenhall, can we meet?' It was a request but sounded more of a command.

'Do you have somewhere in mind, Mr Mildenhall?'

'Yes, it is quite close by, Starbucks at The Tower of London. Can we say one p.m.?'

One o'clock seemed fine to Mickey so he agreed and then Mildenhall clicked off. As Mickey finished his coffee he glanced up at the Shard: the impressive glass structure gleamed in the bright sunlight. He had a thought that at this very moment Mildenhall was up there looking down at the city from his window high in the sky.

Mildenhall turned from the window, with the phone still in his hand, and looked at Lee Chiang, sitting comfortably in the leather armchair.

'Did he agree?' Chiang asked.

'Yes,' Mildenhall replied softly, before dropping his eyes to the floor.

'Good,' said Chiang, getting out of the chair. 'I will have a few people follow you, Mister Mildenhall, to your meeting with this Mister Ross. They will be discrete, so you will not be able to see them, but they will be there for your protection.'

'I really don't think this is necessary, Mr Chiang,' replied Mildenhall.

Chiang smiled as he moved towards the door.

‘As I said, Roger, it is for your own protection and that of the company’s.’

As Chiang left, Mildenhall turned back to the window, staring out towards the horizon, before looking down at the river, wishing he could dive into the water below and disappear beneath its surface, like a fish, and swim outwards to the sea beyond.

London is a city for all seasons, and caters for as many visitors and tourists in winter as it does in summer. As Carol had left early for her parents taking Lucy with her, Mickey spent the next hour and a half wandering through Spitalfields and Brick Lane, before jumping on the number fifteen bus travelling towards the Tower of London.

When Mickey arrived, a coach-load of Japanese tourists along with their guide were making their way down the hill to its entrance. The guide, a middle-aged woman of around five feet tall, held a small red flag raised above her head and marched briskly in front of them. As he reached the bottom of the hill Mickey spotted Roger Mildenhall with his back to him. Mildenhall, with both hands on the wall of the river bank, leaned forward slightly, as if looking down at the water’s edge. He was still impeccably dressed and became aware of Mickey’s presence.

‘This is where they brought them ashore, you know. Traitors’ Gate, their final view of freedom, before they spent the remainder of their lives behind those walls,’ he said, as he nodded towards the high outer wall of the Tower.

The Japanese coach party had reached the entrance and each of them held a white admission ticket in their hand, as the guide walked up and down the line, still holding the silly little red flag, barking orders.

'Anne Boleyn and Catherine Howard entered through there and never returned,' he said, continuing with the history lesson.

Mickey returned the nod and watched as the greasy water lapped at the inlet running under their feet and under the walls of the Tower.

Mildenhall suddenly snapped out of the sixteenth century and suggested, 'Shall we grab a coffee and then talk as we walk.'

'Of course,' Mickey replied.

They stood in line behind the tourists and many office workers making use of the good weather to get away from their desks. Once outside, Mickey and Mildenhall walked a slow leisurely pace, as if on a Sunday stroll, licking ice cream. Surprisingly it was Mildenhall who started the ball rolling.

'How did you become aware of the $10 million payment, Mr Ross?' he asked, as casually as one would enquire about the health of a wife or child.

'I became aware of it after in-depth research,' Mickey lied, 'but Mr—'

'Roger, and can I call you Michael?'

'Sure, Roger. My concern and that of my client is not the Swiss bank accounts of you and your fellow directors. It is why Lee Chiang was so interested in joining the board of PetroUK.'

'Are you able to tell me who your client is?' he asked.

'Sorry, Roger,' Mickey replied, shaking his head.

Mildenhall said nothing and looked down at the stone cobbles as they continued their walk.

'How much do you know about Zone 7?' Mickey asked.

Mildenhall looked surprised. 'How the hell do you know about Zone 7?' he replied, his voice rising.

Mickey looked around, and smiled as he caught the eye of a passer-by. 'Is it true?' he asked.

'Of course it's bloody true; that will be the downfall of this company,' he said.

'You were against it?'

'Damn right I was.'

'Then why did you sign up to it?'

He shrugged his shoulders.

'This is all about Chiang, isn't it?'

Mildenhall was silent.

Nearby was an empty bench facing the river.

'Shall we sit?' Mickey suggested.

They took a seat, with the sandstone wall of the Tower behind them and the sun sparkling on the water in front. Two women in business suits walked slowly towards them, one had her jacket folded across her arms, and both carried similar throw-away coffee cups.

As they weren't within earshot, Mildenhall said, 'Michael, Lee Chiang owning a large chunk of our company means that he has a stake in the energy resources of the world, especially oil.'

'Yes, but why?'

'So he can control the price of oil.'

Mickey stared at him. 'But the supply is set by OPEC and to a certain degree the price.'

'That's correct, Michael, but Chiang wants to force the price higher for the longer term.'

Mickey was unmoved. 'He may be a large shareholder but he doesn't have the ability to raise the price of crude.'

Mildenhall sat looking at Mickey; there was sadness in those big blue eyes, but he was contemplating about how to word his next sentence. The two women sat on a bench slightly down and across from them. Mildenhall waited until a young couple passed by. He sighed, then continued, 'The price of crude will rise if there is a war in the Middle East.'

'War? Chiang couldn't start a war,' Mickey said incredulously. 'You can't be serious, Roger?'

A smile began to appear on Mildenhall's face, as if he couldn't quite believe it himself, but he added, 'I'm afraid so, Michael.'

'It's impossible. With who?'

'Israel,' Mildenhall replied calmly.

'China and Israel?'

'Not China, Michael, Iran.'

Mickey was delving deep into his memory, before he asked, 'Was Chiang behind the movement of oil the other week?'

'The figures out of China were false, Michael.'

'But it was a government release?'

'True, but Chiang has his own man in there.'

'Triad?'

'The family, as he likes to call them, but then the Chinese Government released a new set of economic figures claiming the previous one was a miscalculation and the commodities market recovered,' Mildenhall said.

'Did David Harrison know about Chiang's plans?' Mickey asked.

'David knew very little; he didn't like Chiang, didn't trust the little bastard. I wish I'd listened to him, but I only saw the pound signs, Michael, and got greedy.'

'Was he responsible for David's death?'

Mildenhall didn't seem surprised at the question, but dodged the answer slightly. 'We were all very shocked at David's death.'

'Why didn't you go to the police or the Stock Exchange?' Mickey asked, trying to keep the anger from his voice.

Mildenhall looked to his left and smiled at a woman with a pram passing nearby and whispered, 'I didn't have any proof, Michael.'

A reflection from the sun on an opened window or sliding door from the apartments across the river caught Mickey's eyes, dazzling him slightly.

'Okay, Roger. Then what proof do you have that Chiang is trying to start a war?'

'Last week an executive from an Israeli software company was killed by a bomb planted underneath his car right here in London.'

'Yes, I heard about that.'

Mildenhall looked at him and said nothing.

Mickey stared back at him, open-eyed. 'Did Chiang have something to do with that?'

Mildenhall glanced down at his hands and fiddled with the lid of his cup. He looked up again at Mickey and said, 'Some of Chiang's family followed me here today. They're probably watching as we speak.'

Mickey couldn't help but glance around. 'You need to go to the police, Roger,' he said.

'It's too late for that now, Michael.'

Mickey leaned forward slightly onto his elbows, puffing out his cheeks and poking a hole in the side of his empty coffee cup. He was about to ask Mildenhall about Black Castle, but didn't get the chance. Instead, he felt a slight draft as something buzzed past his left ear, then a sprinkle of something warm and wet on his face tasting sweet on his lips. He looked across at the two women on the bench opposite, and then the world slowed down.

The woman with the jacket across her arms put one hand to her mouth. At the same time the other woman dropped her coffee cup and Mickey's gaze followed its fall as it tumbled to the ground with the lid coming off and its contents spilling out, before the woman let out a piercing scream.

Mickey turned to look at Mildenhall, but his brain wasn't functioning correctly. He was picturing and deciphering something entirely different. It was as if he was staring at the three hundred and fourteenth frame of Abraham Zapruder's 8mm film on Dealey Plaza, of President John F Kennedy's motorcade, as the assassin's third bullet struck the President's head and exploded it like a watermelon. Except this was not 1963, Mickey was sure of that, and he was certain he was not in Dallas, Texas, and the mush of red flesh and bone which confronted his eyes was not that of the thirty-fifth President of the United States.

The reaction side of Mickey's brain eventually kicked into gear and he dived onto the ground, crawling towards the wall of the riverbank just as a second bullet slammed into the wall of the Tower behind where he had been sitting. The two women opposite were also on the ground, thankfully uninjured, but whimpering in shock as other people in the area dived for cover. Mickey put a finger to his face and felt a sticky wetness. Looking at it, he saw the colour of crimson, not of his own blood, but that of Mildenhall's, who lay slumped to one side, lifeless, with half of his face missing. Mickey stayed where he was for what seemed like an eternity, tucked in against the cold stone wall, as if any further shots would find him. The shooting, though, had stopped, and as the distant sirens of the emergency services approached, he realised that the second bullet which had chipped a large piece from the Tower's outer wall, had been intended for him.

'Let's try again, Mr Ross. In what capacity, did you know, the now deceased Mr Mildenhall?' asked the detective.

Mickey was sitting in the interview room of Bethnal Green Police Station. The room was small, not much larger than twelve feet square and a virtual cube, with a young uniformed constable standing by the door. From the ceiling an old twin fluorescent light, supported by two chains, gave off a glow not much brighter than a couple of candles, with the dimness creating shadows against the grey-painted London Met standard walls. A letterbox window close to the ceiling, that had filtered in a little light from earlier, was now just a darkened void. The detective's patience was wavering, as he drummed the fingers of his right hand on the old wooden table while sitting opposite Mickey.

Mickey had answered the same question three times and for the fourth time he repeated the same answer, 'If you contact Lauren King, she will be able to provide you with all the information that you require, detective.'

'And who is this Lauren King?' he asked again.

The detective had a Scottish brogue that sounded Glaswegian; he was mid-fifties, out of shape and called McGregor, and he reminded Mickey of a cop out of the Scottish television series Taggart.

'I don't know who Miss King is, except I think she works for MI5,' Mickey replied.

Although when he thought about it, Mickey didn't really know who the hell Lauren was. She was paying him, but he had only met her once, and for all he knew, she herself could be working for some terrorist network. He had given McGregor her direct-line telephone number, but she hadn't picked up, so at that moment he was beginning to feel very much alone.

McGregor brought his hand down hard on the table and the sound vibrated around the small room. From the corner of his eye, Mickey saw the young uniformed officer at the door twitch, possibly awakened from a daydream.

The second detective, sitting beside McGregor and slightly younger with a Geordie accent, whose name Mickey had missed during the introductions, said, 'Mr Ross, you have told us that you think Miss King works for MI5, an organisation called Chameleon, which we have checked out and unfortunately it does not appear to exist.'

'What are you, Mr Ross, some kind of James Bond?' mocked McGregor.

'No comment, Moneypenny,' he replied.

'Don't you get smart with me, sonny, or I'll throw a conspiracy to murder in your lap,' yelled McGregor.

Mickey was getting pissed off with the good cop, bad cop routine. He took a mouthful of coffee which the good cop had been good enough to fetch for him. It was the colour of mud, tasted something similar and came in a flimsy brown plastic cup, the type you would get from an old vending machine, but the caffeine was beginning to kick in.

Mickey leaned forward on his elbows, almost reaching half way across the table, making McGregor pull back, and said, 'You're full of shit, detective!'

McGregor looked as if he was going to explode, but his colleague stepped in, calming the situation. 'Mr Ross, you need to see it from our position…'

The young constable reacted to a knock at the door, and as he pulled it open a third plain-clothed officer poked his head around it. 'Sarge,' he said, motioning for McGregor to leave the room.

McGregor scraped his chair violently across the floor, staring down Mickey as he got up, and stormed out of the room.

'Mr Ross,' continued the second detective, 'we have a situation. There has been a shooting at one of London's most popular tourist attractions, with one person dead, the person you were talking to, and the mayor is busting our balls to find out why.'

'I have told you everything I know,' Mickey repeated for the umpteenth time.

'I understand that, Mr Ross, but what was the reason that you needed to meet with Mr Mildenhall?' the detective asked.

Thankfully for Mickey, he didn't get the chance to answer, because McGregor threw open the door, almost taking the young constable's head off. He sat down and pulled in his chair, breathing heavily. He clasped his hands in front of him and then took a drink of water, before rubbing his eyes and blowing out his cheeks.

'Well, Mr Ross,' he said, glancing at his colleague, 'it looks like your young lady Miss King came through; you are free to go,' he sighed.

'Thank you,' replied Mickey, getting up immediately from his chair.

As the young constable escorted him out of the room, McGregor added, 'Don't be planning any foreign trips, Mr Ross; we may need to speak to you again.'

Mickey was relieved to feel the cold air on his face, once he had stepped outside of the police station, having spent five hours inside a stuffy interview room. The outside air may not have been fresh as the early evening commuter traffic clogged the main road, but he was relieved to be free of the continual questioning by McGregor.

Frustration was beginning to grow with drivers as they leaned on their horns as a van with its hazards blinking blocked one lane of traffic. The city was cloaked in darkness and a light drizzle had replaced the bright sunshine of the daylight hours. Although office units were locked and shuttered, several convenience stores remained open and their bright stores brought a little relief to the grimness of the evening. Mickey walked a few hundred yards from the police station and took out his phone and dialled Lauren's number; he let it ring seven or eight times before ending the call and putting the phone back into his pocket. He crossed over the road and saw the underground station in the distance, but as he passed a fast-food store he suddenly became hungry and was about to double back when his phone vibrated. He immediately took it out and answered it.

'Michael, are you out?' she asked.

'Yes, Lauren, they have just this moment released me.'

'Where are you?' There was concern in her voice.

'Lauren, what the hell is going on?'

'Michael, listen to me, it's too dangerous for you to go home.'

'Why, Lauren, what the hell have you gotten me into?' he asked, putting a finger in his ear, while at the same time looking for somewhere quiet to speak. 'Why didn't you tell me that you worked for MI5?'

'How do you know that?' she asked, surprised.

'You hired me, Lauren. I'm a private investigator.'

Ignoring the inquisition, she asked, 'What did Mildenhall say to you?'

'Not very much, because someone blew his brains out,' Mickey spat.

'Michael, I need to know where you are; your life could be in danger.'

He stopped and looked behind him: the only people around were commuters and shoppers hurrying home through the rain.

'I'm walking towards Bethnal Green tube station,' he said.

Mickey heard her flicking through paper; then, as if she transferred the phone from one hand to the other, said, 'Michael, make your way to…'

A heavy goods vehicle trundled past and Mickey missed what Lauren had said. A block of maisonettes sat back from the road, where there was parking and a green area with shrubbery. He walked towards it, with the road traffic quieter now, stopping beside a parked car, and said, 'Sorry, Lauren, you cut out.'

'Michael, get on the tube and go one stop east to Mile End. Have you got that?'

'Mile End, okay,' he said.

'When you exit the station, turn left and make your way towards…'

He didn't hear any more: something or someone hit him on the back of the neck. He slumped forward with a thump, onto the bonnet of the car, and watched as his mobile phone bounced and slid along the metal before disappearing out of sight and finally hearing it fall to the ground. He felt a pair of hands on him, possibly two, and then a cloth or handkerchief being placed over his nose and mouth. Mickey couldn't help but breathe in: it had a sweet and pungent smell both at the same time as he was overcome with nausea, and the sound of the street becoming more distant. With much effort, he tried to fight, but at the same time he felt heavy and weak, before his body finally fell limp as he slipped into a state of unconsciousness.

Chapter 25

He opened his eyes and found the room spinning. He closed them again, waited a few seconds, before reopening them slowly. Mickey found himself upright in a chair, hands tied behind his back, minus his coat, with the sleeves of his shirt rolled to his biceps. With blurred vision, he focused on a dark object roughly twenty feet in front. As the mist cleared, the shape was that of a young Oriental man who was dressed in a black suit sitting facing him. The young man, realising that Mickey was awake, got up from his chair and walked towards him. Mickey tensed, as he waited for the first strike, but instead the young man lifted an unopened bottle of water from the table beside him, cracked the top, and held it in front of Mickey's face. It wasn't until the first swallow that Mickey realised he was thirsty, and then he was looking for more. He was allowed three more gulps, before the bottle was set back on the table, minus its lid. The young man, who hadn't said a word the whole time, then turned towards the door, opened it and left the room, leaving Mickey alone.

The room, with curtains drawn floor to ceiling along two of its walls, contained five large circular tables that sat randomly across the floor, each with white linen upon them and large enough to comfortably sit eight people. A hatch or dumb-waiter sat in a wall to Mickey's left and when he managed to crane his neck around, he saw that behind him a bar counter stood locked and shuttered, with upturned bottles on optics and beer taps on the counter. He heard noise from above, the sound of feet and more than a couple of pairs, then chairs moving, more feet and voices with inaudible conversation and laughter. He was in a restaurant, a private function room and probably a basement.

After a few minutes, the young Oriental man returned, he closed the door and once more took his place on the chair in front of Mickey.

Mickey looked towards the table with the bottle of water, and then back to the young man. 'Can I have more water, please?' he asked.

The young man said nothing; he didn't blink or raise an eyebrow, only that he continued to stare at Mickey.

Mickey tried again. 'Water, please,' he said, motioning to the bottle beside him.

The young man didn't reply.

'Where am I?' Mickey asked.

But the young man wasn't playing. Maybe he didn't speak English,' thought Mickey.

'Wo zai nali?' Mickey repeated in Mandarin.

There was a slight flicker in the young man's eyes, as he recognised his native tongue, but again he didn't answer.

Mickey had previously worked at Lehman's with a few guys from Hong Kong, and he'd picked up enough words to pass himself if he ever visited the former British colony, which at this moment seemed very unlikely.

It wasn't long before Mickey heard footsteps on a flight of stairs, coming closer with every step. The door opened and in walked two men dressed the same as Mickey's babysitter, but slightly older. Behind them came Lee Chiang and following Chiang, was the man Mickey had driven to Edgware Road.

'Did you have a good sleep, Mr Ross?' Chiang asked.

'I've had better.'

‘I trust you enjoyed the company of my young nephew,’ he said, pointing at the young man seated.

‘He’s not too good at making conversation,’ Mickey replied.

Chiang clicked his fingers, and his nephew stood, gave a slight bow and left the room.

‘I am sorry about the limitations on refreshments, Mr Ross,’ Chiang said, pointing at the bottle of water, ‘but the bar, as you can see, is currently closed.’

‘Thanks, but I’ve already had a mouthful,’ Mickey returned.

Chiang smiled. He was educated, probably at a university here in England, before he eventually returned to Hong Kong to graduate in fraud, extortion and murder.

‘Excuse my manners, Mr Ross,’ he said, turning to the other man. ‘This is Mr Mohammed Shakiba, and these are two more of my nephews,’ as he pointed at the two younger men. ‘And I believe you are well acquainted with me,’ he continued.

Mickey was grateful Shakiba hadn’t remembered him from his journey in the cab, as he’d only seen the back of Mickey’s head and fleeting glances of his face.

Chiang placed on the table beside Mickey two enlarged black and white photographs. Mickey recognised the first one immediately: it was of him looking up at the camera outside Leila’s apartment; but he cursed himself silently on seeing the second photograph, which was a shot of his face from the webcam on Chiang’s laptop, most likely activated when he logged on with Chiang’s passwords. He had been careless and should have placed a piece of black tape across the lens.

Chiang smiled again. ‘Mr Ross, the Chinese have a saying. Dismantle the bridge, shortly after crossing it.’ He leaned in towards Mickey's face. 'Tell me, Mr Ross, why are you so interested in me?'

'David Harrison,' he replied.

'It was terrible, what happened to David; a heart attack in a quiet street, I believe,' said Chiang, moving away.

'It may have been a heart attack, but one that was inflicted upon him,' Mickey returned, nodding at Chiang's two nephews.

Chiang again smiled, before it disappeared, becoming more serious, and then he asked, 'Mr Ross, where is the information that you stole from my computer?'

'It's safe… for now,' he replied. Mickey had given Carol the memory stick and Vinnie held on to a second copy.

'We searched your house, but we didn't find it,' he said.

'You broke into my house, you bastard.'

'I didn't break in to it personally, Mr Michael William Ross,' he replied, holding Mickey's driver's licence in front of him.

Mickey's first thought was of Lucy, but luckily Carol had taken her to Norfolk. Chiang's men would have searched his house, possibly trashed it, but wouldn't have found anything. They had his driver's licence and that meant the key to his cab.

'If anything happens to me, the information will be handed to the police,' Mickey bluffed.

Chiang laughed, as did Shakiba, while the two goons stood stony-faced at the door. 'Mr Ross, no one knows where you are. You should have gotten hand relief from the whore and walked away, happy!'

'Maybe he did,' Shakiba commented, speaking for the first time.

'Maybe it's time you went back to sand land,' Mickey responded.

The smile from Shakiba disappeared.

'Now, Mr Ross, you should be more respectful to Mr Shakiba; he is a prominent Iranian, doing business in the UK,' continued Chiang.

'Well, Mr Shakiba, or whatever the fuck your name is, you should be more careful who you do business with; your pal here is planning on starting a war.'

Chiang was enjoying himself, as he walked circles around Mickey's chair.

'Mr Ross, the English have a saying, if I am correct. Out of little acorns, great oaks will grow. Well, one great oak is about to fall, while its acorns will be scattered in the wind.'

'You're mad,' Mickey replied, refusing to follow Chiang's movement.

'I don't want to start a war, Mr Ross. I just want the price of oil to increase, and this is the ideal time, with the northern hemisphere gripped in winter. The higher the price, the richer we become,' said Chiang, glancing at Shakiba, who was becoming restless and uncomfortable with Chiang's performance.

'What shall we do with him?' the Iranian asked firmly.

'Mr Ross is going to be very useful to us, Mr Shakiba.'

Chiang clicked his fingers and his two nephews walked over and stood at the back of Mickey's chair. They each took hold of a shoulder, forcing him back into his seat. Mickey struggled until he received a fist to the back of his head. Chiang took a syringe from his pocket, held it in the air, and like a nurse or a doctor, squeezed the end so that a droplet of liquid squirted from the needle. He bent in front of Mickey and said, 'You will only feel a slight prick, Mr Ross.'

Mickey strained and tensed.

'Relax, Mr Ross,' Chiang added, 'you are just going for another short sleep.'

Mickey watched helplessly as Chiang jabbed him with the syringe and the cool liquid emptied into his arm. He felt nothing for a few seconds, before his head became light and the room once more began to spin. He focused on the door in front of him before it blurred, his shoulders relaxing as the two guys released them. He found talking impossible as his facial muscles numbed, and his eyes burned as he forced them open. Mickey didn't remember closing them, because soon after he blacked out.

Luke Radcliffe opened his eyes: it was 2.59 a.m. Reaching across, he switched off the alarm, one minute before it was due to sound. He had been in bed six hours and awake for one, rested and alert. His wife Kirstin was asleep across the hall in the master bedroom with their six-month-old son Adam, his mop of blond hair and bright blue eyes gave him the Aryan looks of his German mother. Luke showered in the main bathroom, avoiding the ensuite so as not to waken Kirstin or Adam. Once dressed, he quietly made his way downstairs for a light breakfast of tea and toast, checking emails as he ate. Fifteen minutes later, with his sports bag in the foot well of the back seat, he reversed the Golf GTI out of the garage, swinging the car around on the driveway, and with stones crunching beneath its tyres, pulled out onto the suburban street.

The muster point was a 1950s five-storey former office block with ample parking in south London and not far from The Elephant and Castle. It had been purchased as a repossession during the collapse of the property market and snapped up at a rock-bottom price by the security services.

This morning it was to be used by the specialist firearms unit of the London Metropolitan Police.

Luke's drive from Pinner on the outskirts of northwest London at this time on a Friday morning would be around thirty-five minutes. Four hours from now the same journey could take up to two hours. He set his wipers to flick as a fine mist of rain settled on the windscreen as he joined the A40 Western Avenue at Northolt, just east of the aerodrome. As he eased through Hanger Lane, the car's interior was a comfortable 21C, with the cruise control set to sixty. He reduced his grip on the steering wheel and relaxed into his seat, increasing the volume slightly on the car stereo, as the local station played a favourite Gerry Rafferty track.

Luke had joined the police at the age of twenty-one. Eight years later he applied for the firearms unit CO19 and excelled in training for firearms and covert operations. Shortly after, CO19 merged with the Central Operations and Specialist Crime Unit and became known as SCO19, a member of the UK's elite forces. He had been with SCO19 for just over a year, and at thirty years of age, he was one of the unit's youngest members. He turned south at White City, stopping at his first red light, and reached across to the glove box for a tin of energy drink that would provide him with increased alertness, but at the same time he found the taste refreshing. He had a few night buses and London cabs for company as he drove along the embankment at Chelsea, while the Thames was inky black as he crossed at Vauxhall Bridge; then, after negotiating a few more sets of traffic lights he arrived.

Luke showed his pass to the security guard on the gate, who crossed out his name, before lifting the barrier and allowing him to enter. He parked at a right angle to the rear of the building among a dozen or so cars of various makes. A pair of charcoal unmarked Renault people carriers with darkened windows sat side by side close to a doorway where a warm glow of yellow light emanated from it. A young uniformed constable unknown to Luke, wearing Hi-Viz waterproofs, stood guard outside. As Luke approached carrying his sports bag, he saw the constable stamping his feet and blowing into his gloved hands.

'Good morning, sir,' the constable said.

Luke returned the early morning greeting. Regardless of rank, the constable greeted everyone as sir, due to the arrivals in plain clothes.

'Lovely morning,' added Luke, making conversation as the constable double-checked his identification.

The constable smiled at the sarcasm. 'We drew lots at the station, and guess what?'

'You won,' Luke replied.

The constable laughed. 'Yeah, you could say that. There's coffee in the briefing room, sir, room two.'

'Thanks, have you had any?' Luke asked, suddenly feeling for the poor guy.

'Another half hour and my relief arrives.'

'Good. Make sure you get warm, before going out again.'

'Thank you, sir.'

Luke went inside and turned right into a long corridor, feeling an immediate rise in temperature. The corridor's walls were painted battleship grey, with the floor laid with large black square tiles that had probably been part of the original flooring. He could hear a hubbub of noise as he reached the briefing room, which was much the size of a school classroom, with the same type of furniture, plastic chairs and rectangular Formica tables. A whiteboard had been screwed to the wall at the far end of the room and a dozen or so people congregated around an industrial coffee dispenser. Various greetings were made with a smile or a nod as Luke helped himself to coffee. He could not help to notice that every member present was a white male, which was not part of the Met's persona of a multicultural police force. An assortment of biscuits had been placed on an oval-shaped plate, and while helping himself to one to dunk into his coffee he heard his name called.

'Hello, Luke.'

Glancing up, he saw that it was Leslie Shaw, a bloke he had buddied with on a previous shout.

'Hi, Les, what's going down?'

'Don't know, mate, probably another drug bust.'

A woof whistle pierced the air as a short-haired, attractive, slim, blonde woman entered the room. She quickly produced her middle finger in the direction of the abuser.

Les was eyeing her up. 'You like blondes, Luke, don't you?' he asked.

'Yeah, I'm married to one, Les, happily.'

'Did you not fancy tackling her?'

'Who, Alice? You're kidding, aren't you?'

'What's wrong with her? She's a hard-on heaven. Look at her, great tits, tight ass, all lean and no fat, and she's what, thirty-nine?'

Smiling at him, Luke paused, before he asked, 'Did you not hear about the last bloke who hit on her?'

'Go on,' he said eagerly.

Luke leaned in towards Les and whispered, 'She walked seductively up to him, stuck her tongue down his throat, dropped her hand and squeezed his nuts, then whispered into his ear, you're all man.'

Les looked puzzled, but Luke kept smiling.

‘No way, man, she’s not a dyke, is she?’ a disappointed Les asked.

Luke nodded and said, ‘One hundred percent.’

‘Shit! I’m gutted, what a waste.’

‘Never mind, mate,’ Luke laughed, offering him the plate of biscuits, ‘have a bourbon cream.’

The room grew quiet as three senior officers wearing police standard fire-retardant cover-all’s walked in, their zips drawn up three quarters of the way exposing white crewneck tee shirts. Each had Police embroidered in large letters on their breast pocket while on their feet a pair of RF/1s, Tactical Patrol Boots, and carrying full face combat helmets. Luke knew two of the men. The lead one, carrying a black leather folder, he didn’t know, but like the other two, he was early-fifties, with cropped greying hair and appeared fit enough to put any man half his age to shame.

The three of them took their seats behind a table facing out onto the floor. The first man looked up and gestured for the person nearest to shut the door, a signal for everyone else in the room to take a seat and pay attention. Luke did a quick head count of fifteen, plus the three senior officers, the usual size for an Op, as he and Les took a seat beside two other officers.

The first senior officer stood and said, ‘Firstly, thank you all for arriving promptly at this hour of the morning. For those of you who don’t know me, I am Deputy Chief Inspector Elliot Yorke. And for those of you who do know me, I am still Deputy Chief Inspector Elliot Yorke.’

There was a brief chuckle around the room as the joke reduced a little tension. ‘You all know Sergeant Croft and Sergeant Woods,’ continued the DCI, as the two men acknowledged the room with faint smiles.

Luke glanced at Les, who raised his eyebrows, obviously thinking the same thing, about why a DCI would be going on a shout so early in the morning.

'Okay, people, let's get started,' announced the DCI, unzipping the leather folder, handing the two sergeants each a brown A4-size envelope.

'Sergeant Croft and Sergeant Woods will each distribute colour photographs of the target property and suspect.'

The first photograph was of a well-maintained early twentieth century three-storey detached property, which had a matching low garden wall with black painted railings. Luke observed that the building was obviously in an area of high property prices. The second photograph was a blown-up passport style of an elegant-looking woman aged late thirties or early forties, with olive skin, dark hair and eyes as black as night. She was stunningly beautiful and a murmur went around the room as her beauty sunk in.

'Anyone in love yet?' joked Sergeant Croft, before he got serious. 'This lady could love you to death and the emphasis is on death. Meet Safra Mazdaki, also known as Leila. She is of Iranian origin and a suspected sleeper linked to Islamic State. The terrorist group have adapted. They now employ former professionals with extremist beliefs to work as individuals, who are hired out for large amounts of money, to other terrorist networks and Mafia-style groups to attack their enemies in the West. Mazdaki is a suspect in the death of PetroUK Director David Harrison, either directly or indirectly, and worked covertly as an escort, before seducing the unfortunate Harrison.'

'No shit!' someone said.

Sergeant Wood added, 'There is also circumstantial evidence linking Mazdaki to the murder of Benjamin Levy, an

Israeli software executive killed by a booby-trap bomb placed under his car at his home in Notting Hill.'

'Circumstantial?' Les asked.

'She was picked up numerous times on traffic cameras and other CCTV on the evening before the explosion and in the vicinity of the property, although further investigations are still ongoing,' the DCI announced.

'Where is the target property?' asked another in the group.

'It's in the upmarket area of Holland Park, which is close to Notting Hill, and the reason we stress circumstantial,' the DCI answered.

'However, we could be dealing with a very dangerous lady,' Sergeant Croft warned.

'I second that,' whispered Luke, studying Mazdaki's photograph, whose dark eyes, he felt, seemed to stare right through him.

'The property is under surveillance, and as far as we are aware, Mazdaki entered the property at 6.15 p.m. yesterday evening and has not exited it since,' Sergeant Croft continued.

'Are there any other residents of the apartments?' Luke asked.

'There are twelve numbered apartments: eight are occupied by private owners, who we have been able to contact and provide alternative accommodation for, one is the suspect's and three are currently vacant,' the DCI replied.

'You will be split into three groups of five, with one lead group, the second as back-up and the third watching the rear,' Sergeant Woods added.

'Are there any other questions?' asked Sergeant Croft, looking around the room.

There were a few shakes of the head, but most of the team remained silent.

'Good! Get changed and be back here in twenty minutes, so we can sign out your weapons,' added the DCI.

'Let's go, guys!' shouted Sergeant Croft.

Everyone pushed back their chairs and slowly left the room. Luke made a face at Les, who shrugged and said, 'Let's get it done and be home before breakfast, mate.'

Chapter 26

He was moving; well, he thought he was. He could feel a vibration through his body and hear sounds associated with movement, but he had been sitting before, before what? Mickey was trying to remember, but his brain remained foggy. He was lying down, with his hands and feet bound; now his memory was becoming clearer. The chair and the men, his hands tied, still tied, and then the needle. He wasn't dead, that was a relief, but where the hell was he, or more to the point, where was he going?

The movement was not the smoothness of a train rocking from side to side, nor of the sound it makes travelling over tracks. This was more of a hum, such as tyres on tarmac and freshly laid, not dug up by utility companies. The vehicle was travelling fast, not the speed for a motorway or slow enough for the twists and bends of the country, and yet it wasn't city traffic.

Mickey opened his eyes and saw that he was in the back of a van, a roller shutter at its rear, with its sides a light metal and the roof opaque as if made of plastic. Every couple of seconds the van's interior brightened and then darkened as it sped past what he believed to be street lighting. A cloth or a blanket lay beneath him, which felt coarse on the side of his face like an old sack. The van's interior smelt of linen, and a few black oblong shapes lay behind and in front of him. He inched himself forward slightly and kicked one: it was soft and rustled on impact, like a laundry bag. The smell: linen, laundry. He was in a laundry van, but how long had he been unconscious and how far had he travelled? Mickey licked his top lip and found a day's stubble and was thankful that he hadn't been missing for days, but the question was, did anyone know that he was missing?

The vehicle lurched and then slowed, with the engine straining as the driver changed down a gear. Mickey slid to the right into the laundry bags as the van took a sharp left. There were a few more turns and then the driver drove straight for a couple more minutes, before he again slowed, with Mickey feeling a thump as the van drove over a speed ramp. After more thumps and turns, the vehicle finally came to a stop. Mickey heard a rattle as if an automatic shutter was being raised, before the van shot forward and up a short slope, moving slowly a few feet, before it stopped again. The driver cut the engine and the noise died.

Nobody got out. It was darker now and Mickey heard a gentle tick as the vehicle settled on its suspension, then he heard a muffled voice beyond the bulkhead, either two people inside the driver's cab or a single person talking on a phone; but apart from that, the only other noise was of his heart thumping in his ears.

He heard another set of tyres approaching and on the road they sounded as if they belonged to a light vehicle, possibly a saloon or an estate, moving slowing. It was low to the ground because he heard its mud flaps scrape the surface of the road as it rode up the ramp before coming to a stop beside the van. Now there was movement up front within the van, as one door opened and then the other. He heard two pairs of feet hitting the ground and both doors slamming shut, with the sound echoing around the cavernous space. Another vehicle door opened and then closed, a more solid sound, probably from the saloon. There was a flicker of light, and above him the sky lit up as if it was a summer's day. Voices appeared at the rear of the van, with the conversation not in English. The van's shutter rattled as someone fumbled with the lock, clattering as it was pushed up, before two men climbed in, the same two men from the restaurant that Chiang claimed to be his nephews. They manhandled Mickey and hauled him onto his feet, while a third person remained outside.

'Did you have a pleasant journey, Mr Ross?' asked Chiang.

'You could improve the cabin service,' Mickey replied.

Chiang chuckled and nodded at one of his nephews, who withdrew a knife and cut the binds to Mickey's legs, before ushering him down out of the rear of the van.

He was in an empty warehouse, one the size of a football pitch, and newly constructed. Its concrete floor was fresh and clean like virgin snow, the steel leg supports were painted with red undercoat equally spaced across the large expanse, reaching upwards all the way to the arched roof, which in turn supported the cross-beams that held in place the aluminium sheeting. The saloon was a Mercedes Benz S Class, black in colour, its side windows tinted, with its driver remaining seated behind the steering wheel.

'Do you ever do things for yourself?' Mickey asked Chiang, as he nodded towards the driver.

'I don't see why I should drive, when others can do it for me, Mr Ross.'

The rear door of the Mercedes opened and out climbed Shakiba. He looked tired and obviously was not enjoying Chiang's game, but Chiang seemed to be the one in total control.

‘No show without Punch, eh,’ Mickey said, motioning towards Shakiba.

The humour was lost on both Chiang and Shakiba.

‘Are you sure it is a good idea to use him?’ Shakiba asked impatiently.

‘Of course, Mr Shakiba,’ answered Chiang. ‘Mr Ross is well used to driving this type of vehicle; in fact, it is his.’

Mickey was looking from one to the other, as if watching a tennis match on centre court at Wimbledon.

‘We will not keep you in suspense any longer, Mr Ross,’ continued Chiang. ‘Please, follow me.’

Mickey stayed put. Chiang frowned and then both of his nephews gripped Mickey by the shoulders, but he stood firm.

‘Now, Mr Ross, we can do this the easy way or the hard way; it is entirely up to you,’ Chiang said.

‘You, choose, it’s your party.’

Chiang nodded to the nephew on Mickey’s right, who slowly and steadily reached into his jacket and withdrew a gun.

Mickey stared at it. He had an idea about guns, having attended an anti-terrorist seminar not long after the 2005 London terror attacks. Lehman Brothers had sent all their staff over a period of months to attend the course, and pistol training had been one of the modules. So, Mickey knew he was looking down the barrel of a 9mm handgun, and when fired at close range, could cause a lot of damage or death to the bullet’s receiver.

‘It’s just a precaution, Mr Ross. I don’t want you to come to any harm, at least not yet,’ laughed Chiang.

Mickey followed Chiang around to the front of the van, and a few feet in front of him was his own black taxi, sitting a little low on its suspension, as if full of luggage.

‘Was it not good of us to bring the taxi to you?’ Chiang asked.

Mickey said nothing.

‘I have a job for you,’ Chiang added.

‘I think I’ll pass on the offer, thanks,’ Mickey replied sarcastically.

Chiang smiled and said, ‘You are going to drive and follow the instructions on the Satellite Navigation.’

Mickey was cold, hungry and pissed off, so he said, ‘Fuck off, Chiang. Drive it yourself or get one of your family to do it.’

The nephew with the gun prodded him in the side.

‘Please, Mr Ross, I am not a violent man,’ Chiang pleaded.

‘Are you going to tell him?’ Shakiba asked impatiently.

Chiang raised his hand to Shakiba and opened the driver’s door, while his nephew guided Mickey towards it, before pushing him. Mickey, still with his hands tied, was unable to prevent his head colliding with the door frame, opening a gash above his left eyebrow.

‘You bastard!’ he yelled, turning around, air kicking as the nephew stepped back.

The one with the gun pushed Mickey onto the driver’s seat, swinging him round, while the other cut his hands free with the knife, before slamming the door.

Mickey could feel blood trickling down the side of his face. He wiped it away, but more returned.

Chiang, dialled a number on his mobile phone and spoke for a few seconds, before the driver of the Mercedes got out carrying a small briefcase and walked the twenty yards to Chiang, who unzipped it, taking out a small laptop. He placed an earpiece into his ear and the other end he attached to the laptop. He then spoke into the microphone and Mickey heard his voice boom out of the taxi's speakers.

'Mr Ross, can you hear me?' he asked.

Mickey said nothing.

'Mr Ross, make this easy on yourself and you may live.'

'Oh, I intend to live, you bastard.'

'Thank you, I now know that the two-way communication is working. Mr Ross, at the bottom of the windscreen to the left you will see a small pen-size camera; this camera will record everything that happens within the cab. There is also a second camera behind the rear view mirror watching the road ahead. Any deviation from the set route will be recorded.'

'And what happens if I do... deviate?'

Chiang laughed. 'I had hoped you would ask; this is the part I have been looking forward to.'

Mickey had a sickly sensation in the pit of his stomach.

'Underneath the rear seats of your black taxi, Mr Ross, are 500lbs of explosives.'

Mickey tried the door handle, but it wouldn't open. He tried the windows but they also were locked.

'What type of game are you playing, you sick fuck?' Mickey shouted. 'I could be diverted due to an accident.'

'It will be picked up by the front camera,' Chiang responded smugly.

'Or I could drive it into the Thames.'

'Then you will die.'

'You're going to kill me anyway,' Mickey said, glancing around the cab, looking hopelessly for an escape.

'Mr Ross, when the device is set...' he said glancing at Shakiba, who could only hear the one-way conversation, 'you will have approximately ten seconds until the device is fully armed. I think that is a fair bargain considering what you have stolen from me.'

Shakiba frowned; he was not enjoying the pantomime.

It was a quiet suburban street and the two dark people carriers sat either side of the target property, approximately two hundred feet apart. The curtains of the property had been drawn, although a halo of light drifted outwards from the first-floor apartment, but the rest of the block remained in darkness except for the emergency lighting.

Luke had been assigned to Alpha 2, along with four other members, including Les Shaw and Sam Smith, who was the senior officer. They were sitting in one of the darkened people carriers having changed into their protective clothing, which offered roughly one minute of protection from flammable liquids such as petrol bombs. On top of this, each officer wore a 2.5 kilogram Kevlar protective vest, which would prevent injury from a 9mm handgun, knives or spikes. When worn, it was easy to manoeuvre in, and one of the top body armour protection vests available. Luke's helmet, fitted with a portable camera, was light and provided the same amount of comfort and protection. He also had his personalised weapon holstered, a 9mm Glock, and along with the rest of his team, was further armed with a Heckler and Koch MP5 sub-machine with a torch attached to the fire grip.

A third people carrier containing Alpha 4 drove slowly into the street and parked further along, being the back-up for Alpha 2, while Alpha 3 was on garden duty securing the rear of the property. An armour-plated Land Rover contained the comms. along with Alpha 1, which consisted of the DCI and the two sergeants, who sat opposite the property.

The radio under Luke's ear protectors crackled. 'Alpha teams, clear to go.'

Sam Smith opened the door and Luke with the rest of his team silently exited. Two members of the team, with their MP5s shouldered, carried between them the Enforcer, a steel tubular battering ram, weighing sixteen kilos, which, when used correctly, could apply three tonnes of kinetic energy to door locks.

The apartments' exterior door had been left ajar by the leasing agent, and two members of Alpha 4 now stood either side of the doorway. Once inside, each officer of Alpha 2 switched on their torches, and beams of light swayed back and forth as if searchlights scanning the sky for an enemy bomber, while the shadows on the wooden staircase danced against the far wall as they climbed. The apartment stood directly at the top of the stairs, with the number five on its door catching the light of the torches. The two men with the Enforcer took position in front of the door, while Luke stood behind and to the right, with Les and Sam to the left.

Sam spoke softly into his mic, 'Alpha 2 in positon.'

'Roger, Alpha 2,' replied Sergeant Croft.

'Alpha 3, you are clear to proceed,' said the DCI.

A few seconds later, Luke heard a window smashing within the apartment and an object bouncing and rolling on the floor. Shortly after, there was a flash of light and a deafening sound as the Flashbang stun grenade exploded. The 160 decibels of sound and blinding flash would disorientate, temporarily deafen and blind any occupant of the apartment. The two men with the Enforcer charged the door, smashing the lock at the first attempt, dropping the battering ram and reaching around for their weapons. Sam Smith kicked open the door and entered the apartment with his weapon raised and yelled, 'Armed police!'

Les spotted a sports bag on the floor, close to the now-busted door and immediately sensed fear.

'Shit!' he shouted, throwing himself across the hall, landing on top of Luke, as the blast and massive fireball exploded outwards from the apartment. Sam Smith and the second officer vaporised almost immediately, while the third member of Alpha 2 was thrown backwards downstairs on fire. The shockwave shot out across the hallway as shrapnel, masonry and pieces of wood rained down in all directions, with glass showering the officers outside as they threw themselves to the ground.

Luke remained still, with his eyes shut, but could feel Les on top of him.

'What the fuck,' Les said quietly.

'Are you okay, mate?' asked Luke.

'Yeah, I think so, what about you?'

'The same, I think. What about the others?'

'I don't hear them,' replied Les.

'Shit!'

Luke and Les stayed where they were, until they heard voices from below. They got to their feet slowly, ensuring that all limbs were intact. Then, with guns at eye level and safety off, they both quietly stepped towards the apartment's blown-away door frame, debris crunching under their feet. What they saw was total devastation: a gaping hole was all that remained of the apartment's far wall and beyond they could clearly see the outline of the trees in the gardens of the properties behind. Anyone who had been in the apartment could not have possibly survived.

Les turned to Luke and said, 'I think breakfast is cancelled.'

Chapter 27

Luke heard the back-up team from Alpha 4 enter the building and find the officer who had been blown backwards by the blast on the ground floor with severe burns. Two of them stayed with the injured officer and called for medical back-up, while the rest of the team cautiously climbed the remains of the wooden staircase, with the only light being that of their torches.

'Anyone else injured?' asked an officer.

'We're okay,' Luke replied.

'What about the rest of your team?'

'This is it,' Les said, 'the other two are missing after the explosion.'

'And the suspect?'

'Dead, I presume. That blast took out the back of the building,' Luke said.

But Leila hadn't been in the apartment. She had been planning her escape for months and had become aware of the recent surveillance. Shortly after three a.m., dressed in black, a hood over her head and a balaclava covering her face, she exited through the rear ground-floor fire escape. She crawled on her elbows along the wet ground to a mature cherry tree close to the back wall. Easing herself up through the bare branches as lightly as a cat stalking its prey and ensuring that the small backpack she was carrying did not snag on the branches, she dropped quietly onto the grass in the garden of the property next door. She repeated the exercise again, this time crawling the width of the garden until she reached a concrete wall treated with pitch that allowed her clothing to blend. She did not expect company at this hour of the morning, and knew that the occupiers of this property and the one next to it did not own dogs, but at the same time she was being careful not to startle any animals that she had not accounted for.

As she climbed the wall, her black plimsolls gripped its rough façade and she permitted herself a smile. Such an easy task, entering one garden and then the other. As easy a task as it was when she climbed the wall where the Zionist lived to plant the little surprise under his car.

When she cleared the final property, she slid down the wall into a thicket of brambles. The winter months had been kind to her, providing little growth, as the gap near to the ground that she had widened over the weeks by late-night visits hadn't narrowed. Removing her backpack and pushing it forward in front of her she crawled under the hedge. On reaching the other side, she stood up, opened her bag and took out the loaded .40 calibre SIG228 pistol and screwed on its suppressor. With its pinpoint accuracy, anyone in the vicinity with enough ambition to confront her would receive a quick double tap for their troubles. She had a look behind her, paused for any sound and then began making her way through the park and down the hill towards the street lights which marked the main road. The path was soft with mud but not boggy, as the grass trail she encountered had been worn by cyclists on mountain bikes and the frequent off-road runner.

She was making good progress along the trail as it merged from a fork into a wider path set with gravel. A few trees and shrubs marked either side of the path and she was within a few hundred yards of the road when she was startled by something striking her on the shoulder before it made a light metallic sound as it fell to the ground. She turned, looking down, and saw a squashed beer can lying a few feet away, with laughter coming from under one of the trees. The laughter belonged to three figures and they moved from the darkness, while she took a position standing her ground, slipping her right arm around her back and shielding the SIG from view as they moved closer.

'Who the fuck are you?' the first one demanded.

He was young, maybe late teens or early twenties, and Leila made a calculated guess that his two friends would be of similar age. They were within twenty feet of her now, although it was difficult to judge in the poor light, but now she was beginning to feel threatened.

'Go away, please, I don't want to hurt you!' she shouted.

'Hurt us? Did you hear that, man?' the second one said.

'It's a bird,' said the third. 'I won't hurt you,' as he gyrated his hips, 'I've got a big cock that's hungry for some company.'

The other two laughed.

With animal instinct and without talking, the three started moving towards her, slowly outwards, in a semi-circle, as if trying to outflank her, with the middle guy the closest. Slowly, she moved the SIG around in front of her, and levelled it at chest height. When he was within ten feet, she gave a quick double tap, and the SIG made a puff, puff as he went down.

'What the fuck was that!' yelled the guy to the right, before he was the next to fall with a double tap.

'She's got a…' That was the last thing the third one would say, before he went down with the third double tap.

Leila walked over to him; he was still breathing, but making a gurgling sound, having been shot in the throat.

'You want to show me your cock now, big boy?' she asked, before shooting him once in the groin and once in the head.

She left the three of them lying there. By daylight they would be found, probably by a dog walker or a jogger, but they were not any longer a concern of hers: if they had not interfered with her plans they would still be alive. It was the choice they had made and now they were in hell.

She quickly covered the remaining few hundred yards of the park and before reaching its railings she removed her dark clothing, unscrewed the suppressor from the SIG and put everything into her backpack. Checking her watch, she saw that the earlier incident had only held her up by a few minutes. She couldn't believe the endorphin release as she fired the SIG, killing the three young men, the adrenaline rush and the enjoyment experienced at pulling the trigger. Leila exited the park and crossed over the road, keeping to the shadows to avoid being spotted by any police patrols, and walked the short distance to a row of shops. She knew of a twenty-four-hour store that sold coffee and a regular haunt for some night-time cab drivers, and decided to wait there until she was able to hail a cab.

The store was empty, and the Asian guy behind the counter gave her the once-over as she entered. The self-service coffee machine stood at the back of the shop and she helped herself to a shot of hot black. She paid the guy and he allowed her to wait inside for a taxi. One arrived within ten minutes and Leila was surprised to see that the driver was a woman. She thought that this woman took a risk by driving at night, but it wasn't any business of hers and least of all her interest. The woman talked incessantly before telling a story about a previous passenger, and Leila was relieved to reach her destination. She paid the driver, got out and was briefly tempted to put a bullet in the woman's head to spare any future passengers the grief of listening to her.

Leila approached the rear of the building cautiously. Before leaving the previous day, she had inserted a small electronic device to the emergency exit which would show that it was shut and secure, when in fact it was slightly ajar. She was then able to manipulate her fingers around the edges and pull open the door. The surrounding streets had been empty and without sound, while the railings of the school were low and easy to climb, but she had kept to the shadows wherever possible until she reached her entry point.

The door led to a small assembly hall that the school also used as the breakfast room for early arrivals. At the front of the hall was a stage with a wooden surround. She unscrewed a panel and crawled in, before setting it back in place. Over the past number of weeks, she had brought with her the accessories that she would need for this morning. Today, Friday, was to be the final day of term, before the Zionists broke for the culmination of the Jewish holiday of Hanukkah, the Festival of Lights: a holiday which coincided with the Christian holiday called Christmas; therefore, today was to be a special day for the children and their teachers.

Leila also taught dance, as well as assisting the teachers in the classroom. This morning was to be a display of dancing that the children would be performing, but Leila had already decided that she herself would take centre stage. She would first tell them her real name, not Leila, as they called her, or as the Englishman had known her by, but Safra, a true Persian name, meaning golden one. A name she was proud of, and one her father had chosen for her, and as she had grown up her father had often referred to her as the Golden Girl.

Today would be a performance none of the Zionists present would ever forget, the ones, if any, that lived. She had, though, been surprised at the similarities in culture between her people and the Jews, whether it be language, tastes in food, music or dance. Dancing had at one time been her life, in a former life, a happier life, before that life had been taken from her.

They had met on his first night home. He had studied physics and chemistry at the Universite Pierre et Marie Curie in Paris, and five years later he returned with a PhD. Amir was his name, meaning King. He was tall, handsome and could speak three languages: his native Iranian, French and English.

Safra had been with a group of female friends at an outdoor café, on a warm summer's evening, in her home city of Esfahan, in the southwest of Iran, a beautiful ancient city on the banks of the Zayandeh River. Amir had arrived with three of his friends and sat a few tables away. Safra was captivated by him and kept stealing glances in his direction, until ultimately their eyes met and her heart melted. They stared at each other, maybe a second too long, with him smiling and she returning it, before she shyly looked away. Eventually, Amir approached Safra's table and spoke to her. They then spent the rest of the evening chatting, before taking a stroll that led them across the Khaju Bridge with its two levels of terraces overlooking the river.

A year after they were married, the Government sought men with physics degrees for its project to build a nuclear power plant outside Tehran. Amir applied and was offered a position, leading to him and Safra moving to the capital. They were supplied a house on a tree-lined suburban street, in a middle-class area of northeast Tehran. It was a lush and green area, close to the foothills and mountain trails of the Darband district.

It was September now; how could she forget, the day and date, forever etched in her mind. She had stood at the door and waved him off, watching as he pulled away in their Korean SUV, Amir smiling back, waving and giving a light toot of the horn.

The early autumn air had been cool that morning and Amir dropped the driver's side window so he could take advantage of the freshness, before the sun reached its point in the sky, where the earth below would once again be scorched.

Safra had gone inside, closed the door and at the time it hadn't registered, but later she knew that she had heard it, the growl of the engine, different from the other two-stroke engines that the many young men and women now rode around Tehran.

Amir had reached the intersection and turned right onto the six-lane road. He filtered into the middle lane and eased to a stop three cars from the front as the traffic lights changed to red. The motorcycle had been a Japanese variety, with a maximum speed of 210kph, and ideal for the various road surfaces that could be found throughout the country. The blacktop it currently travelled on was smooth and flat, but on rougher roads and stony tracks it would provide easy and agile handling. Amir heard the purr of its engine and glanced in his wing mirror as it pulled alongside him. He had been accustomed to that type of motorcycle while studying in Paris, but mopeds and scooters were mostly what were used on the city roads around Tehran.

The rider and pillion passenger both wore black leathers with tinted full-face helmets. Amir turned to give the two riders a friendly wave, but watched as the pillion passenger removed something from inside his jacket and point it directly at him. Realising it was a gun, Amir turned his body and tried to move the car forward, but as the lights were still red he didn't have anywhere to go.

The first shot hit Amir in the shoulder, forcing him to recoil, before the assassin fired twice more, the second bullet entering his left cheekbone, exiting through the back of his neck, while the third was a coup de grace through the centre of his forehead which confirmed the ending of Amir's life.

The .22 calibre bullets belonged to a Beretta model 70 that was synonymous with Mossad, the national intelligence agency of Israel, who feared that Iran's nuclear power programme was cover for a more sinister project, developing instead an atomic bomb. The continued elimination of scientists working on the programme would, they believed, delay future development of any nuclear device.

Under the stage, Safra struck a match taken from a small box sitting beside her. She smelt the sulphur burn as the little stick ignited. Holding the point of it downwards, she created a larger flame as it lit up the surrounding space, making it appear like a large tomb. She had arranged in a wide circle six tea lights and lit each one individually before blowing out the match. She then removed her clothes, sat down naked and cross-legged on a neatly laid out white towel, which she had placed over one of the large blue gym mats taken from the large pile at the side of the room.

A plastic basin of water was within arm's reach, covered with a white cloth to prevent contamination by dust or insects. The water had been sitting for around thirty-six hours and was now at room temperature; it wasn't ideal, but Safra believed Allah would understand and forgive her. She began washing with a flannel that she had brought with her. The water was cool. She soaked the cloth, bringing it to her face, holding it there for a few moments before sliding it to her neck and shoulders, as far down her back as she could reach, then along the length of her arms, gently stroking and allowing the water to drip from her body onto the towel. She soaked the cloth again, then applied it to her chest, washing under each breast, her tummy and lower back. She paused slightly, before applying water to her thighs and in between her legs, raising herself up slightly to wash her buttocks, before finishing off with her calves and feet.

When she was finished, she lay down on the mat to allow the flow of air to dry her naturally. She shivered slightly as her body chilled, while goose bumps flowed over her skin. Safra felt cleansed, and she breathed in slow, deep breaths in through her nostrils, before pushing the air out through her mouth, creating a sense of calm, peace and relaxation. She closed her eyes, with the only sound that of her breathing, but making herself aware that she must not sleep, because there was more to do, although allowing herself a few minutes of peace was greatly pleasurable.

Safra's journey had been long. She had spent many nights camped in the mountains near to Mazar-I-Sharif in northern Afghanistan, an environment which originally had been alien to her, but soon became familiar, before she eventually called it home. A place where she had been taught to use the same high-velocity rifles that were fired by snipers. Adjusting the sight, lining up the target in the crosshairs, turning the tiny screw a little to the left or to the right. Using the smallest screwdriver that she had ever seen and allowing for wind direction. She was good; she knew that and they had been pleased with her progress. The feeling she experienced exploding watermelons from three hundred metres away was nothing compared to the pleasure she had felt the day before, when she had pulled the trigger and watched from across the river as the man's head also exploded. Her only disappointment was that her second shot had missed the man seated next to him, the one who had come asking about David.

She had attended lessons in large camouflaged tents with the other women she had been grouped with, watching and listening with great interest in how to make and assemble bombs, ensuring that the correct amount of high explosive was used. She then spent three years learning Hebrew, perfecting the accent and living as Leila, until her trainers believed she was ready.

She opened her eyes. Above her the floor of the stage had strips of wood running in a horizontal direction. During the summer in Afghanistan they slept outside under the stars, where she became accustomed to the smells and sounds of the mountains. Then she had been assigned to the Oriental man and Shakiba as her handler. He was a grotesque man, overweight and always smelling of sweat. Whenever she was in close proximity to him she wanted to vomit. But the assignment suited her: it brought her close to the Zionists and whatever plans the Oriental man had, were not of her concern.

She sat up and slipped on her underwear, and from a shallow zipped pocket of the backpack she took out a small black and white photograph. It was passport size, and a photograph of Amir; though slightly creased, she did her best to smooth out the lines.

She kissed his face and whispered, 'Soon, my love,' before tucking it into her bra underneath her left breast and as close to her heart as possible.

As calm as if she was reaching for a coat, Safra picked up the vest and held it out so she could view it over the light of the candles. It was more of a waistcoat than a vest, consisting of twelve small pockets, six on either side of the zip fastener, three above, and three below, wide enough to carry a packet of ten cigarettes. Except these pockets held something more deadly than tobacco. Each of the pockets contained between fifty and sixty grams of plastic explosives that were lined with small ball bearings, which made the vest effective but light enough not to be obtrusive.

She slipped one arm through and then the other, gently attaching both ends of the fastener together and pulling the zip up as far as it would go. It felt more like a life jacket, as if there was enough buoyancy within to keep her afloat in water. But this wasn't a life jacket, it was an end of life jacket. With duct tape, she wrapped the command wire to her right arm, making a double loop before attaching the detonator just above her wrist. When the time came, she would be able to slide the detonator into her hand and, with her thumb around it, enter paradise.

When she had finished dressing, she prepared a hot drink from a small flask, brought in her backpack. She breathed the aroma as she drank, remembering that before martyrdom many soldiers of Allah behaved irrationally and showed signs of nervousness. She wanted to ensure that the same would not happen to her. Currently, her breathing was stable and her heart rate low to a point where she wanted it to remain.

Beside her rested a small copy of the Koran; she picked it up and flicked through its pages until she found the one she wanted. It was a book that she had read many times, and one that had been given to her as a child. Like then, she was reading by candlelight, but unlike then this was by choice, because as a child many nights were spent in blackout, as the eight-year war raged on with Saddam. She would often be lifted from her bed in the middle of the night by her father, as the air raid siren sounded, and along with her mother and older sister, they'd huddle for shelter under the stairs, as the Iraqi air force thundered overhead, en-route to release their bomb cargo over Tehran.

It was an hour before the school caretaker would arrive and another hour before the children would appear and twenty minutes after that her performance would begin. Very shortly she would exit the school and walk a few streets to a quaint café, one that had pleasant décor and a Parisian theme. She had never been to Paris, but it reminded her of Amir and his stories of how beautiful and romantic the French capital could be. There, she would eat a simple breakfast, and then return to the school for the final time.

Chapter 28

Mickey was in an industrial estate. Which one, he didn't know, but the woman's voice on the Satnav informed him to take the third exit off the roundabout. He drove slowly, aware that every manoeuvre was being watched by Chiang. Mickey wasn't sure what was going through his head, but he didn't intend to be blown up in the cab, along with whatever destination that had been programmed into the seven-inch screen on the dashboard.

A pair of headlights approached from the opposite side of the road, bright and blurred, and a road sign he had just passed was unreadable. The vehicle sounded a long piercing blare of its horn as it went by, shaking Mickey from his daze. He flicked the wipers, clearing the falling rain from the windscreen, seeing that he had almost drifted into the oncoming traffic lane, and added to that he was driving without lights. Switching them on, they immediately illuminated the road in front.

'I am pleased you remembered your lights, Mr Ross,' laughed Chiang, his voice eerie through the speakers, now that he was alone on the open road.

Mickey didn't reply; he needed to remain calm if he had any chance of survival.

'Take the third exit,' the Satnav repeated.

Mickey swung the wheel around and negotiated the roundabout as the traffic sign directed him towards London. He was a little over nine miles from the destination, or twenty-five minutes according to the Satnav with its digital clock reading 6.50 a.m. The drive, though, into central London, if that was where he was going, could take a lot longer.

He now had a throbbing headache from being unconscious, made worse by the gash above his eyebrow, but the blood had now dried into a crust. It was less than a day since Mildenhall's murder, but it felt like a week since then and his own interrogation in the police station. He was still angry at his stupidity for forgetting the webcam on Chiang's computer and now, as a proxy human bomb, all he could think of was that, maybe, Sophie had been right after all: he should have stayed in the city.

In the sky to the east, as dawn began to break, he saw a bright star, then another beside it not quite as bright. The stars were getting closer, but that was impossible, unless they weren't stars, but instead aircraft! Approaching from the east, and making for a westerly landing. He was too close to London for them to be landing at Stansted or Gatwick, so it must be Heathrow. If he was correct, the airport was behind him and he was being directed towards West London, then a few minutes later he spotted a sign directing him onto the M4 east. Turning onto the motorway slip road, he noticed headlights behind him, maybe three car lengths back, but keeping a good distance, travelling at the same speed, and were most likely to be Chiang's goons.

The rain became heavier and the wipers quickened, as the traffic slowed into Chiswick and the outskirts of West London. The M4 morphed into The Great West Road, which ran parallel with a sweeping bend of the Thames before reaching the Hammersmith Flyover. A combination of the Friday before Christmas and a wet morning at commuter time equalled shit traffic. As he sat at the traffic lights, he was overcome with a sense of calmness: maybe it was because he now understood his predicament: no matter what he did, he couldn't prevent the bomb from exploding; whether it exploded with him still in the cab, well, he wouldn't know much about that if it did. One minute he'd be here, the next he'd be gone. But Chiang could explode it anywhere. He was sitting by his laptop, as if playing some computer game, and Mickey was the main character. One press of a button and it would be game over. But Chiang had a sick sense of humour; he would enjoy Mickey frantically trying to make his escape, before the device exploded. Counting off ten seconds in your head seems quite long and watching Usain Bolt power through 100 metres on the track in a little under ten seconds appears pretty damn quick, but trying to smash your way out of a locked London black taxi in the same amount of time is no time at all.

He followed the Satnav's instructions and turned right onto Kensington High Street, with Chiang's goons becoming stuck a few vehicles behind, but the nutter of a driver was weaving in and out of traffic trying to catch up. Gradually, the night time darkness gave way to daylight, but on a dull morning such as this, brightness was at a premium. With just under a mile to go, Mickey wondered how it would happen. Would he experience pain before being blown to oblivion, or would that millisecond of light and sound which followed an explosion be the last his brain would interpret? He tried not to focus too much on that and still believed there was a means to escape, but time was running out.

The target of the bomb was becoming clearer; ultimately, he would be near to Hyde Park, but closer to Kensington Park, but where? Kensington Palace was close by, but Mickey didn't believe Chiang would achieve his ambitions by attacking

Royalty. There were, though, a few embassies based in this leafy part of the city, and the little Satnav was telling him to make a left turn three hundred yards ahead, with only two hundred yards after that until his destination. He was familiar with the street, and began running the embassies through his head: Estonia, Portugal, Chile… Then it hit him like a bolt of lightning. There would be a large detached building on the right, sitting on its own and contained within a boundary wall, and that building was the embassy of The State of Israel.

It was coming together now, what Chiang had said, about toppling the great oak. Israel was the oak, but he spoke of scattering acorns. Acorns were small and grew into oaks. Little acorns, he ran it through his mind. He didn't have much time; he turned into the street, one hundred and eighty yards to go. Maybe another two minutes of his life remained. Children were small and grew… like acorns. He looked around for a crèche or a… 'Shit!' he yelled. 'The school! Leila!' He had to get the hell out.

The embassy was ahead on the right and the lights of Kensington Palace appeared on a rise at the end of the road. Fifty yards from where he was and along on the left stood an old brown brick building. It had a slate roof but its windows had long since disappeared, though someone had taken time to paint cottage panes and window boxes with flowers, to bring a little colour and attractiveness to it. Halfway along was a barn style door made of wood, as old as the building itself and most probably the building's original. It had a rusty padlock and looked as if it hadn't been opened in years. In a former life, the building could have been used for storing cars or as a mechanic's workshop. There were a few cars parked in the tree-lined street, but apart from that it was empty, and more importantly empty of pedestrians.

Mickey thought if he could take Chiang by surprise it would maybe buy him a few extra seconds. He swung the cab out into the centre of the road, creating a wide arc, then with his foot to the floor drove straight at the door. It burst open on impact, a large wooden splinter crashing down onto the windscreen, creating a bull's-eye crack. He slammed on the brakes and preformed a handbrake turn, just before he crashed into the rear wall. The building thankfully was empty. The only glass was that of an interior office, which had probably once been used as a reception area or for doing account work. He had barely stopped but had his feet up, kicking at the glass on the passenger door. Chiang screamed something through the speakers, which sounded like good bye or you die! A loud beep sounded from somewhere within the cab, then a ten second countdown appeared on the car stereo. He was dead. He couldn't get out. Mickey was about to kick again, when the glass on the driver's door shattered around him and a huge arm reached in and grabbed him around the midriff and hauled him out.

'What the fuck, Mickey?' shouted a shocked Vinnie.

'Bomb!' he gasped. Mickey reckoned they had about five seconds. Vinnie supported him as they ran to the entrance of the building. Carol was sitting in her car. 'Bomb!' he yelled at her. 'Get back!'

She slammed the Mercedes into reverse and shot up the street, as Vinnie and Mickey dived for cover behind a Royal Parks maintenance van. A flash of light lit up the street and an explosion rocked the ground as brick, slate and wood was thrown outwards from the building. The force of the blast set off several car alarms as glass shattered in the surrounding area. Other pieces of debris rained down, striking parked cars. Mickey heard a metallic sound and watched as a mangled door handle from his taxi bounced on the ground a few feet from his head.

They didn't move for what seemed like an eternity, then Vinnie got to his feet first. 'Fuck, man!' he said.

Mickey heard a pair of feet running towards them. He looked up, smiled and said, 'I thought you were in Norfolk.'

'And I thought you were dead,' Carol replied.

It had stopped raining, but the cold and wet ground was beginning to ooze through Mickey's shirt. Both held out their hands and pulled him up.

'You, saved my life, Vinnie,' he said, gratefully.

Vinnie shrugged and said, 'You look like shit, mate.'

'What happened to you?' Carol asked.

Mickey was beginning to shiver. 'I'll tell you in the car. I'm starting to freeze.'

He began with the abduction while he was on the phone to Lauren and then wakening up in the restaurant. He told them about Chiang, the Iranian and then the warehouse. He was almost finished, when he asked, 'How did you find me?'

'After you got cut off from Lauren, she telephoned me, then I contacted Vinnie,' replied Carol.

'Do you remember that GPS disc in your shoe?' Vinnie asked.

'Yeah.'

'Luckily for you it's still producing a signal, though faint, but as we got closer we narrowed down your position. It eventually led us to that industrial estate near Heathrow,' Vinnie said.

Mickey reached down and touched the heel of his shoe, and felt the dried glue. Of course, it was still there. 'Thank God.'

'It was only when you were driving the cab, that we got an exact hit, then we tailed you,' continued Carol.

'So it was you! I saw headlights weaving in and out of the traffic. I was thinking it was Chiang's people.'

'Mickey, this lady is one hell of a driver,' laughed Vinnie.

'Former champion rally driver, don't forget,' she reminded them both.

A crowd was beginning to gather, alerted by the explosion, and then they spotted blue lights moving down the hill from Kensington Palace.

'I think we should get out of here,' Mickey said, nodding towards the hill.

'Right, you're going to the hospital,' Carol said, noticing Mickey's gashed head and the dried blood.

'No, we need to get to the school,' Mickey insisted.

'We're taking you to the hospital, Mickey,' she replied with a bit more force, 'you've a nasty cut above your eye.'

'It'll come off with wet wipes if you have any. I'm fine, honest; we need to get to the school!'

'Why?' she asked, pulling a packet of wet make up wipes from her bag.

'Leila is working for Chiang.'

'What makes you think that?'

'Chiang and the Iranian were having great fun with cryptic clues, great oaks and little acorns.'

She gave him a puzzled look.

'The bomb,' he said. 'It was intended for the Israeli Embassy.'

'Oh my God, we should wait for the police,' she said.

'No, you better drive, lady,' Vinnie added, glancing up the road at the approaching sirens. 'We'll have too much explaining to do and if Mickey's hunch is right, by the time the cops let us go, it will be too late.'

She screwed up her face and looked at Mickey. 'Okay,' she said, putting the car into drive and swinging it around, 'but I think you should phone Lauren,' Carol added, as she pulled out onto the main road.

'Good idea.'

Turning to Vinnie, Mickey said, 'We can drop you somewhere, if you wish.'

'No way, man,' he replied, 'I'm having the time of my life.'

The further they got away from the blast scene, the more Mickey relaxed. Carol turned the car's heater system to high, and the air began to warm him. Mickey pulled down the sun visor and saw himself in the vanity mirror. Blood-shot eyes, but the wipes had cleaned the blood from his face. Vinnie passed him a bottle of water and he drunk half in a couple of gulps, realising it had been the first liquid he had consumed since being tied to the chair in the restaurant. 'Anyone got chewing gum?' he asked. Carol pointed to the car's unused ashtray. She then put her phone onto speaker and dialled Lauren's number. It rang half a dozen times before she answered.

'Hello,' she said, sounding stressed.

'Lauren, it's Mickey Ross.'

'Michael, where the hell are you?'

'I've just left the Israeli Embassy.'

'What were you doing there?'

'Leaving a car bomb, Lauren.'

'Michael, I'm not in the mood for jokes.'

'It's not a joke, Lauren. Put on a news channel, you'll soon hear all about it, because it's just exploded. And if it hadn't been for Carol and Vinnie, I'd have exploded with it.'

'Michael, this has got out of control; you need to come in… all of you.'

Carol shook her head and Vinnie grunted.

'I'm at Leila's apartment,' she continued. Except her real name is Safra and I've got two dead officers and one critical.'

'She's at the school, Lauren. Have you sent a team there?'

'Bullshit! She's dead; there was an explosion and she hasn't left the apartment.'

'She's at the school,' Mickey stressed again.

'How do you know?' she asked.

'I have a feeling.'

'Come on, Michael, I can't send an armed response unit to a primary school just because you have a feeling.'

'Did you find her body?'

She was quiet for a spell.

'Well! Did you?'

'Not yet,' she said, 'but she didn't leave the apartment.'

'No, you didn't see her leave the apartment,' he said.

'We had the apartment watched!'

'We are heading for the school, Lauren,' Mickey said, ignoring Lauren's last statement.

'No, Michael! One Charlie Foxtrot is enough for one day,' she said.

'We'll be careful.'

He heard her sigh. 'Okay, I'll fill you in. Safra is Iranian, a widow. Her husband was killed by Mossad, Israeli intelligence. That's what this is about; everything else is a decoy.'

'You better send back-up, Lauren.'

'I'll see what I can do.'

They said their goodbyes, and Carol blew out her cheeks.

Vinnie whistled. 'That's one wound-up lady we have there.'

'Too right,' said Carol. 'What's Charlie Foxtrot?' she asked.

'It's military speak for… fuck up,' replied Vinnie.

'Okay,' said Carol. 'Well, she's right about one thing.'

'What's that?' they both asked.

'We don't need another Charlie Foxtrot at the school.'

Chapter 29

The drive to the school was slow, as they were hitting peak commuter traffic into central London. Carol did a loop around the eastern edge of Hyde Park through the upmarket area of Park Lane, but after that it was a straight drive to Kilburn. When they arrived, it appeared to be just another ordinary day at the school: parents were dropping children off, oblivious of the possible threat within, and those same children were running and playing inside the school grounds. Mickey was beginning to think he had got it wrong. They parked a short distance from the school and the three of them walked through the gate. A sign for reception directed them left towards a single storey building, not unlike most of the primary schools across the country. The heavy automatic door was locked, and a metallic buzzer with an intercom was attached to a nearby wall. Pressing it, Carol inched forward as the door clicked and began to open.

'By the look of you two, I'd better go first,' she said, as they entered the foyer.

Photographs of children of years gone by hung on one of the walls and a woman at reception behind Perspex glass watched as they approached.

'Can I help you?' she asked.

The school had known Safra as Leila, so Carol was careful to keep it as normal as possible. 'Hi, I'm looking for a member of your staff called Leila.'

‘And who might you be?’ the receptionist asked suspiciously.

‘We are… friends of hers,’ replied Carol, somewhat unconvincingly.

‘I’m sorry, but it’s not school policy to admit friends of staff members during school hours,’ the woman said.

Mickey moved closer to the desk. ‘Madam, my name is Michael Ross. It is my belief that the children at this school are in grave danger.’

‘How do you mean?’ she asked, startled.

‘Leila is an Iranian national,’ he continued. ‘In fact, Leila is not her real name. Her husband was killed by Israeli Intelligence.’

‘That’s impossible. We did thorough checks. I carried them out myself,’ she said, her face now ashen.

‘If you want confirmation, contact Lauren King on this number, she works for MI5,’ continued Mickey, scrawling Lauren’s number down with a pen and a scrap of paper he found sitting on the desk.

‘Lady, show us where she is, please,’ Vinnie asked firmly.

The woman, seeing Vinnie’s bulk and coming to terms with the possible seriousness of the situation, led them along the corridor.

‘She’s in the assembly hall; that’s where we hold a breakfast club for some of the children who arrive early. It’s the last day of term and Leila… I mean, she is giving a special dance class for the children.’

‘How many children are with her?’ enquired Carol.

‘Ten, fifteen, I really don’t know, but they’re aged from five to ten,’ she said, almost tearfully.

There were empty classrooms either side as they walked. Soon they would be filled with children and their happy chatter. A few of the walls were decorated with course work, drawings and writings, and on window sills were small models made from velvet pipe cleaners. It was a scene reminiscent of Mickey's own junior school life and most likely one that hadn't changed for decades. When they reached the assembly hall, the door was locked and the curtains drawn across to prevent anyone from outside seeing in.

The receptionist looked at Mickey in panic. 'The doors are never locked,' she said.

'Is there another entrance?' he asked, trying to keep her thinking.

Nothing had happened, yet, but the woman was seeing the ramifications if anything did. It had been her responsibility for the security check. She was thinking, what it was she had missed.

'Sorry, what? Another entrance?' She was in a daze.

'Yes, another entrance. Quickly, please,' urged Carol.

'Through the kitchen, this way.'

They walked what would have been the length of the hall, turning left and entering the school kitchen. The ovens were on, but it was eerily empty.

'Where is everyone?' the receptionist asked.

A sound was coming from a large walk-in fridge, fists banging heavily on the door. Vinnie pulled on the handle, opened the fridge and found two frightened women in cooking whites. They staggered out, with the cold air from the fridge pouring into the warm kitchen.

'It was Leila,' one of them said, barely able to speak, 'She had a gun.'

'Oh my God,' the receptionist said, putting a hand to her mouth.

'Where is the door?' asked Vinnie.

‘Over there behind the dishwasher,’ she said, pointing at a large machine with steam rising from it.

Vinnie tried the door; he could push it slightly, but something heavy had been set against it on the other side. With his shoulder, he managed to open it a few more inches. ‘There’s something blocking it,’ he said. ‘I think it’s a couple of tables.’

‘Can you get it wide enough for me to squeeze through?’ Mickey asked.

‘Oh no, Mickey! You’re not going in there,’ Carol said.

‘Why not?’

‘Because she’s armed.’

‘What, so we just stay here and do nothing?’

‘No, we wait for the police.’

Mickey said, ‘It will take ages for them to arrive and if they come with all sirens blaring, who knows what could happen.’ He looked at Vinnie.

‘One in, all in,’ Vinnie said, looking at her.

‘Oh, for goodness sake,’ relented Carol.

‘I’ll go first,’ Mickey said.

He squeezed through the gap. To his left was a short hallway, which led to the side of a stage and then on into the room. He signalled for Vinnie and Carol to stop and poked his head around the corner. He saw Leila standing in the middle of the room, with her back to him, but what he also saw made his heart jump into his throat. She was wearing what appeared to him to be a waistcoat or vest.

‘Shit!’ he whispered.

In her right hand, she held a small rectangular shaped device, much like an old television remote control, that was connected to wiring which ran up her arm and back to the vest. There were three female teachers and at least a dozen children, all under the age of ten, seated in a semi-circle, with one of the teachers sobbing quietly, holding a young child in each arm, while the two other teachers had their eyes fixed on the bomber.

Mickey tiptoed back to Carol and Vinnie, re-entered the kitchen and spoke first to the receptionist. 'Go back to your front office and telephone the number I gave you, ask for Lauren King, tell her Michael Ross told you to call, and explain to her that Safra is holding several children and teachers' hostage and that…' he took a deep breath, '… she is wearing a bomb vest.'

The woman gasped and took a step back, steadying herself. She didn't speak, but nodded and then left with the two cooks.

'Bomb vest?' Carol asked, unbelievingly. 'She's a suicide bomber?'

Mickey didn't reply, but his expression said it all.

'We can't go back in there, Mickey; she's unstable and if she sets it off we'll all be killed.'

He looked at her, but she knew that he was going back in.

'Okay, what about you, Vinnie?' she asked.

'I'm cool.'

The three of them crept back into the hall. Mickey took a deep breath as he reached the corner. Leila still had her back to him; she hadn't moved and appeared rooted to the spot.

Mickey took a deep breath and spoke softly. 'Safra.'

Her back stiffened at the mention of her name. She took a step back towards the wall and turned slightly, so she could see the three newcomers and the children.

'Why are you here and how do you know my name?' she asked sadly.

'Do you recognise me?' Mickey asked.

'Yes. It was you who came asking about David, and you were with the man at the river.'

'You killed Roger!'

'I was ordered to kill him,' she said.

'By whom?'

'The Oriental man,' she replied.

'Were you ordered to kill me also?' Mickey asked.

'Yes.'

Mickey took a step back, as his legs wobbled. It was a surreal moment to find he was talking to the woman who had tried to take his life. He took another deep breath to calm his mind, careful not to make any sudden movement that would startle Safra.

She was watching him. Mickey showed that his hands were empty, but his eyes were fixed on her thumb, which still hovered above the button that would detonate the vest and kill her, along with everyone else in the room. He often wondered what went through the mind of a suicide bomber just before they set off their device. It was something that he couldn't comprehend, but had been close to experiencing something similar earlier that morning, which was a detached feeling of unreality.

Vinnie and Carol moved slowly into the room behind Mickey and began walking in a wide circle away from Safra.

'Who are they?' she asked.

'They are my friends,' Mickey replied.

'The woman, she is not very good at following.'

Carol gave Mickey a startled look.

He gave a slight shake of the head in return, before replying to Safra, 'It was her first time.'

'They trained us well in Afghanistan,' she said, 'how to watch for surveillance, to be aware of faces that kept reappearing. I saw her in the car, on the bus, in the café and how she followed me from the train station to here. I could have killed her, but I decided to let her live, because I knew she was an amateur.'

It was good she was talking. Mickey wanted to keep her mind off the detonator, but Carol had turned a shade paler.

'Shall we let the children out to play?' he asked, glancing at Carol, giving her a sympathetic smile.

'They killed my husband,' Safra said.

'The children didn't kill your husband,' he offered.

'They are Zionists. The enemy of my people.'

'They are only children,' added Mickey.

'I loved him, he was the beat of my heart.'

'I'm sorry.'

'An eye for an eye,' she said.

'No, Safra, this is what Chiang wants. It's all a game to him.' Mickey took a step forward, moving slowly between her and the children, creating a barrier. He flicked a look at Vinnie, who picked up on his intentions, seeing the emergency exit behind.

Safra's focus was still on the children with her thumb hovering precariously above the detonator which would send everyone in the room to heaven… or hell.

'I wanted children. Amir wanted children,' she shouted.

At that moment, Mickey hated the Israeli Government. He hated his own government and he hated Lauren along with her MI5 spooks. Here was a woman, also a victim, who had lost everything and now was rudderless in the sea of life, and if she died here today and wherever her soul ended up, it would not be in a worse place than the hell she was living in at this moment.

'Safra,' he said softly, 'if you kill yourself and everyone here, then Chiang and Shakiba win.'

Then something happened; maybe it was the mention of Shakiba's name. It was as if she was slowly awakening from a trance or some form of hypnosis. Her gaze moved slightly from the children to Mickey.

'What do you know about the man called Shakiba?' she asked.

Mickey knew shit-all, to be honest, but he said, 'Chiang and Shakiba plan to increase the price of oil by starting a Middle Eastern war between Israel and Iran.'

She nodded ever so slightly, listening to every word that he said.

'A war could start by killing these children,' Mickey continued, thinking on his feet. 'Oil will increase in price, making Chiang and Shakiba very rich people. They don't care about you or Amir, or these children or the children of Iran. They only care for the wealth that they will create for themselves.' Mickey paused and, without realising, put out his hand and pleaded, 'Please, Safra, let the children go.'

The room was very quiet; even the children were silent. Mickey could feel his heart in his chest and the back of his shirt soaked in sweat. From the corner of his eye he could see Carol and Vinnie standing as still as statues.

Safra returned her gaze to the children, and she smiled slightly at them, before she said, 'Children, I think the rain has stopped. It's time to go outside.'

Mickey breathed a sigh of relief as he signalled to Vinnie to open the emergency exit. Carol with tears in her eyes, began to usher the children outside along with the teachers. Mickey moved backwards towards the exit, but watching for any sudden movement from the bomber. He spotted a pile of gym mats to his right, but nothing else was close by for cover.

Suddenly, one of the children broke from the group. 'No, Ruth!' shouted one of the teachers. Carol made a move to grab the child, but failed to stop her. The little girl ran to Safra and took hold of her hand. Carol took a step forward, but Mickey put out his hand to stop her, urging her to clear the building.

'Come with us, Leila,' the little girl said. 'I want you to play too.'

The child aged around six had dark hair and olive skin, with eyes the colour of onyx. The similarity was striking, because in another world and another time, the child could have been holding the very hand of her mother.

Tears were rolling now from Safra's eyes. As he looked behind him, Mickey saw that everyone was out of the building. Then in the distance he heard the faint sound of sirens, which meant police. Armed police.

Safra heard them too and must have thought the same, because her head jolted up and her body again tensed. Mickey was ten feet from her, leaning forward, his arm out, trying to coax the little girl to him.

'Please, go,' Safra said, smiling, letting go of the little girl's hand.

The sirens were closer now, almost screaming.

Ruth hesitated as Safra released her hand.

'Please, Ruth,' Mickey whispered. He was almost within touching distance of her.

There were tyres on the gravel outside.

He watched as Safra tightened her grip around the detonator.

The little girl took a step closer to Mickey, but then turned back to look at Safra, whose thumb was now touching the detonator. Mickey inched forward and grabbed the little girl around her waist, swinging himself around as if on a sixpence and lifting her off her feet. He heard voices. Men's voices. Mickey was transfixed on Safra's right hand. He saw her thumb bend slightly over the detonator, and then she looked at him, locking her eyes onto Mickey's for what seemed an eternity. It was then he knew. Smiling, she closed her eyes.

With the little girl under his right arm he dived behind the gym mats, pulling a number on top of them as they fell. The explosion was deafening. The shockwave ripped across the room. Shrapnel whizzed through the air, striking with force everything in its path and peppering the walls when it couldn't go any further. Windows shattered, with pieces of glass crashing to the floor. It was as if a machine gun had been set to automatic and let loose. He heard and felt the thump, thump, as debris hit, but thankfully did not penetrate where they were lying. For the second time that morning he remained still, until the noise had ceased and all he could hear was the breathing of the little girl uninjured and curled up beside him.

Mickey heard heavy footsteps and more than one pair with glass crunching underfoot and then someone removing the gym mats from on top of them. He looked up and saw two rifles pointed directly at him which were held by two men in dark uniform with head protection, Police emblazoned across their chests and reading their names as Radcliffe and Shaw above their left breast pocket.

'Sir, are you or the little girl injured?' Radcliffe asked.

'I think we're okay,' Mickey replied.

The second officer, Shaw, bent down and picked up Ruth, putting her over his shoulder before carrying her outside. Radcliffe then helped Mickey to his feet.

Mickey surveyed the room: it was a scene of utter carnage. Tables and chairs had been blasted across it. Curtains were strewn and every window had been smashed. Pieces of masonry were missing from the walls and blood was splattered against the rear wall, close to where Safra had been standing. The macabre scene worsened as his eye caught something on the floor by the stage: it looked like the face of a mannequin, except this one had hair and eyelashes, but he knew immediately what it was. The sight made him stagger in shock and he needed to be supported by the officer.

'It's usually the only part of them which remains intact,' Radcliffe said. 'The explosive force goes upwards and out and it's not uncommon for the head to become detached from the body, which of course is blown apart.'

Pieces of Safra's clothing were scattered across the room. Near to the emergency exit was a piece of white material, concave or cup shape. Mickey recognised it to be a part of a woman's bra. Inside was a crumpled black and white photograph that was passport in size and he bent down to pick it up.

'Sir, please don't touch anything, we need to keep the crime scene clean,' scolded Radcliffe.

It was a photograph of a handsome young man with a full head of hair, smiling for the camera.

'Amir,' Mickey said, almost in a whisper.

'Sir?'

Mickey handed Radcliffe the photograph. 'Do you have children, Officer?' he asked.

'A six-month-old son, sir.'

'Safra wanted children but she was unable to, because her husband Amir was killed by Israeli intelligence.'

'I know, sir.'

'She may have been a terrorist, but I think his murder drove her to this.'

He looked at Mickey sympathetically and said, 'Sir, it is best we leave now.' Radcliffe stopped as Mickey stepped outside and looked at the bloody mess on the far wall. He sighed and spoke under his breath, quite possibly to himself, 'She is at peace now.'

Chapter 30

'Mickey, if you don't hurry, we're going to hit the traffic,' shouted Carol, from somewhere downstairs.

'I'll be there in a minute,' he shouted back.

It had been five days since that morning at the school, in which he had spent two of those days in hospital. Mickey felt rested and was beginning to feel back to his old self. The house had been set back in order after Chiang's mob had trashed it. They hadn't taken anything, as they didn't find what they came for, but Mickey was happy that Carol was driving them both to her parents for Christmas. He was looking forward to a few days in the country and seeing Lucy again. He came downstairs carrying a large sports bag, with Carol at the bottom smiling and shaking her head.

'What?' he asked.

'We're only going for a few days,' she replied.

'Yes, but I might need all this, plus I have to bring food for Lucy.'

'Yeah, she's such an enormous dog; it'll take loads to feed her. Mickey she's a West Highland Terrier, for goodness sake; she'll have plenty of food at my parents' house and don't forget they also have dogs, much larger ones.'

'Okay,' he said, walking towards the kitchen.

'Where are you going now?'

'My laptop.'

'It's in. As is my tablet, and the back of the house is locked. I watched you lock up before you went upstairs and you've switched off all the sockets.'

'Okay, smarty,' he said, 'let's go.'

Carol opened the door and Mickey followed, locking it behind him. He watched as a dark-coloured Bentley, with tinted rear windows, travelled slowly along the street. When it reached the end of the cul-de-sac, it eased to a stop, blocking the driveway.

'Who do you think it is?' Carol asked nervously.

'I don't know, but be prepared to run,' he answered.

The driver's door opened and a tallish grey haired middle-aged man wearing a dark suit got out. In one hand, he held a military style cap, before placing it on his head and straightening it. He then moved to the rear door and opened it.

'A chauffeur?' Carol asked quizzically.

A man around the same height as the driver, though much older, climbed out. He was wearing a dark fedora hat and a dark grey overcoat to protect him against the cold morning air. He began walking slowly towards the house.

'It's Sir John Warricker,' said Carol, almost in a whisper.

'Are you sure?'

'Absolutely. I worked there for long enough,' she replied, as she walked down to greet him. 'Sir John, it's so good to see you.'

'Good morning, Ms Freeman,' he returned, and like the true gent that he was, tipped his hat.

Mickey joined Carol and she did the introductions.

'I'm pleased to see you are in one piece, Mr Ross.'

'How can we be of help, Sir John?' Carol asked.

'I wanted to visit you personally to thank you for what you both did, not only for my company but for those children and their teachers at the school.'

'Thank you, sir,' Mickey said.

Warricker sighed. 'You no doubt have heard that PetroUK faces a difficult future,' he said glumly.

On Friday evening, Harold Goodwin and his wife were hosting a dinner party at their large estate near Aylesbury in Buckinghamshire. They had hired silver service for the eighty or so guests and the party was in full swing until around eleven p.m., when the police arrived and arrested Goodwin on charges of fraud and insider dealing. Geoffrey Burbridge's freedom lasted until Saturday morning, as he was lining up a tee shot on the eleventh green at the Royal Musselburgh Golf Course in Edinburgh. The arresting officers arrived and departed the course, along with Burbridge in a golf buggy. The same charges of fraud and insider dealing had been put to him. Unfortunately, Chiang and Shakiba had both disappeared. Then on Monday morning the London Stock Exchange suspended all trading of PetroUK's shares, due to the current police investigation.

'I'm very sorry, Sir John,' Mickey offered sympathetically.

'This has been a ghastly business altogether, along with David Harrison's death. I was too ill to travel for his funeral, you know. He was a man I always thought of as a son.'

'It's not your fault, Sir John, you weren't to know,' added Carol.

'Sir John, have you heard anything more on our two friends, Chiang and Shakiba?' Mickey asked.

'That's a question which would be better answered by my daughter,' he said.

Warricker nodded to the chauffeur, who walked around to the passenger side rear door and opened it. When the woman got out she looked across at Mickey and smiled.

Mickey smiled in return, shaking his head, and said, 'I might have known. I'm actually disappointed with myself that I hadn't worked it out.'

Carol looked at him perplexed.

'Carol, allow me to introduce Lauren King.'

'You're Sir John's daughter?' Carol asked.

'That's right. I needed to use my mother's maiden name to avoid a conflict of interest.'

'That was why we needed your help, Mr Ross. Lauren's contacts in the city referred you to us,' continued Warricker.

'Really,' Mickey said, surprised.

'Yes, we were told that not only were you one of the top analysts in Lehman's, but also in the city. The fact that you were doing a little PI work swung the offer in your direction,' added Lauren.

'Thank you,' Mickey replied.

'Mr Ross, the city would be a much healthier place if you were to return to work there. Which brings me to the second reason why I am here today.'

Mickey was looking from Warricker to Lauren and then back to her father again, unsure of what the old man was getting ready to say.

'My company is now short of a board of directors, Mr Ross, and as you have proved your in-depth knowledge, I would like to invite you to be one of PetroUK's new directors.'

'Thank you. I'm very flattered that you would think of me, Sir John,' he replied.

He then turned to Carol. 'Ms Freeman, you were treated very harshly after David Harrison died. You are also someone who knows the company inside out, probably much more than the members on my previous board, so I would like you to return to work, not to your previous job, but to join the board alongside Mr Ross.'

'I am very honoured that you would consider me, Sir John,' she said.

'I hope both of you think it over during the Christmas holidays and that we can arrange a meeting early in the New Year,' Warricker added. He then turned to Lauren. 'Mr Ross was asking about this Chiang fellow and his partner.'

'Shakiba was arrested as he tried to board the Eurostar at St Pancras Station dressed as an Arab woman,' she said, trying to keep a straight face.

'Really,' laughed Carol.

Lauren then checked her watch and with a wink said, 'Whereas Chiang should be getting picked up any moment now.'

Warricker and his daughter were about to leave when Sir John asked, 'Aren't we forgetting one thing, Lauren?'

She looked at her father, smiled, and said, 'Oh yes, sorry.' She signalled to the chauffeur, who brought over a padded envelope and handed it to Lauren, before turning and walking back to the car.

'Here you are, Michael, this is the rest of the money that I promised you.'

'Thank you,' he said.

Reaching into his coat, Warricker brought out two smaller envelopes. 'This is a thank you from me, Mr Ross and Ms Freeman.'

'That is very kind of you, Sir John, thank you,' said Carol.

‘Right, I think we should go, Lauren,’ said Warricker. ‘I wish you a Happy Christmas and I hope I shall see you both in the New Year.’

They said their goodbyes, shaking hands, then Warricker and Lauren made their way back to the car. The chauffeur helped both father and daughter in before he also tipped his hat to Mickey and Carol. He got into the driver’s seat, turned the car and slowly moved off down the street.

They both stood rooted to the spot until they were gone from view. ‘How about that!’ she said.

‘I would never have thought Lauren was his daughter, did you not have an inkling?’ Mickey asked.

‘Not one. I knew Sir John had a daughter, but I didn’t know her name.’ Then she asked, ‘What do you think of the job offer?’

‘I’m very interested,’ Mickey replied, ‘but I want to think about it, I quite enjoy the maverick lifestyle that I have, even though I’m now minus my London taxi. What about you?’

‘I am very tempted,’ she said, wrapping her arms around his neck. ‘Well, Mr Ross, looks like you got the bad guys, the reward, a directorship and the girl.’

‘Hmm,’ he said.

‘What?’

‘What exactly should I do with these?’ he asked, showing her the two flash drives.

‘Maybe we should chuck them in the river,’ she replied. ‘We don’t need them and the police have Chiang’s and PetroUK’s computers.’

‘You’re right. We’ll take a detour and toss them. I’ll phone Vinnie and tell him to do the same with his copy.’

‘Okay, Mickey, we’d better get going or we really are going to get stuck in traffic,’ she said, checking her watch.

Mickey was still holding her by the waist when a little snowflake fell and landed on her nose. 'Well, how about that? It looks like we're going to have a white Christmas after all,' he said, before kissing her.

Chapter 31

Lee Chiang stood in front of a mirror in the bathroom of a grimy upstairs flat in Chinatown. He had lain low for the past week, remaining out of sight and only straying from these walls wearing a disguise to which he was now putting the finishing touches to. He delicately placed the little grey beard onto his chin, smoothing it down with his fingers. His eyebrows had been shaved and replaced with greyer versions. The previous night he had dyed his hair a silvery grey and, using an old trick he had perfected with clear nail varnish, enhanced the effect of crow's feet around his eyes. He heard the toot of a horn from the taxi in the street below and then, as if it was natural, he turned slowly and walked slightly lame into the living room and collected his small bag. He picked up the fake passport of his pseudonym Hui Kwok, an elderly farmer of the Hani ethnic group in Yunnan province close to the Red River, who had died six years previous at the age of eighty-four. Chiang had used Kwok's fake passport several times on his travels and today would be no different.

It would be a short flight from the Denham Aerodrome in northwest London to the Weston private airfield on the outskirts of west Dublin and the light aircraft he would be using was ideal as there wasn't any need to log a flight plan. He would then live and work in the kitchen of one of the many Chinese restaurants that the family owned in the Irish capital. Then in January, once the Christian festival was over, he would fly back to Hong Kong and disappear.

The taxi tooted again. Chiang picked up an old wooden walking stick and made his way slowly down the narrow staircase. Once outside, he introduced a slight stoop as he walked. He shuffled to the taxi with the driver reaching behind and opening the rear door. Chiang thanked him with a shaky voice and told the driver where he wanted to go.

The driver spoke into his radio, informing his base that he had picked up his passenger and confirmed the destination. He then moved off and at the end of the street stopped, before turning left.

Chiang tapped his stick on the Perspex partition. 'The airport is to the right,' he said.

'Sorry, Guv, there's been an accident at Charing Cross and the traffic's backed up,' the driver replied, looking at him through the rear-view mirror.

Satisfied with this, Chiang nodded in return.

The driver drove straight for a few hundred yards along a narrow one-way street, before turning left again, taking them out of Chinatown and the theatre district. He cut across Tottenham Court Road into a short two-way street, before turning right into a narrow cobbled lane between two office buildings. The driver stopped when he reached the end of the lane and checked for traffic approaching from the crossroad.

Two men in dark suits and shades stood either side of the taxi as it came to a stop. The driver gave the one closest to him a slight nod and as he made to move off stalled the vehicle. The two rear doors opened simultaneously while a third man seemed to appear from nowhere. The first two men sat either side of Chiang, flanking him, while the third took a seat facing.

Having been taken by surprise, Chiang forgot his act. 'This taxi is occupied,' he protested.

'Relax, Mr Chiang,' the man facing said. 'We would just like to ask you a few questions.'

The man was much older than the two sitting either side of him and there was something to this man's voice. His accent, though his English was excellent, he sounded foreign.

'My name is Hui Kwok,' replied Chiang unsteadily, suddenly remembering who he was supposed to be.

The man sitting opposite smiled and said, 'Allow myself and my colleagues to introduce ourselves.'

The man opened his wallet, showing Chiang his identification, but Chiang wasn't absorbing any of it. What he found disturbing was the large writing above that set his pulse racing: the words that read, *Israeli National Intelligence Agency.*

'Mossad,' he said to himself. Chiang swallowed hard and tried to regain some composure. 'I have a flight to catch,' he said, but his mouth was dry, and the sound came out high-pitched and scratchy.

'Oh, do not worry, Mr Chiang, we have a flight to catch also; in fact, we are all going to the same airport,' the agent opposite replied.

Chiang noticed that the two younger men either side of him had yet to utter a word. 'Driver, please stop the taxi,' Chiang pleaded.

'Tim?' The man opposite said, nodding in the driver's direction. 'He's one of us!'

Chiang tried to get up, but was slammed back into his seat by the two men on either side of him.

Chiang, now breathing hard, was trying to get to grips with the situation. 'Okay,' he said. 'How much money do you want?'

The man opposite smiled, before glaring at him. He leaned forward into Chiang's face and said, 'No amount of money will repay your evil deeds, Mr Chiang,' before he gave a discreet signal to the man to Chiang's right.

Chiang didn't see the needle until he felt the prick as it entered his leg. He watched helplessly as the man squeezed the syringe, injecting whatever liquid it contained into him.

'Now sit back and relax, Mr Chiang,' the man opposite said.

But Chiang didn't want to relax, he wanted to get up and out of the taxi; he tried to fight his way off the seat, but the two men were holding him down. He used both hands to push himself off the seat, but his muscle strength had all but disappeared. It was then he realised he wasn't being held down into his seat. He tried to speak, but found that his tongue moved loosely in his mouth. He was trying to form words, but his brain didn't know what words were. His limbs went numb and his eyes began to close, but he fought to keep them open while his head was silently screaming at him to close them. It was impossible, the strength within him was gone. He sat back and felt as if his body was sinking into the seat. The man opposite was just a blur of colour while the sounds around him were indistinguishable.

Chiang managed to tell himself that it would be okay to sleep, just until he got to the airport. Then he could straighten out what must be a misunderstanding. This was what his brain was telling him repeatedly. Silence enveloped him, and all he could hear was the beat of his heart within his ears. He felt himself slipping into unconsciousness, a deeper and darker unconsciousness than he had ever experienced before. It was this deep darkened sleep that frightened Chiang, because it was then he knew: it was a sleep that he wouldn't ever again awaken from.